Elephant Small goes to a party

Sally Grindley • Andy Ellis

little ORCHARD

Elephant Small was very excited because he had been invited to Jolly Dog's birthday party.

"Time to get ready," said Elephant Mum.
"WHOOPEE!" said Elephant Small.

Elephant Mum began to wrap up Jolly
Dog's present.
"Can I do it?" asked Elephant Small.

"Put your trunk there," said Elephant Mum. "OUCH!" cried Elephant Small. "You stuck me as well."

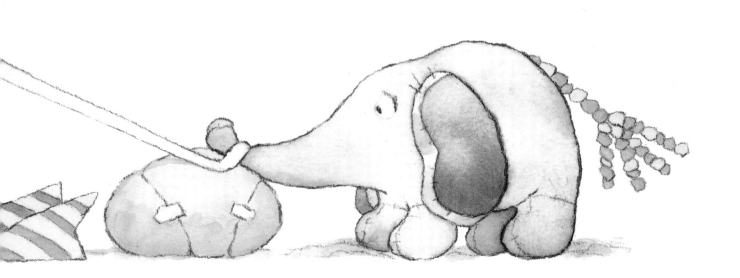

Elephant Mum took Elephant Small
over to the party. Jolly Dog bounced up
to greet them.

"Give Jolly Dog his present," said
Elephant Mum.
"Can't I keep it?" said Elephant Small.
"It's not your birthday," said
Elephant Mum.

"Aren't you staying with me?" asked Elephant Small.
"No," said Elephant Mum, "but all your friends are here."

"I'll be scared without you," whispered
Elephant Small.
"You'll have fun," said Elephant Mum,
"and I'll be back soon."

"Don't be shy," said Jolly Dog. "Come and have a fizzy drink."
Elephant Small sucked with his trunk.
SLEUCH!

But the bubbles made him sneeze
– ATISHOO! – and he blew
Plastic Penguin's hat off.

"Time for musical chairs," said Jolly Dog.

Elephant Small watched, then he joined in, then he got so excited, he missed the chair and sat on Loppy Rabbit.

"Now it's time for my birthday cake,"
said Jolly Dog.

Elephant Small was so excited, he waved his trunk — SPLAT! — and sploshed cream all over Clockwork Mouse.

"Did you miss me?" said Elephant Mum
when she came to collect him.

Elephant Small was so excited, he didn't know what to tell her about first.
"We had games and food and cake and . . . and . . . when can I have a party, Mummy?"

Collins

Year 7, Pupil Book 2

NEW MATHS FRAMEWORKING

Matches the revised KS3 Framework

Kevin Evans, Keith Gordon, Trevor Senior, Brian Speed

Contents

Introduction

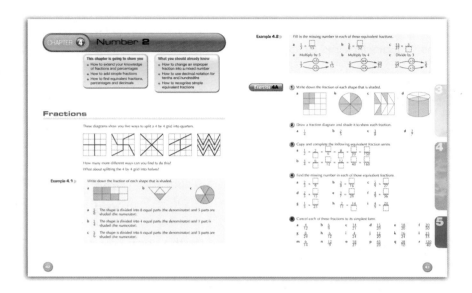

Learning objectives

See what you are going to cover and what you should already know at the start of each chapter. The purple and blue boxes set the topic in context and provide a handy checklist.

National Curriculum levels

Know what level you are working at so you can easily track your progress with the colour-coded levels at the side of the page.

Worked examples

Understand the topic before you start the exercises by reading the examples in blue boxes. These take you through how to answer a question step-by-step.

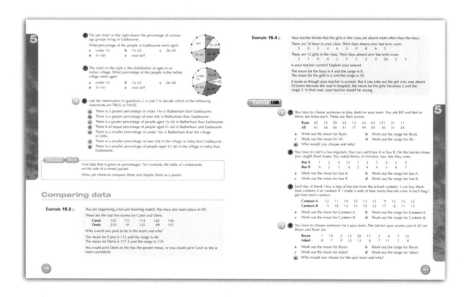

Functional Maths

Practise your Functional Maths skills to see how people use Maths in everyday life.

 Look out for the Functional Maths icon on the page.

Extension activities

Stretch your thinking and investigative skills by working through the extension activities. By tackling these you are working at a higher level.

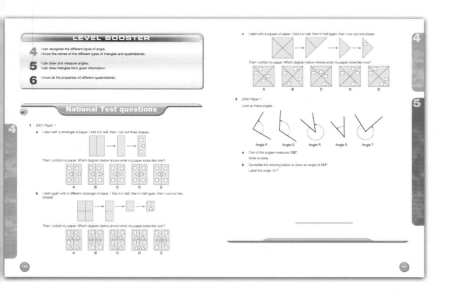

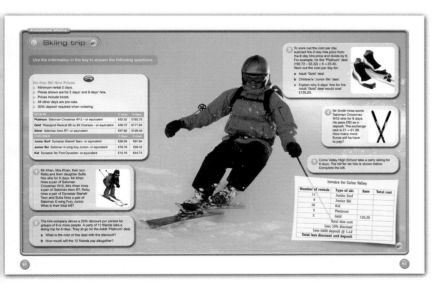

Level booster

Progress to the next level by checking the Level boosters at the end of each chapter. These clearly show you what you need to know at each level and how to improve.

National Test questions

Practise the past paper Test questions to feel confident and prepared for your KS3 National Curriculum Tests. The questions are levelled so you can check what level you are working at.

Extra interactive National Test practice

Watch and listen to the audio/visual National Test questions on the separate Interactive Book CD-ROM to help you revise as a class on a whiteboard.

 Look out for the computer mouse icon on the page and on the screen.

Functional Maths activities

Put Maths into context with these colourful pages showing real-world situations involving Maths. You are practising your Functional Maths skills by analysing data to solve problems.

Extra interactive Functional Maths questions and video clips

Extend your Functional Maths skills by taking part in the interactive questions on the separate Interactive Book CD-ROM. Your teacher can put these on the whiteboard so the class can answer the questions on the board.

See Maths in action by watching the video clips and doing the related Worksheets on the Interactive Book CD-ROM. The videos bring the Functional Maths activities to life and help you see how Maths is used in the real world.

 Look out for the computer mouse icon on the page and on the screen.

CHAPTER 1 Algebra 1

This chapter is going to show you

- Some simple number patterns that you may have seen before, and how to describe them
- How to create sequences and describe them in words
- How to generate and describe simple whole-number sequences

What you should already know

- Odd and even numbers
- Times tables up to 10×10

Sequences and rules

You can make up many different sequences with integers (whole numbers) using simple rules.

Example 1.1

Rule ⟨add 3⟩ Starting at 1 gives the sequence 1, 4, 7, 10, 13, …

Starting at 2 gives the sequence 2, 5, 8, 11, 14, …

Starting at 6 gives the sequence 6, 9, 12, 15, 18, …

Rule ⟨double⟩ Starting at 1 gives the sequence 1, 2, 4, 8, 16, …

Starting at 3 gives the sequence 3, 6, 12, 24, 48, …

Starting at 5 gives the sequence 5, 10, 20, 40, 80, …

So you see, with *different* **rules** and *different* **starting points**, there are very many *different* **sequences** you may make.

The numbers in a sequence are called **terms** and the starting point is called the **1st term**. The rule is often referred to as the **term-to-term rule**.

Exercise 1A

1 Use each of the following term-to-term rules with the 1st terms **i** 1 and **ii** 5.

Create each sequence with 5 terms in it.

a	add 3	**b**	multiply by 3	**c**	add 5	**d**	multiply by 10
e	add 9	**f**	multiply by 5	**g**	add 7	**h**	multiply by 2
i	add 11	**j**	multiply by 4	**k**	add 8	**l**	add 105

2 Give the next two terms in each of these sequences. Describe the term-to-term rule you have used.

    a 2, 4, 6, …   **b** 3, 6, 9, …   **c** 1, 10, 100, …   **d** 1, 2, 4, …

    e 2, 10, 50, …   **f** 0, 7, 14, …   **g** 7, 10, 13, …   **h** 4, 9, 14 , …

    i 4, 8, 12, …   **j** 9, 18, 27, …   **k** 12, 24, 36, …   **l** 2, 6, 18 , …

3 Give the next two terms in these sequences. Describe the term-to-term rule you have used.

    a 50, 45, 40, 35, 30, …   **b** 35, 32, 29, 26, 23, …

    c 64, 32, 16, 8, 4, …   **d** 3125, 625, 125, 25, 5, …

    e 20, 19.3, 18.6, 17.9, 17.2, …   **f** 1000, 100, 10, 1, 0.1, …

    g 10, 7, 4, 1, –2, …   **h** 27, 9, 3, 1, $\frac{1}{3}$, …

4 For each pair of numbers find at least two different sequences, writing the next two terms. Describe the term-to-term rule you have used.

    a 1, 4, …   **b** 3, 7, …   **c** 2, 6, …

    d 3, 6, …   **e** 4, 8, …   **f** 5, 15, …

5 Find two terms between each pair of numbers to form a sequence. Describe the term-to-term rule you have used.

    a 1, …, …, 8   **b** 3, …, …, 12   **c** 5, …, …, 20

    d 4, …, …, 10   **e** 80, …, …, 10   **f** 2, …, …, 54

Extension Work

1 Choose a target number, say 50, and try to write a term-to-term rule which has 50 as one of its terms.

2 See how many different term-to-term rules you can find with the same 1st term that get to the target number. (Try to find at least five.)

Finding missing terms

In any sequence, you will have a 1st term, 2nd term, 3rd term, 4th term and so on.

Example 1.2 ▶

In the sequence 3, 5, 7, 9, …, what is the 5th term, and what is the 50th term?

You first need to know what the term-to-term rule is. You can see that you add 2 from one term to the next:

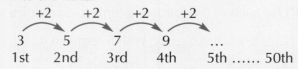

To get to the 5th term, you add 2 to the 4th term, which gives 11.

To get to the 50th term, you will have to add on 2 a total of 49 times (50 – 1) to the first term, 3. This will give 3 + 2 × 49 = 3 + 98 = 101.

Exercise 1B

1 In each of the following sequences, find the 5th and the 50th term.

a	4, 6, 8, 10, …	**b**	1, 6, 11, 16, …	**c**	3, 10, 17, 24, …
d	5, 8, 11, 14, …	**e**	1, 5, 9, 13, …	**f**	2, 10, 18, 26, …
g	20, 30, 40, 50, …	**h**	10, 19, 28, 37, …	**i**	3, 9, 15, 21, …

2 In each of the sequences below, find the 1st term, then find the 50th term.

In each case, you have been given the 4th, 5th and 6th terms.

a	…, …, …, 13, 15, 17, …	**b**	…, …, …, 18, 23, 28, …
c	…, …, …, 19, 23, 27, …	**d**	…, …, …, 32, 41, 50, …

3 In each of the following sequences, find the missing terms and the 50th term.

Term	1st	2nd	3rd	4th	5th	6th	7th	8th	50th
Sequence A	…	…	…	…	17	19	21	23	…
Sequence B	…	9	…	19	…	29	…	39	…
Sequence C	…	…	16	23	…	37	44	…	…
Sequence D	…	…	25	…	45	…	…	75	…
Sequence E	…	5	…	11	…	…	20	…	…
Sequence F	…	…	12	…	…	18	…	22	…

4 Find the 40th term in the sequence with the term-to-term rule ADD 5 and a 1st term of 6.

5 Find the 80th term in the sequence with the term-to-term rule ADD 4 and a 1st term of 9.

6 Find the 100th term in the sequence with the term-to-term rule ADD 7 and 1st term of 1.

7 Find the 30th term in the sequence with the term-to-term rule ADD 11 and 1st term of 5.

Extension Work

1 You have a simple sequence where the 50th term is 349, the 51st is 354 and the 52nd is 359. Find the 1st term and the 100th term.

2 You are building patterns using black and yellow squares.

  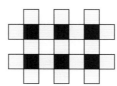 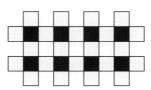

| **Pattern 1** | **Pattern 2** | **Pattern 3** | **Pattern 4** |

You have 50 black squares. How many yellow squares will be in the pattern?

Functions and mappings

Example 1.3 ▷ Complete the function machine to show the output.

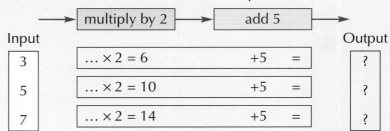

Input			Output
3	... × 2 = 6	+5 =	?
5	... × 2 = 10	+5 =	?
7	... × 2 = 14	+5 =	?

The output box can be seen to be:

11

15

19

Exercise 1C

1 Complete the input and output for each of the following function machines:

a add 3

input	output
4	?
5	?
8	?
11	?

b subtract 2

input	output
4	?
5	?
8	?
11	?

c multiply by 5

input	output
4	?
5	?
8	?
11	?

d divide by 10

input	output
100	?
80	?
60	?
50	?

e add 4

input	output
3	?
?	9
8	?
?	15

f multiply by 3

input	output
4	?
?	18
8	?
?	36

2 Express each of these functions in words:

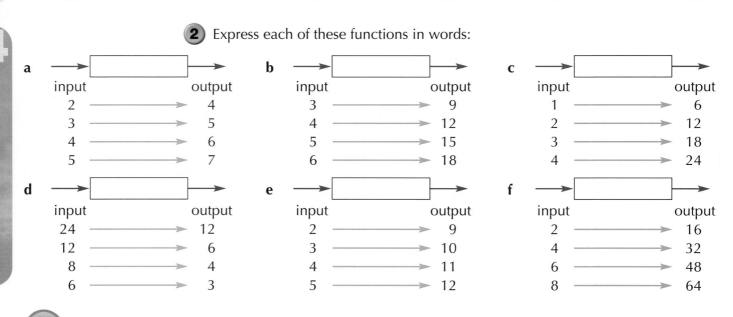

a

input	output
2	4
3	5
4	6
5	7

b

input	output
3	9
4	12
5	15
6	18

c

input	output
1	6
2	12
3	18
4	24

d

input	output
24	12
12	6
8	4
6	3

e

input	output
2	9
3	10
4	11
5	12

f

input	output
2	16
4	32
6	48
8	64

3 Fill in the missing values in the following double function machines.

a $\xrightarrow{4}$ $\boxed{\times \dots}$ $\xrightarrow{8}$ $\boxed{+ \dots}$ $\xrightarrow{11}$

b $\xrightarrow{5}$ $\boxed{\times \dots}$ $\xrightarrow{15}$ $\boxed{- \dots}$ $\xrightarrow{9}$

c $\xrightarrow{4}$ $\boxed{+ \dots}$ $\xrightarrow{6}$ $\boxed{\times \dots}$ $\xrightarrow{18}$

d $\xrightarrow{3}$ $\boxed{+ \dots}$ $\xrightarrow{\dots}$ $\boxed{\times 2}$ $\xrightarrow{18}$

4 Each of the following functions is made up from two operations, as above.

Find the **combined functions** in each case.

a 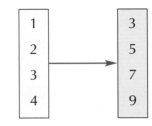   b 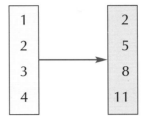   c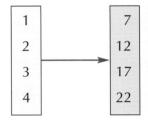

1 Work backwards from each output to find the input to each of the following functions:

a $\boxed{?, ?, ?, ?}$ ⟶ $\boxed{\times 3}$ ⟶ $\boxed{+ 4}$ ⟶ $\boxed{7, 13, 16, 25}$

b $\boxed{?, ?, ?, ?}$ ⟶ $\boxed{+ 5}$ ⟶ $\boxed{\times 2}$ ⟶ $\boxed{14, 16, 20, 26}$

c $\boxed{?, ?, ?, ?}$ ⟶ $\boxed{\times 4}$ ⟶ $\boxed{- 3}$ ⟶ $\boxed{9, 17, 33, 37}$

2 From the following single functions, see how many different combined functions you can make.

$\boxed{\times 3}$ $\boxed{+ 4}$ $\boxed{- 1}$ $\boxed{\times 2}$ $\boxed{+ 5}$

Using letter symbols to represent functions

Here is some algebra shorthand that is useful to know:

$2x$ means two multiplied by x

$2g$ means two multiplied by g

$5h$ means five multiplied by h

The idea of algebra is that we use a letter to represent a situation where we don't know a number (value) or where we know the value can vary (be lots of different numbers).

Each of these is an **expression**. An expression is often a mixture of letters, numbers and signs. We call the letters **variables**, because the values they stand for vary.

For example, $3x$, $x + 5$, $2x + 7$ are expressions, and x is a variable in each case.

When the variable in an expression is a particular number, the expression has a particular value.

For example, in the expression $x + 6$, when $x = 4$, the expression has the value $4 + 6$, which is 10.

Example 1.4 ▷ Given that $n = 5$, write down the value of the following expressions:

a $n + 6$ **b** $4n$ **c** $n - 2$

In each case, substitute (replace) the letter n with the number 5.

a $n + 6 = 5 + 6 = 11$

b $4n = 4 \times 5 = 20$

c $n - 2 = 5 - 2 = 3$

Example 1.5 ▷ Draw mapping diagrams to illustrate each of the following functions:

a $x \rightarrow x + 5$ **b** $x \rightarrow 3x$ **c** $x \rightarrow 2x + 1$

a $\xrightarrow{\quad x \quad}\boxed{+\,5}\xrightarrow{\quad x+5 \quad}$

b $\xrightarrow{\quad x \quad}\boxed{\times\,3}\xrightarrow{\quad 3x \quad}$

c $\xrightarrow{\quad x \quad}\boxed{\times\,2}\xrightarrow{\quad 2x \quad}\boxed{+\,1}\xrightarrow{\quad 2x+1 \quad}$

Exercise 1D

1 Write down what the expression $\boxed{n + 5}$ is equal to when:

i $n = 3$ **ii** $n = 7$ **iii** $n = 10$ **iv** $n = 2$ **v** $n = 21$

2 Write down what the expression $\boxed{3n}$ is equal to when:

i $n = 4$ **ii** $n = 8$ **iii** $n = 11$ **iv** $n = 5$ **v** $n = 22$

3 Write down what the expression $\boxed{x - 1}$ is equal to when:

i $x = 8$ **ii** $x = 19$ **iii** $x = 100$ **iv** $x = 3$ **v** $x = 87$

4 Write each of the following rules in symbolic form (for example, $x \rightarrow x + 4$).

a add 3   **b** multiply by 5   **c** subtract 2   **d** divide by 5

5 Draw mapping diagrams to illustrate each of the following functions.

a $x \rightarrow x + 2$ **b** $x \rightarrow 4x$ **c** $x \rightarrow x + 5$ **d** $x \rightarrow x - 3$

6 Express each of the following functions in symbolic form as in Question 4.

a
```
2 →  9
3 → 10
4 → 11
5 → 12
```

b
```
2 → 10
3 → 15
4 → 20
5 → 25
```

c
```
2 → 1
3 → 2
4 → 3
5 → 4
```

d
```
2 →  8
3 → 12
4 → 16
5 → 20
```

e
```
12 →  4
15 →  5
21 →  7
30 → 10
```

f
```
2 →  7
3 →  8
4 →  9
5 → 10
```

g
```
2 → 20
3 → 30
4 → 40
5 → 50
```

h
```
12 →  9
13 → 10
14 → 11
15 → 12
```

7 Draw mapping diagrams to illustrate each of these functions.

a $x \rightarrow 2x + 3$ **b** $x \rightarrow 3x - 2$ **c** $x \rightarrow 5x + 1$ **d** $x \rightarrow 10x - 3$

8 Describe each of the following mappings as functions in symbolic form, as above.

a
```
1 → 1
2 → 3
3 → 5
4 → 7
```

b
```
1 →  7
2 → 11
3 → 15
4 → 19
```

c
```
1 →  1
2 →  4
3 →  7
4 → 10
```

d
```
1 → 11
2 → 21
3 → 31
4 → 41
```

Extension **Work**

Put the same number through each of these function machines:

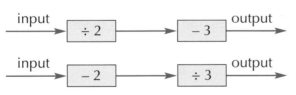

Repeat with other numbers.

Can you find an input that gives the same output for both function machines?

The general term (*n*th term)

We can describe sequences by giving a rule for any term. This is called the *n*th term and is an algebraic expression.

Example 1.6 ▷

The *n*th term of the sequence 7, 11, 15, 19, 23, … is given by the expression $4n + 3$.

a Show this is true for the first three terms.

b Use the rule to find the 50th term of the sequence.

a Let $n = 1$: $4 \times 1 + 3 = 4 + 3 = 7$

Let $n = 2$: $4 \times 2 + 3 = 8 + 3 = 11$

Let $n = 3$: $4 \times 3 + 3 = 12 + 3 = 15$

b Let $n = 50$: $4 \times 50 + 3 = 200 + 3 = 203$

So, the 50th term is 203.

Example 1.7 ▷

The *n*th term of a sequence is given by $3n - 1$.

a Find the first three terms of the sequence.

b Find the 60th term of the sequence.

a Let $n = 1$: $3 \times 1 - 1 = 3 - 1 = 2$

Let $n = 2$: $3 \times 2 - 1 = 6 - 1 = 5$

Let $n = 3$: $3 \times 3 - 1 = 9 - 1 = 8$

So, the first three terms are 2, 5, 8, ….

b Let $n = 60$: $3 \times 60 - 1 = 180 - 1 = 179$

So, the 60th term is 179.

Exercise 1E

1 Find **i** the first three terms and **ii** the 100th term, of sequences whose *n*th term is given by:

a $2n + 1$	b $4n - 1$	c $5n - 3$
d $3n + 2$	e $4n + 5$	f $10n + 1$
g $\frac{1}{2}n + 2$	h $7n - 1$	i $\frac{1}{2}n - \frac{1}{4}$

Extension **Work**

Find **i** the first three terms and **ii** the 100th term, of sequences whose *n*th term is given by:

a n^2 b $(n + 2)(n + 1)$ c $\frac{1}{2}n(n + 1)$

An *n*th term investigation

Here is a list of three sequences and their *n*th term.

$$4, 9, 14, 19, 24, \ldots \quad 5n - 1$$
$$2, 6, 10, 14, 18, \ldots \quad 4n - 2$$
$$8, 11, 14, 17, 20, \ldots \quad 3n + 5$$

Make up at least three more *n*th terms of the form $an \pm b$, for example $2n + 5$, and work out the first five terms.

Copy and complete the table below using the three sequences above and the ones you made up.

Sequence			*n*th term	
Sequence	Difference between terms	First term	Coefficient of *n*	Constant term
4, 9, 14, 19, 24	5	4	5	−1
2, 6, 10, 14, 18	4	2	4	−2
8, 11, 14, 17, 20				

1. What is the connection between the difference between the terms and the coefficient of *n*?

2. What is the connection between the difference between the terms, the first term and the constant term?

3. Without working out the terms of the sequences, match these sequences to the *n*th term expressions.

	Sequence	*n*th term
a	3, 9, 15, 21, 27, …	$6n + 1$
b	10, 13, 16, 19, 22, …	$3n - 1$
c	7, 13, 19, 25, 31, …	$3n + 7$
d	2, 5, 8, 11, 14, …	$6n - 3$

4. Can you write down the *n*th terms of these sequences?
   a 4, 11, 18, 25, 32, …
   b 5, 7, 9, 11, 13, …
   c 9, 13, 17, 21, 25, …
   d 5, 13, 21, 29, 37, …
   e 11, 21, 31, 41, 51, …

3 I can work out the value of expressions like $3a - 4b$ for values of a and b such as $a = 5$ and $b = 3$, i.e. 3.

I can find the output value for a function machine like the one below when I know the input value.

4 I can write down a sequence given the first term, say 3, and a term-to-term rule such as 'goes up by 4 each time', i.e. 3, 7, 11, 15, 19, …

I can give the term-to-term rule for a sequence such as 4, 7, 10, 13, 16, …, i.e. 'goes up by 3 each time'.

I can write an algebraic expression for a rule such as 'add 3', i.e. $x + 3$.

I can find the operation in a function machine like the one below when you are given the inputs and outputs, i.e. $\times 4$.

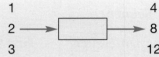

5 I can find any term in a sequence given the first term, say 5, and the term-to-term rule such as 'goes up by 6 each time', i.e. the 20th term is 119.

I can write a double operation rule using algebra, i.e. $\frac{x}{2} - 3$ for the function machine below.

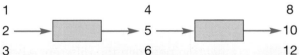

6 I can find the operations in a double operation function machine like the one below given the inputs and outputs, i.e. $+ 3$ and $\times 2$.

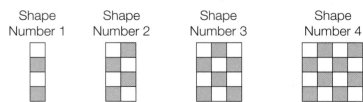

I can find any term in a sequence given the algebraic rule for the nth term, i.e. a sequence with an nth term of $6n - 5$ has a 10th term of 55.

National Test questions

1 *2004 4–6 Paper 2*

Here is a sequence of shapes made with grey and white tiles.

| Shape Number 1 | Shape Number 2 | Shape Number 3 | Shape Number 4 |

The number of grey tiles = 2 × the shape number
The number of white tiles = 2 × the shape number

a Altogether, how many tiles will there be in shape number **5**?

b Altogether, how many tiles will there be in shape number **15**?

c Write down the missing number from the following sentence:

The **total** number of tiles = ☐ × the shape number.

2 *2000 Paper 2*

a Write down the next two numbers in the sequence below:

281, 287, 293, 299, …, …

b Write down the next two numbers in the sequence below:

1, 4, 9, 16, 25, …, …

c Describe the pattern in part **b** in your own words.

3 *2000 Paper 2*

You can make 'huts' with matches.

1 hut needs
5 matches

2 huts need
9 matches

3 huts need
13 matches

A rule to find how many matches you need is:

$m = 4h + 1$

m stands for the number of matches

h stands for the number of huts

a Use the rule to find how many matches you need to make 8 huts.
(Show your working.)

b I use 81 matches to make some huts. How many huts do I make?
(Show your working.)

FM Valencia Planetarium

Use this key to answer the following questions.

Ladders and grids are made from combinations of:

'L' links   'T' links   'X' links   'R' rods

Each combination can be expressed algebraically.

For example

4L + 2T + 7R4   L + 6T + 2X + 17R

1 Look at the ladders on the right.

    a Write down algebraic expressions for each of them.

i

ii

iii

    b Copy and fill in this table.

Ladder	L links	T links	R Rods
1	4	0	4
2	4	2	7
3			
4			
5			

    c Write down an algebraic expression for the links and rods in ladder 10.

2 Look at the following rectangles that are 2 squares deep.

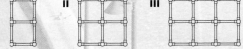

i   ii   iii

    a Write down algebraic expressions for each of them.

    b Copy and complete the following table.

Rectangle	L links	T links	X links	R Rods
2 × 1	4	2	0	7
2 × 2	4	4	1	12
2 × 3				

    c Write down an algebraic expression for the links and rods in a 2 × 10 rectangle.

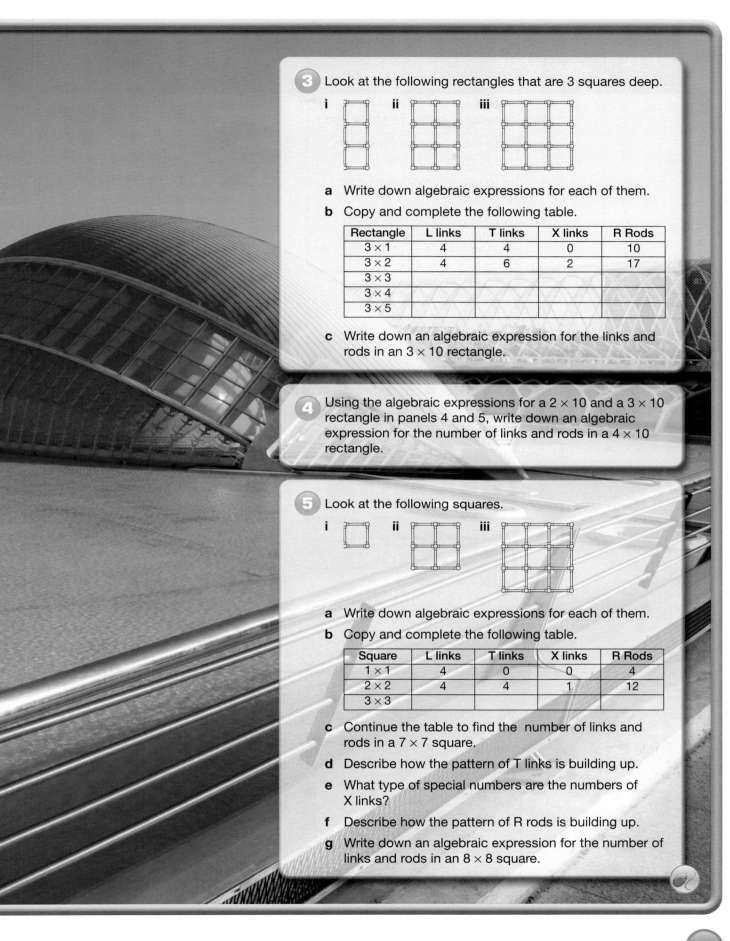

3 Look at the following rectangles that are 3 squares deep.

i   ii   iii

a Write down algebraic expressions for each of them.

b Copy and complete the following table.

Rectangle	L links	T links	X links	R Rods
3 × 1	4	4	0	10
3 × 2	4	6	2	17
3 × 3				
3 × 4				
3 × 5				

c Write down an algebraic expression for the links and rods in an 3 × 10 rectangle.

4 Using the algebraic expressions for a 2 × 10 and a 3 × 10 rectangle in panels 4 and 5, write down an algebraic expression for the number of links and rods in a 4 × 10 rectangle.

5 Look at the following squares.

i   ii   iii

a Write down algebraic expressions for each of them.

b Copy and complete the following table.

Square	L links	T links	X links	R Rods
1 × 1	4	0	0	4
2 × 2	4	4	1	12
3 × 3				

c Continue the table to find the number of links and rods in a 7 × 7 square.

d Describe how the pattern of T links is building up.

e What type of special numbers are the numbers of X links?

f Describe how the pattern of R rods is building up.

g Write down an algebraic expression for the number of links and rods in an 8 × 8 square.

This chapter is going to show you	What you should already know
● How to work with decimals and whole numbers	● How to write and read whole numbers and decimals
● How to use estimation to check your answers	● How to write tenths and hundredths as decimals
● How to solve problems using decimals and whole numbers, with and without a calculator	● Times tables up to 10×10
	● How to use a calculator to do simple calculations

Decimals

Look at this picture. What do the decimal numbers mean? How would you say them?

When you multiply by 100, all the digits are moved two places to the left.

Example 2.1 ▷ Work out 3.5×100.

Thousands	Hundreds	Tens	Units	Tenths	Hundredths	Thousandths
			3	5		
	3	5	0			

The digits move one place to the left when you multiply by 10, and three places to the left when you multiply by 1000.

When you divide by 1000, all the digits move three places to the right.

Example 2.2 ▶

Work out 23 ÷ 1000.

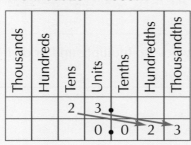

In the same way, the digits move one place to the right when you divide by 10, and two places to the right when you divide by 100.

Exercise 2A

1 Without using a calculator work out:

    a 34×10 **b** 89×100 **c** 7×100

    d 4×1000 **e** $34 \div 10$ **f** $89 \div 100$

    g $7 \div 100$ **h** $4 \div 1000$ **i** $58 \div 1000$

2 Find the missing number in each case.

    a $3 \times 10 = \boxed{}$ **b** $3 \times \boxed{} = 300$

    c $3 \div 10 = \boxed{}$ **d** $3 \div \boxed{} = 0.03$

3 Without using a calculator work out:

    a 4.5×10 **b** 0.6×10 **c** 5.3×100

    d 0.03×100 **e** 5.8×1000 **f** 0.7×1000

    g $4.5 \div 10$ **h** $0.6 \div 10$ **i** $5.3 \div 100$

    j $0.03 \div 100$ **k** $5.8 \div 1000$ **l** $0.04 \div 10$

    m $5.01 \div 10$ **n** 6.378×100

4 Find the missing number in each case.

    a $0.3 \times 10 = \boxed{}$ **b** $0.3 \times \boxed{} = 300$ **c** $0.3 \div 10 = \boxed{}$

    d $0.3 \div \boxed{} = 0.003$ **e** $\boxed{} \div 100 = 0.03$ **f** $\boxed{} \div 10 = 30$

    g $\boxed{} \times 1000 = 30\,000$ **h** $\boxed{} \times 10 = 300$

5 Fill in the missing operation in each case.

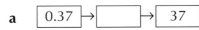

    a $0.37 \to \boxed{} \to 37$ **b** $567 \to \boxed{} \to 5.67$

    c $0.07 \to \boxed{} \to 70$ **d** $650 \to \boxed{} \to 65$

    e $0.6 \to \boxed{} \to 0.006$ **f** $345 \to \boxed{} \to 0.345$

6 Copy, complete and work out the total of this shopping bill:

1000 chews at £0.03 each = ...

100 packets of mints at £0.23 each = ...

10 cans of pop at £0.99 each = ...

Extension Work

Design a poster to explain clearly how to multiply and/or divide a number by 10, 100 or 1000.

Ordering decimals

Name	Leroy	Myrtle	Jack	Baby Jane	Alf	Doris
Age	37.4	21	$32\frac{1}{2}$	9 months	57	68 yrs 3 mths
Height	170 cm	1.54 m	189 cm	0.55 m	102 cm	1.80 m
Weight	75 kg	50.3 kg	68 kg	7.5 kg	85 kg	76 kg 300 g

Look at the people in the picture. How would you put them in order?

When you compare the size of numbers, you have to consider the **place value** of each digit.

It helps if you fill in the numbers in a table like the one shown on the right.

The decimal point separates the whole-number part of the number from the decimal-fraction part.

Thousands	Hundreds	Tens	Units	Tenths	Hundredths	Thousandths
			2	3	3	0
			2	0	3	0
			2	3	0	4

Example 2.3 ▷ Put the numbers 2.33, 2.03 and 2.304 in order, from smallest to largest.

The numbers are shown in the table. Zeros have been added to make up the missing decimal places.

Working across the table from the left, you can see that all of the numbers have the same units digit. Two of them have the same tenths digit, and two have the same hundredths digit. But only one has a digit in the thousandths. The order is:

2.03, 2.304 and 2.33

Example 2.4 ▷ Put the correct sign, > or <, between each of these pairs of numbers.

    a   6.05 and 6.046   **b**   0.06 and 0.065

    a   Both numbers have the same units and tenths digits, but the hundredths digit is bigger in the first number. So the answer is 6.05 > 6.046.

    b   Both numbers have the same units, tenths and hundredths digits, but the second number has the bigger thousandths digit, as the first number has a zero in the thousandths. So the answer is 0.06 < 0.065.

Exercise 2B

1 **a**   Copy the table on page 16 (but not the numbers). Write the following numbers in the table, placing each digit in the appropriate column.

        4.57, 45, 4.057, 4.5, 0.045, 0.5, 4.05

   b   Use your answer to part **a** to write the numbers in order from smallest to largest.

2 Write each of these sets of numbers in order from smallest to largest.

   a   0.73, 0.073, 0.8, 0.709, 0.7

   b   1.203, 1.03, 1.405, 1.404, 1.4

   c   34, 3.4, 0.34, 2.34, 0.034

3 Put these amounts of money in order from smallest to largest.

   a   56p   £1.25   £0.60   130p   £0.07

   b   £0.04   £1.04   101p   35p   £0.37

4 Put these times in order: 1 hour 10 minutes, 25 minutes, 1.25 hours, 0.5 hours.

5 Put the correct sign, > or <, between each of these pairs of numbers.

   a   0.315 … 0.325   **b**   0.42 … 0.402   **c**   6.78 … 6.709

   d   5.25 km … 5.225 km   **e**   0.345 kg … 0.4 kg   **f**   £0.05 … 7p

6 Write each of the following statements in words.

   a   3.1 < 3.14 < 3.142

   b   £0.07 < 32p < £0.56

7 One metre is 100 centimetres. Change all the lengths below to metres and then put them in order from smallest to largest.

        6.25 m, 269 cm, 32 cm, 2.7 m, 0.34 m

8 One kilogram is 1000 grams. Change all the weights below to kilograms and then put them in order from smallest to largest.

        467 g, 1.260 kg, 56 g, 0.5 kg, 0.055 kg

Choose a set of five consecutive integers (whole numbers), such as 3, 4, 5, 6, 7.

Use a calculator to work out the **reciprocal** of each of the five numbers. The reciprocal is the number divided into 1. That is:

$$1 \div 3, \ 1 \div 4, \ 1 \div 5, \ 1 \div 6, \ 1 \div 7$$

Put the answers in order from smallest to largest.

Repeat with any five two-digit whole numbers, such as 12, 15, 20, 25, 30.

What do you notice?

Directed numbers

Temperature 32 °C
Latitude 17° South
Time 09 30 h GMT

Temperature −13 °C
Latitude 84° North
Time 23 24 h GMT

Look at the two pictures. What are the differences between the temperatures, the latitudes and the times?

All numbers have a sign. Positive numbers have a + sign in front of them although we do not always write it. Negative (or minus) numbers have a − sign in front of them. We *always* write the negative sign.

The positions of positive and negative numbers can be put on a number line, as below.

$$-10 \ -9 \ -8 \ -7 \ -6 \ -5 \ -4 \ -3 \ -2 \ -1 \ 0 \ 1 \ 2 \ 3 \ 4 \ 5 \ 6 \ 7 \ 8 \ 9 \ 10$$

This is very useful, as it helps us to compare positive and negative numbers and also to add and subtract them.

Example 2.5 ▷

Which is bigger, −7 or −3?

Because −3 is further to the right on the line, it is the larger number, we can write −7 < −3.

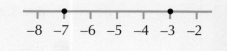

$$-8 \ -7 \ -6 \ -5 \ -4 \ -3 \ -2$$

Example 2.6 ▷

Work out the answers to   **a**   3 − 2 − 5   **b**   −3 − 5 + 4 − 2

a   Starting at zero and 'jumping' along the number line gives an answer of −4.

b   −3 − 5 + 4 − 2 = −6

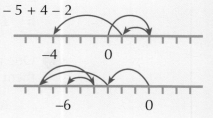

Example 2.7 ▷

Work out the answers to   **a**   −2 − +4   **b**   −6 − − 3 + −2

a   Rewrite as −2 − 4 and count along a number line: −2 − 4 = −6

b   Rewrite as −6 + 3 − 2 and count along a number line: −6 + 3 − 2 = −5

1 Put the correct sign, > or <, between each pair of numbers.

a −5 ... 4 **b** −7 ... −10 **c** 3 ... −3 **d** −12 ... −2

2 Find the number that is halfway between each pair of numbers.

a −8 −2 **b** −6 +3 **c** −9 −1

3 Work out the answer to each of these.

a $6 - 9$ **b** $4 - 3$ **c** $2 - 7$ **d** $3 + 9$ **e** $1 - 3$ **f** $4 - 4$

g $-6 + 9$ **h** $-4 - 1$ **i** $-7 - 3$ **j** $-1 + 8$ **k** $-2 - 3$ **l** $-14 + 7$

m $-2 - 3 + 4$ **n** $-1 + 1 - 2$ **o** $-3 + 4 - 7$ **p** $-102 + 103 - 5$

4 Copy each of these calculations and then fill in the missing numbers.

a $3 + +1 = 4$
$3 + 0 = 3$
$3 + -1 = 2$
$3 + -2 = ...$
$3 + ... = ...$
$3 + ... = ...$

b $-2 - +1 = -3$
$-2 - 0 = -2$
$-2 - -1 = -1$
$-2 - -2 = ...$
$-2 - ... = ...$
$-2 - ... = ...$

c $4 - +2 = 2$
$3 - +1 = 2$
$2 - 0 = 2$
$1 - -1 = ...$
$0 - ... = ...$
$... - ... = ...$

5 Work out the answer to each of these.

a $+3 - +2$ **b** $-4 - -3$ **c** $+7 - -6$ **d** $-7 + -3$ **e** $+7 - +3$

f $-9 - -5$ **g** $-6 + +6$ **h** $+6 - -7$ **i** $-6 + -6$ **j** $-1 + -8$

k $+5 - +7$ **l** $7 - -5$ **m** $-2 - -3 + -4$ **n** $- +1 + +1 - +2$

6 Find the missing number to make each of these true.

a $+2 + -6 = \boxed{}$ **b** $+4 + \boxed{} = +7$ **c** $-4 + \boxed{} = 0$

d $+5 + \boxed{} = -1$ **e** $+3 + +4 = \boxed{}$ **f** $\boxed{} - -5 = +7$

g $\boxed{} - +5 = +2$ **h** $+6 + \boxed{} = 0$ **i** $\boxed{} - -5 = -2$

j $+2 + -2 = \boxed{}$ **k** $\boxed{} - +2 = -4$ **l** $-2 + -4 = \boxed{}$

7 a A fish is 10 m below the surface of the water. A fish eagle is 15 m above the water. How many metres must the bird descend to get the fish?

b Alf has £25 in the bank. He writes a cheque for £35. How much has he got in the bank now?

8 In a magic square, the numbers in any row, column or diagonal add up to give the same answer. Copy and complete each of these magic squares.

a

−7	0	−8
−2		−3

b

−2		−4
		−3
		−8

c

0		−13	−3
	−5		
−7	−9	−10	
−12			−15

A maths test consists of 20 questions. Three points are given for a correct answer and two points are deducted if an answer is wrong or not attempted.

- Show that it is possible to get a score of zero.

- Show clearly that all the possible scores are multiples of 5.

- What happens when there are four points for a correct answer and minus two for a wrong answer? Investigate what happens when the points awarded and deducted are changed.

Note: A computer spreadsheet is useful for this activity.

Estimates

UNITED v CITY

CROWD	41 923
SCORE	2 – 1
TIME OF FIRST GOAL	42 min 13 sec
PRICE OF A PIE	95p
CHILDREN	33% off normal ticket prices

Which of the numbers above can be approximated? Which need to be given exactly?

You should have an idea if the answer to a calculation is about the right size or not. There are some ways of checking answers. First, when it is a multiplication, you can check that the final digit is correct. Second, you can round numbers off and do a mental calculation to see if an answer is about the right size. Third, you can check by doing the inverse operation.

Example 2.8 ▷ Explain why these calculations must be wrong.

    a $23 \times 45 = 1053$ **b** $19 \times 59 = 121$

    a The last digit should be 5, because the product of the last digits is 15. That is, $23 \times 45 \ = \ \ldots 5$

    b The answer is roughly $20 \times 60 = 1200$.

Example 2.9 ▷ Estimate answers to these calculations.

    a $\dfrac{21.3 + 48.7}{6.4}$ **b** 31.2×48.5 **c** $359 \div 42$

    a Round off the numbers on the top to $20 + 50 = 70$. Round off 6.4 to 7. Then $70 \div 7 = 10$.

    b Round off to 30×50, which is $3 \times 5 \times 100 = 1500$.

    c Round off to $360 \div 40$, which is $36 \div 4 = 9$.

Example 2.10 ▶ By using the inverse operation, check if each calculation is correct.

a $450 \div 6 = 75$ **b** $310 - 59 = 249$

a By the inverse operation, $450 = 6 \times 75$. This is true and can be checked mentally: $6 \times 70 = 420$, $6 \times 5 = 30$, $420 + 30 = 450$.

b By the inverse operation, $310 = 249 + 59$. This must end in 8 as $9 + 9 = 18$, so it cannot be correct.

Exercise 2D

1 Explain why these calculations must be wrong.

a $24 \times 42 = 1080$ **b** $51 \times 73 = 723$ **c** $\dfrac{34.5 + 63.2}{9.7} = 20.07$

d $360 \div 8 = 35$ **e** $354 - 37 = 323$

2 Estimate the answer to each of these problems.

a $2768 - 392$ **b** 231×18 **c** $792 \div 38$ **d** $\dfrac{36.7 + 23.2}{14.1}$

e 423×423 **f** $157.2 \div 38.2$ **g** $\dfrac{135.7 - 68.2}{15.8 - 8.9}$ **h** $\dfrac{38.9 \times 61.2}{39.6 - 18.4}$

(FM) 3 Amy bought 6 bottles of pop at 46p per bottle. The shopkeeper asked her for £3.16. Without working out the correct answer, explain why this is wrong.

(FM) 4 A first class stamp is 27p. I need eight. Will £2 be enough to pay for them? Explain your answer clearly.

(FM) 5 In a shop I bought a 53p comic and a £1.47 model car. The till said £54.47. Why?

6 Which is the best approximation for $50.7 - 39.2$?

a $506 - 392$ **b** $51 - 39$ **c** $50 - 39$ **d** $5.06 - 3.92$

7 Which is the best approximation for 19.3×42.6?

a 20×40 **b** 19×42 **c** 19×40 **d** 20×42

8 Which is the best estimate for $54.6 \div 10.9$?

a $500 \div 100$ **b** $54 \div 11$ **c** $50 \div 11$ **d** $55 \div 11$

9 Estimate the number the arrow is pointing to.

(FM) 10 Delroy had £10. In his shopping basket he had a magazine costing £2.65, some batteries costing £1.92 and a tape costing £4.99. Without adding up the numbers, how could Delroy be sure he had enough to buy the goods in the basket? Explain a quick way for Delroy to find out if he could afford a 45p bar of chocolate as well.

The first 15 **square numbers** are 1, 4, 9, 16, 25, 36, 49, 64, 81, 100, 121, 144, 169, 196 and 225. The inverse operation of squaring a number is to find its **square root**. So $\sqrt{121} = 11$. Only the square numbers have integer square roots. Other square roots have to be estimated or found using a calculator.

For example, to find the square root of 30 use a diagram like that on the right, to estimate that $\sqrt{30} \approx 5.48$. (A check shows that $5.48^2 = 30.03$.)

Here is another example. Find $\sqrt{45}$.

The diagram shows that $\sqrt{45} \approx 6.7$. (Check: $6.7^2 = 44.89$)

Use the above method to find $\sqrt{20}$, $\sqrt{55}$, $\sqrt{75}$, $\sqrt{110}$, $\sqrt{140}$, $\sqrt{200}$.

Check your answers with a calculator.

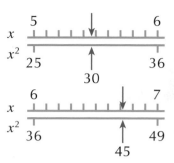

Column method for addition and subtraction

Look at the picture. What is wrong?

You may have several ways of adding and subtracting numbers, such as estimation or using a number line. Here you will be shown how to set out additions and subtractions using the column method. You may already have learnt about 'lining up the units digit'. This is not strictly correct. What you do is 'line up the decimal points'.

Example 2.11 ▷   Work out, without using a calculator: **a** $3.27 + 14.8$ **b** $12.8 - 3.45$

a   Write the numbers in columns, lining up the decimal points. You should fill the gap with a zero.

$$\begin{array}{r} 3.27 \\ + 14.80 \\ \hline 18.07 \\ 1 \end{array}$$

Note the carry digit in the units column, because $2 + 8 = 10$.

b   Write the numbers in columns and fill the gap with a zero.

$$\begin{array}{r} {}^{0\ 1\ \ 7\ 1} \\ \cancel{1}2.\cancel{8}0 \\ - \ \ 3.45 \\ \hline 9.35 \end{array}$$

Note that, because you cannot take 5 from 0, you have to borrow from the next column. This means that 8 becomes 7 and zero becomes 10.

Example 2.12 ▷   Work out 3.14 + 14.5 − 8.72.

This type of problem needs to be done in two stages. First, do the addition and then do the subtraction.

$$
\begin{array}{r}
3.14 \\
+\ 14.50 \\
\hline
17.64
\end{array}
\qquad
\begin{array}{r}
{}^{0\ 16\ 1}\\
\cancel{17}.64 \\
-\ \ 8.72 \\
\hline
8.92
\end{array}
$$

Exercise 2E

1   By means of a drawing, show how you would use a number line to work out the answers to these.

   a   2.4 + 3.7   **b**   5.3 + 7.45   **c**   8.4 − 5.6   **d**   9.4 − 4.86

2   Repeat the calculations in Question 1 using the column method. Show all your working.

3   Use the column method to work out the following additions.

   a   37.1 + 14.2   **b**   32.6 + 15.73   **c**   6.78 + 4.59   **d**   9.62 + 0.7

   e   4.79 + 1.2   **f**   6.08 + 2.16   **g**   1.2 + 3.41 + 4.56

   h   76.57 + 312.5 + 6.08

4   Use the column method to work out the following subtractions.

   a   37.1 − 14.2   **b**   32.6 − 15.73   **c**   6.78 − 4.59   **d**   9.62 − 0.7

   e   4.79 − 1.2   **f**   6.08 − 2.16   **g**   1.2 + 3.41 − 4.56

   h   76.57 + 312.5 − 6.08

Extension Work

$6 \times 8 = 48$ $6 \times 0.8 = 4.8$ $0.6 \times 0.8 = 0.48$

When these calculations are set out in columns, they look like this:

$$
\begin{array}{r}
8 \\
\times\ 6 \\
\hline
48
\end{array}
\qquad
\begin{array}{r}
0.8 \\
\times\ 6.0 \\
\hline
4.8
\end{array}
\qquad
\begin{array}{r}
0.8 \\
\times\ 0.6 \\
\hline
0.48
\end{array}
$$

The column method does not work when we multiply decimals.

Use a calculator to find out the rules for where the decimal point goes in multiplication problems such as:

3×0.2 5×0.7 0.3×0.9 0.2×0.6 0.03×0.5

Solving problems

A bus starts at Barnsley and makes four stops before reaching Penistone. At Barnsley 23 people get on. At Dodworth 12 people get off and 14 people get on. At Silkstone 15 people get off and 4 people get on. At Hoylandswaine 5 people get off and 6 people get on. At Cubley 9 people get off and 8 get on. At Penistone the rest of the passengers get off. How many people are on the bus?

When you solve problems, you need to develop a strategy: that is, a way to go about the problem. You also have to decide which mathematical operation you need to solve it. For example, is it addition, subtraction, multiplication or division or a combination of these? Something else you must do is to read the question fully before starting. The answer to the problem above is one! The driver.

Read the questions below carefully.

Exercise 2F

FM **1** It cost six people £15 to go to the cinema. How much would it cost eight people?

FM **2** Ten pencils cost £4.50. How much would seven pencils cost?

3 30 can be worked out as 33 − 3. Can you find two other ways of working out 30 using three equal digits?

4 Arrange the numbers 1, 2, 3 and 4 in each of these to make the problem correct.

a $\boxed{} + \boxed{} = \boxed{} + \boxed{}$ **b** $\boxed{} \times \boxed{} = \boxed{}\boxed{}$ **c** $\boxed{}\boxed{} \div \boxed{} = \boxed{}$

FM **5** A water tank holds 500 litres. How much has been used if there is 143.7 litres left in the tank?

6 Strips of paper are 40 cm long. They are stuck together with a 10 cm overlap.

a How long would two strips glued together be?
b How long would four strips glued together be?

FM **7** A can of coke and a Kit-Kat together cost 80p. Two cans of coke and a Kit-Kat together cost £1.30. How much would three cans of coke and four Kit-Kats cost?

8 To make a number chain, start with any number.

When the number is even, divide it by 2.

When the number is odd, multiply it by 3 and add 1.

If you start with 13, the chain becomes 13, 40, 20, 10, 5, 16, 8, 4, 2, 1, 4, 2, 1, …

The chain repeats 4, 2, 1, 4, 2, 1. So, stop the chain when it gets to 1.

Start with other numbers below 20. What is the longest chain you can make before you get to 1?

9 If $135 \times 44 = 5940$, write down, without calculating, the value of:
   a 13.5×4.4 **b** 1.35×44 **c** 1.35×4.4 **d** 1350×440

10 Find four consecutive odd numbers that add up to 80.

Using the numbers 1, 2, 3 and 4 and any mathematical signs, make all of the numbers from 1 to 10.

For example: $2 \times 3 - 4 - 1 = 1$, $4 \times 2 - 3 = 5$

Once you have found all the numbers up to 10, can you find totals above 10?

LEVEL BOOSTER

3
I can add and subtract whole numbers.
I can remember simple multiplication facts.
I can solve problems involving whole numbers.

4
I can use and understand place value.
I can remember multiplication facts up to 10×10.
I can add and subtract decimals up to two decimal places.
I can multiply and divide whole numbers by 10 or 100.

5
I can estimate answers and check if an answer is about right.
I can multiply and divide decimals by 10, 100 and 1000.
I can add and subtract using negative and positive numbers.
I can tackle mathematical problems.

National Test questions

1 *2006 Paper 1*

Add **three** to the number on each number line.

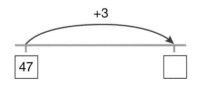 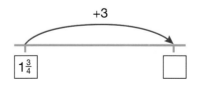 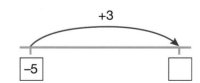

2 *2005 Paper 2*

A meal in a restaurant costs the same for each person.
For **11** people the cost is **£253**.

What is the total cost for 12 people?

3 *2003 Paper 1*

When the wind blows, it feels colder.
The stronger the wind, the colder it feels.

Fill in the gaps in the table.
The first row is done for you.

Wind strength	Temperature out of the wind (°C)	How much colder it feels in the wind (°C)	Temperature it feels in the wind (°C)
Moderate breeze	5	7 degrees colder	–2
Fresh breeze	–8	11 degrees colder	…
Strong breeze	–4	… degrees colder	–20
Gale	…	23 degrees colder	–45

4 *2003 4–6 Paper 2*

The table shows how much it costs to go to a cinema.

Mrs Jones (aged 35), her daughter (aged 12), her son (aged 10) and a friend (aged 65) want to go to the cinema.

They are not sure whether to go before 6pm or after 6pm.

How much will they save if they go **after** 6pm?

Show your working.

	Before 6pm	After 6pm
Adult	£3.20	£4.90
Child (14 or under)	£2.50	£3.50
Senior Citizen (60 or over)	£2.95	£4.90

5 *2006 Paper 2*

A bottle contains 250 ml of cough mixture.

One adult and **one child** need to take cough mixture **four times a day** for **five** days.
Will there be enough cough mixture in the bottle?
Explain your answer.

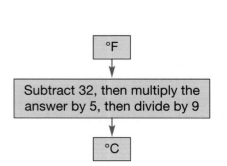

250 ml

Adult: Take **10 ml** four times a day

Child: Take **5 ml** four times a day

6 *2003 4–6 Paper 2*

a The thermometer shows Alan's temperature.

Alan's normal temperature is **37°C**.
How many degrees higher than normal is Alan's temperature?

b On Monday morning, Bina's temperature was **39.2°C**.
By Tuesday morning, Bina's temperature had **fallen** by **1.3°C**.
What was Bina's temperature on Tuesday morning?

c You can measure temperature in °C or in °F.
The diagram shows how to convert °F to °C.
The highest temperature recorded in a human was **115.7°F**.
What is this temperature in **°C**?

Show your working.

°F

↓

Subtract 32, then multiply the answer by 5, then divide by 9

↓

°C

This chapter is going to show you

- How to estimate and calculate perimeters and areas of 2-D shapes
- How to calculate the area of a rectangle
- How to draw 3-D shapes and how to calculate the surface area of a cuboid

What you should already know

- How to measure and draw lines
- How to find the perimeter of a shape
- Area is measured in square centimetres
- How to draw the net of a cube
- The names of 3-D shapes such as the cube and cuboid

Length, perimeter and area

The metric units of length in common use are: the millimetre (mm)
the centimetre (cm)
the metre (m)
the kilometre (km)

The metric units of area in common use are: the square millimetre (mm^2)
the square centimetre (cm^2)
the square metre (m^2)
the square kilometre (km^2)

Example 3.1

The length of this line is 72 mm or 7.2 cm.

Example 3.2

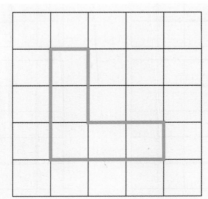

The side of each square on the grid represents 1 cm.

The perimeter of the L-shape = 1 + 2 + 2 + 1 + 3 + 3
= 12 cm

By counting the squares, the area of the L-shape = 5 cm^2.

Example 3.3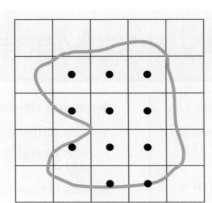

Estimate the area of the shape.

Each square on the grid has an area of 1 cm².

Mark each square which is at least half a square with a dot.

There are 11 dotted squares. So, an estimate for the area of the shape is 11 cm².

Exercise 3A

(1) Measure the length of each of the following lines. Give your answer in centimetres.

a

b

c

d

e

(2) Find the perimeter of each of these shapes by using your ruler to measure the length of each side.

a 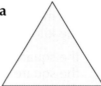   b   c    d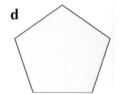

(3) Copy these shapes onto 1 cm squared paper. Find the perimeter and area of each shape.

a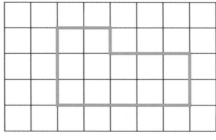

b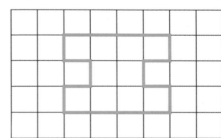

c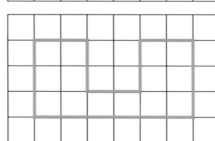

d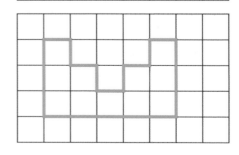

4 Estimate the area of each of these shapes. Each square on the grid represents one square centimetre.

a

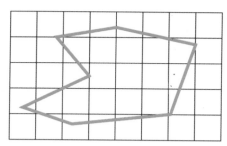

b

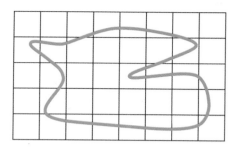

Extension Work

Working in groups, draw the outline of each person's hand (or foot) on 1 cm squared paper. Estimate the area of each hand (or foot).

Make a display of all the hands (and/or feet) for your classroom.

Perimeter and area of rectangles

Length (*l*)

Width (*w*)

The perimeter of a rectangle is the total distance around the shape.

Perimeter = 2 lengths + 2 widths

$$P = 2l + 2w$$ Unit is mm, cm or m.

The area of the rectangle is the amount of space inside the shape.

Area = length × width

$$A = l \times w \text{ or } A = lw$$ Unit is mm², cm² or m².

Example 3.4 ▶ Find the perimeter and area of each of the following.

a

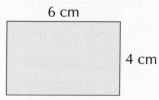

6 cm

4 cm

b

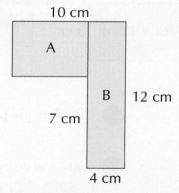

10 cm

A

B 12 cm

7 cm

4 cm

$P = 2 \times 6 + 2 \times 4$
$= 12 + 8$
$= 20$ cm

$A = 6 \times 4$
$= 24$ cm²

$P = 10 + 12 + 4 + 7 + 6 + 5$
$= 44$ cm

Total area = Area of A + Area of B
$= 6 \times 5 + 12 \times 4$
$= 30 + 48$
$= 78$ cm²

Exercise 3B

1 Find the perimeter of each rectangle.

a 5 cm, 5 cm

b 15 cm, 8 cm

c 8 m, 7 m

d 24 mm, 30 mm

FM **2** **a** Find the perimeter of this room.

b Skirting board is sold in 3 m lengths. How many lengths are needed to go around the four walls of the room?

9 m, 6 m

3 A paving slab measures 0.8 m by 0.6 m. Find the perimeter of the slab.

4 Find the area of each rectangle.

a 4 cm, 4 cm

b 12 cm, 7 cm

c 10 m, 6 m

d 25 mm, 16 mm

e 15 cm, 10 cm

f 20 cm, 8 cm

g 9 cm, 6 cm

h 16 cm, 8 cm

5 Find the length of each of the following rectangles.

a Area = 12 cm², 3 cm

b Area = 20 cm², 2 cm

c Area = 24 m², 4 m

d Area = 48 cm², 6 cm

6 Calculate the perimeter of this square. 25 cm²

7 Copy and complete the table for rectangles **a** to **f**.

	Length	Width	Perimeter	Area
a	8 cm	6 cm		
b	20 cm	15 cm		
c	10 cm		30 cm	
d		5 m	22 m	
e	7 m			42 m²
f		10 mm		250 mm²

8 Find **i** the perimeter and **ii** the area of each of the following compound shapes.

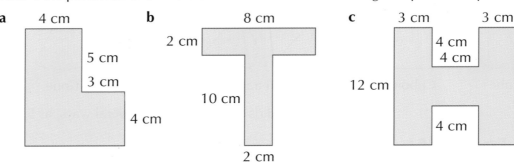

a 4 cm, 5 cm, 3 cm, 4 cm

b 8 cm, 2 cm, 10 cm, 2 cm

c 3 cm, 3 cm, 4 cm, 4 cm, 12 cm, 4 cm

9 Phil finds the area of this compound shape.

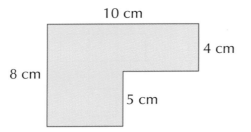

10 cm, 4 cm, 8 cm, 5 cm

This is his working:

Area = 10 x 4 + 8 x 5
= 40 + 40
= 80 cm²

a Explain why he is wrong.

b Calculate the correct answer.

 10 Sandra makes a picture frame from a rectangular piece of card for a photograph of her favourite group.

 a Find the area of the photograph.

b Find the area of the card she uses.

c Find the area of the border.

20 cm, 14 cm, 24 cm, 30 cm

Extension **Work**

1 How many rectangles can you draw with a fixed perimeter of 20 cm but each one having a different area?

 2 **Sheep pens**

A farmer has 60 m of fence to make a rectangular sheep pen against a wall.

Find the length and width of the pen in order to make its area as large as possible.

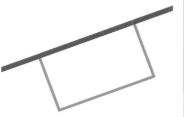

3-D shapes

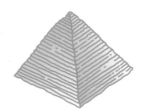

You should be able to recognise and name the following 3-D shapes or solids.

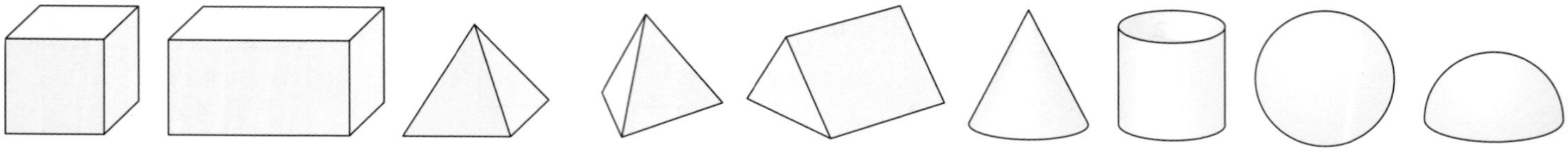

Cube   Cuboid   Pyramid   Tetrahedron   Triangular prism   Cone   Cylinder   Sphere   Hemisphere

Some of these solids can be drawn in several ways, as Example 3.5 shows.

Example 3.5

For a cube

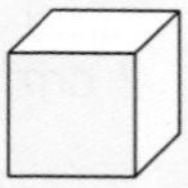

On a square grid

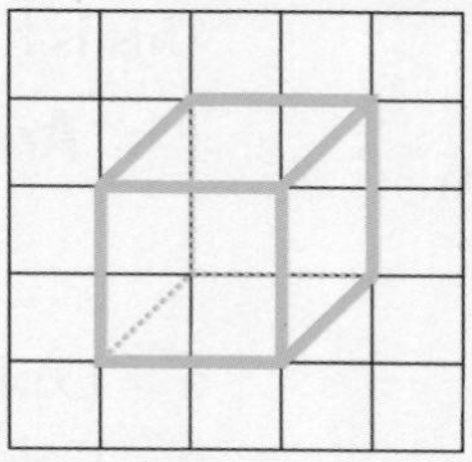

Not easy to draw to scale. Hidden edges can be dotted.

As a net

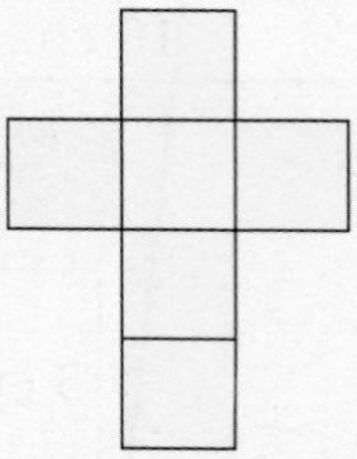

Used to make the shape when tabs are added.

On an isometric grid

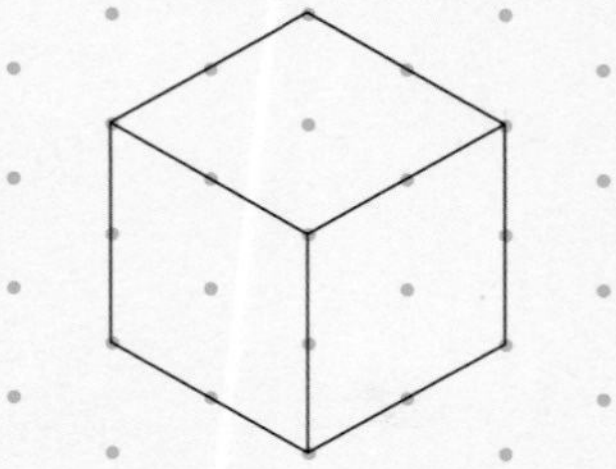

Used to draw accurately. Each column of dots must be vertical.

Exercise 3C

1 A cuboid has six faces, eight vertices and 12 edges.

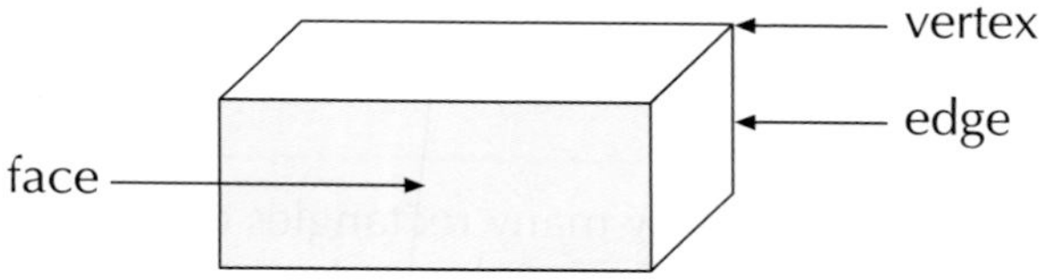

vertex

edge

face

How many faces, vertices and edges do each of the following 3-D shapes have?

a

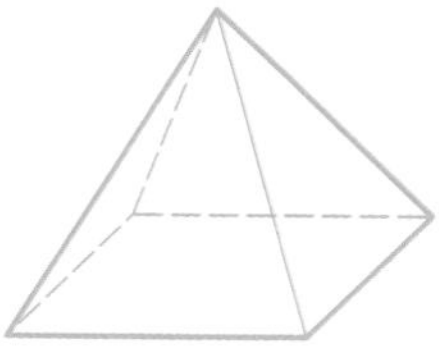

b

c

Square-based pyramid   Triangular prism   Tetrahedron

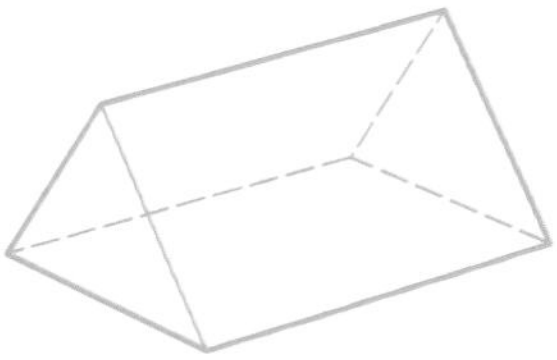

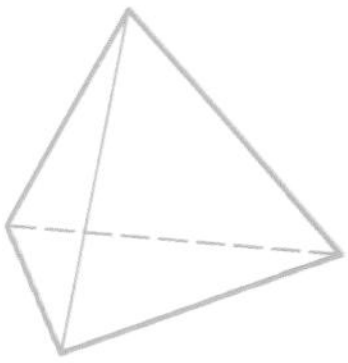

2 On squared paper, draw accurate nets for each of the following cuboids.

a   4 cm

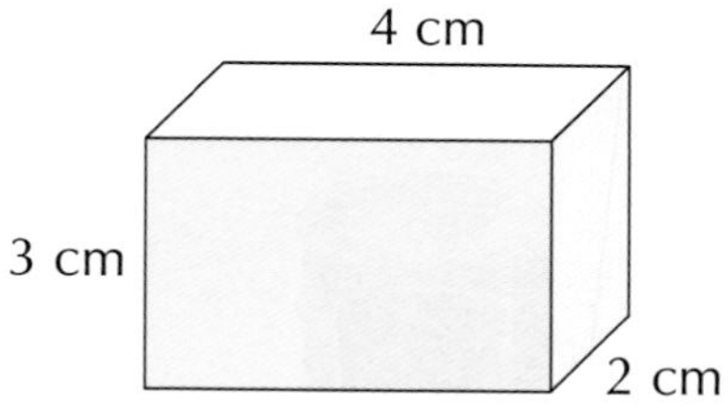

3 cm

2 cm

b   2 cm

2 cm

5 cm

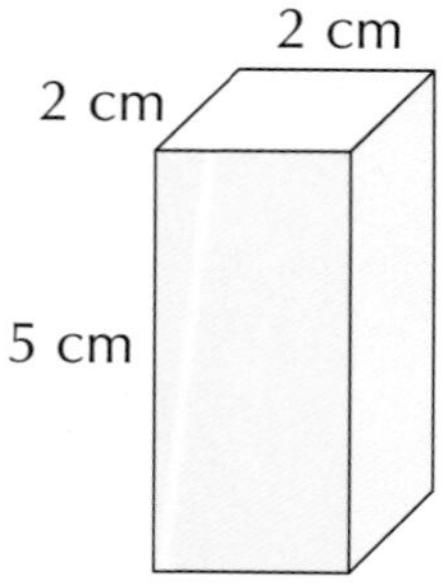

3 The cuboid
below is drawn on an isometric grid.
It is made from three cubes.

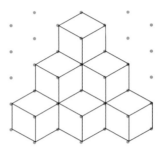

On a copy of the grid:

a add another cube to make an
L shape.

b add another two cubes to make
a T shape.

c add another two cubes to make
a + shape.

4 How many cubes are required to make this solid?

Draw other similar solids of your own on an isometric grid.

5 Draw each of the following cuboids accurately on an isometric grid.

a 6 cm   5 cm   4 cm

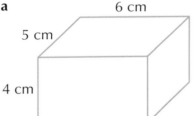

b 2 cm   2 cm   5 cm

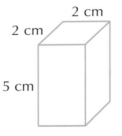

c 5 cm   2 cm   1 cm

Extension **Work**

1 Euler's theorem

Copy and complete the following table for seven different polyhedrons.
Ask your teacher to show you these 3-D shapes.

Solid	Number of faces	Number of vertices	Number of edges
Cuboid			
Square-based pyramid			
Triangular prism			
Tetrahedron			
Hexagonal prism			
Octahedron			
Dodecahedron			

Find a formula that connects the number of faces, vertices and edges.

This formula is named after Léonard Euler, a famous eighteenth-century
Swiss mathematician.

2 Pentominoes

A pentomino is a 2-D shape made from five squares that touch side to side. Here are two examples.

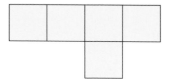 

a Draw on squared paper as many different pentominoes as you can.

b How many of these pentominoes are nets that make an open cube?

3 Four cubes

On an isometric grid, draw all the possible different solids that can be made from four cubes. Here is an example.

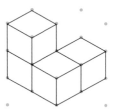

Surface area of cubes and cuboids

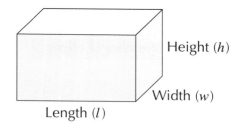

The surface area of a cuboid is found by calculating the total area of its six faces.

Area of top and bottom faces = 2 × length × width = $2lw$

Area of front and back faces = 2 × length × height = $2lh$

Area of the two sides = 2 × width × height = $2wh$

Surface area of cuboid = **$S = 2lw + 2lh + 2wh$**

Example 3.6 ▷ Find the surface area of this cuboid.

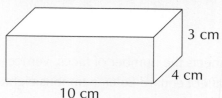

$S = (2 \times 10 \times 4) + (2 \times 10 \times 3) + (2 \times 4 \times 3)$

$= 80 + 60 + 24$

$= 164 \text{ cm}^2$

1 Find the surface area for each of the following cubes.

a 4 cm, 4 cm, 4 cm

b 6 cm, 6 cm, 6 cm

c 8 cm, 8 cm, 8 cm

d 9 cm, 9 cm, 9 cm

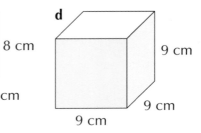

2 Find the surface area of this unit cube.

1 cm, 1 cm, 1 cm

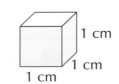

3 Find the surface area for each of the cubes with these edge lengths.

a 2 cm   **b** 5 cm   **c** 10 cm   **d** 12 cm

4 Find the total surface area of this 3-D shape.

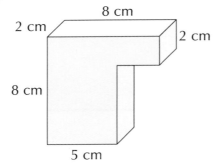

8 cm
2 cm   2 cm
8 cm
5 cm

5 Find the surface area for each of the following cuboids.

a 10 cm, 5 cm, 6 cm

b 3 cm, 12 cm, 2 cm

c 5 cm, 4 cm, 15 cm

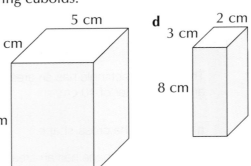

d 2 cm, 3 cm, 8 cm

6 Find the surface area of the outside of this open water tank.
(A cuboid without a top.)

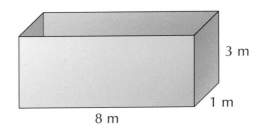

3 m
1 m
8 m

Extension **Work**

Cubes to cuboids

You will need 12 unit cubes for this activity.

All 12 cubes are arranged to form a cuboid.

How many different cuboids can you make?

Which one has the greatest surface area?

LEVEL BOOSTER

4
I can draw and measure straight lines.
I can find the perimeter of a 2-D shape.
I can find the area of a 2-D shape by counting squares.

5
I can find the area of a rectangle using the formula Area = length × width.
I can draw 3-D shapes on an isometric grid.
I can draw the net of a cuboid.

6
I can find the surface area of a cuboid.

National Test questions

1   *2000 Paper 2*

The shaded rectangle has an area of 4 cm²
and a perimeter of 10 cm.

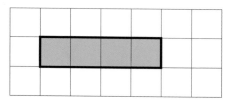

a   Look at the cross-shape.

The cross-shape has an area of ... cm²
and a perimeter of ... cm.

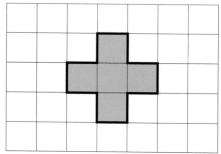

b Draw a shape with an area of 6 cm².

c What is the perimeter of your shape?

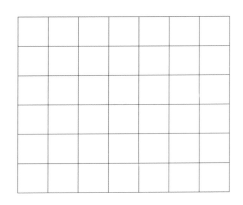

2 *2001 Paper 2*

Alika has a box of square tiles.

The tiles are three different sizes.

1 cm
1 cm
1 by 1 tile

2 cm
2 cm
2 by 2 tile

3 cm
3 cm
3 by 3 tile

She also has a mat that is 6 cm by 6 cm.

36 of the 1 by 1 tiles will cover the mat.

a How many of the 2 by 2 tiles will cover the mat?

b How many of the 3 by 3 tiles will cover the mat?

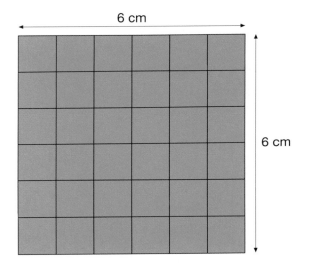

6 cm

6 cm

c Alika glues three tiles on her mat like this. Complete the gaps below.

She could cover the rest of the mat by using another two 3 by 3 tiles and another ... 1 by 1 tiles.

She could cover the rest of the mat by using another two 2 by 2 tiles and another ... 1 by 1 tiles.

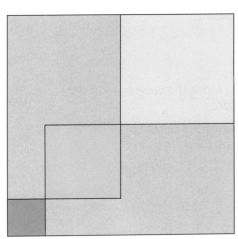

3 *2006 4–6 Paper 1*

I have a square piece of paper.

The diagram shows information about this square, labelled A.

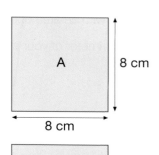

I fold square A **in half** to make rectangle B.

Then I fold rectangle B **in half** to make square C.

Complete the table below to show the area and perimeter of each shape.

	Area	Perimeter
Square A	cm²	cm
Rectangle B	cm²	cm
Square C	cm²	cm

4 *2000 Paper 2*

I make a model with 6 cubes.

The drawings show my model from different views.

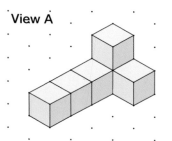

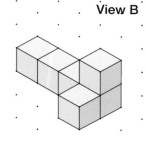

a I join one more cube to my model.

The drawing from view A shows where I join the cube.

Complete the drawing from view B.

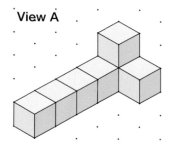

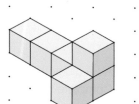

b Then I move the cube to a different position.

Complete the drawing from view B.

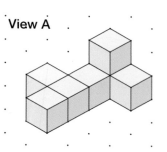

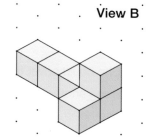

5 *2004 4–6 Paper 2*

Look at this shape made from six cubes.
Four cubes are white.
Two cubes are grey.

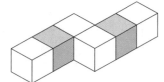

a Part of the shape is rotated through 90° to make the shape below.
Copy this and shade the faces that are grey.

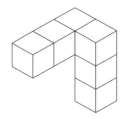

b After another rotation of 90°, the shape is a cuboid.
Draw this cuboid on a grid like the one below.

FM Design a bedroom

1 Here is a sketch of a plan for a bedroom.

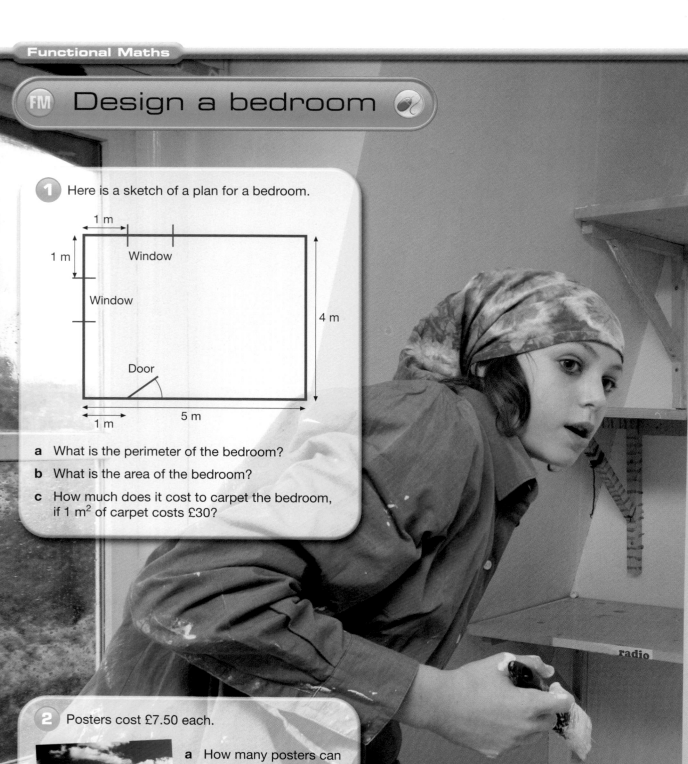

a What is the perimeter of the bedroom?

b What is the area of the bedroom?

c How much does it cost to carpet the bedroom, if 1 m^2 of carpet costs £30?

2 Posters cost £7.50 each.

a How many posters can you buy for £50?

b How much is left over?

Use catalogues or the Internet to find how much it would cost to buy all the furniture for the bedroom.

3 Here are sketches of the door and one of the windows.

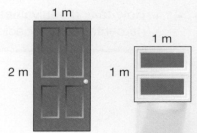

The height of the bedroom is $2\frac{1}{2}$ m.

a Find the area of each wall in the bedroom that needs to be painted.

b What is the total area of all four walls?

c If a one-litre tin of paint covers 12 m², what is the minimum number of tins required to paint the walls?

Furniture challenge

4 Copy the plan of the bedroom onto centimetre-squared paper. Use a scale of 1 cm to $\frac{1}{2}$ m. Decide where you would put the following bedroom furniture. Use cut-outs to help.

Bed
2 m by 1 m

Bedside table
$\frac{1}{2}$ m by $\frac{1}{2}$ m

Wardrobe
$1\frac{1}{2}$ m by $\frac{1}{2}$ m

Chest of drawers
1 m by $\frac{1}{2}$ m

Desk
1 m by $\frac{1}{2}$ m

CHAPTER **4** Number **2**

This chapter is going to show you	What you should already know
• How to extend your knowledge of fractions and percentages • How to add simple fractions • How to find equivalent fractions, percentages and decimals	• How to change an improper fraction into a mixed number • How to use decimal notation for tenths and hundredths • How to recognise simple equivalent fractions

Fractions

These diagrams show you five ways to split a 4 by 4 grid into quarters.

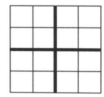 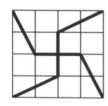 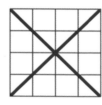 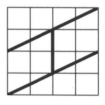 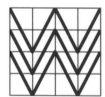

How many more different ways can you find to do this?

What about splitting the 4 by 4 grid into halves?

Example 4.1 ▷ Write down the fraction of each shape that is shaded.

a 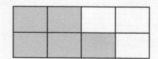 b  c

  a $\dfrac{5}{8}$ The shape is divided into 8 equal parts (the denominator) and 5 parts are shaded (the numerator).

  b $\dfrac{1}{4}$ The shape is divided into 4 equal parts (the denominator) and 1 part is shaded (the numerator).

  c $\dfrac{5}{6}$ The shape is divided into 6 equal parts (the denominator) and 5 parts are shaded (the numerator).

Example 4.2 ▶ Fill in the missing number in each of these equivalent fractions.

a $\dfrac{1}{3} = \dfrac{\square}{15}$　　　b $\dfrac{5}{8} = \dfrac{\square}{32}$　　　c $\dfrac{15}{27} = \dfrac{5}{\square}$

a Multiply by 5　　b Multiply by 4　　c Divide by 3

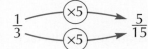　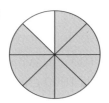　

Exercise 4A

1 Write down the fraction of each shape that is shaded.

a　　　　b　　　　c　　　　d

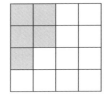

2 Draw a fraction diagram and shade it to show each fraction.

a $\dfrac{1}{4}$　　　b $\dfrac{2}{5}$　　　c $\dfrac{3}{8}$　　　d $\dfrac{1}{7}$

3 Copy and complete the following equivalent fraction series.

a $\dfrac{1}{2} = \dfrac{2}{\square} = \dfrac{\square}{6} = \dfrac{8}{\square} = \dfrac{\square}{20} = \dfrac{\square}{150}$

b $\dfrac{3}{4} = \dfrac{6}{\square} = \dfrac{\square}{12} = \dfrac{12}{\square} = \dfrac{\square}{40} = \dfrac{\square}{160}$

4 Find the missing number in each of these equivalent fractions.

a $\dfrac{2}{3} = \dfrac{\square}{9}$　　　b $\dfrac{3}{8} = \dfrac{\square}{16}$　　　c $\dfrac{5}{9} = \dfrac{\square}{27}$

d $\dfrac{2}{5} = \dfrac{\square}{15}$　　　e $\dfrac{3}{7} = \dfrac{\square}{28}$　　　f $\dfrac{4}{9} = \dfrac{\square}{36}$

g $\dfrac{1}{5} = \dfrac{\square}{25}$　　　h $\dfrac{2}{11} = \dfrac{14}{\square}$　　　i $\dfrac{4}{9} = \dfrac{20}{\square}$

5 Cancel each of these fractions to its simplest form.

a $\dfrac{4}{12}$　　b $\dfrac{6}{9}$　　c $\dfrac{14}{21}$　　d $\dfrac{15}{20}$　　e $\dfrac{18}{20}$　　f $\dfrac{20}{50}$

g $\dfrac{8}{24}$　　h $\dfrac{6}{12}$　　i $\dfrac{4}{24}$　　j $\dfrac{12}{20}$　　k $\dfrac{16}{24}$　　l $\dfrac{25}{35}$

m $\dfrac{6}{14}$　　n $\dfrac{12}{9}$　　o $\dfrac{18}{27}$　　p $\dfrac{45}{20}$　　q $\dfrac{28}{10}$　　r $\dfrac{120}{40}$

6 Clocks have 12 divisions around the face. What fraction of a full turn does:

  a the minute hand turn through from 7:15 to 7:35?

  b the minute hand turn through from 8:25 to 9:25?

  c the hour hand turn through from 1:00 to 4:00?

  d the hour hand turn through from 4:00 to 5:30?

7 This compass rose has eight divisions around its face. What fraction of a turn takes you from:

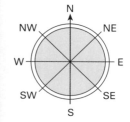

  a NW to SW clockwise?   **b** E to S anticlockwise?

  c NE to S clockwise?   **d** S to NE anticlockwise?

  e W to SE clockwise?   **f** N to NW clockwise?

8 Give each answer in its lowest terms.

  a 1 metre is 100 cm. What fraction of a metre is 35 cm?

  b 1 kilogram is 1000 grams. What fraction of a kilogram is 550 grams?

  c 1 hour is 60 minutes. What fraction of 1 hour is 33 minutes?

  d 1 kilometre is 1000 metres. What fraction of a kilometre is 75 metres?

Extension **Work**

There are 360° in one full turn. 90° is $\frac{90°}{360°} = \frac{1}{4}$ of a full turn.

1 What fraction of a full turn is each of these?

  a 60°   **b** 20°   **c** 180°   **d** 30°

  e 45°   **f** 36°   **g** 5°   **h** 450°

2 How many degrees is: **a** $\frac{1}{8}$ of a full turn?   **b** $\frac{1}{5}$ of a full turn?

3 360 was the number of days in a year according to the Ancient Egyptians. They also thought that numbers with lots of factors had magical properties. Find all the factors of 360.

4 Explain how the factors can be used to work out what fraction of a full turn is 40°.

Fractions and decimals

All of the grids below contain 100 squares. Some of the squares have been shaded in. In each case, write down the amount that has been shaded as a fraction, a percentage and a decimal. What connections can you see between the equivalent values?

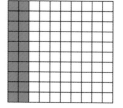 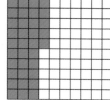 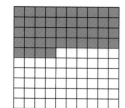 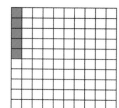 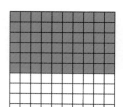 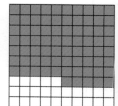

Example 4.3 ▷ Convert each of the following decimals to a fraction: **a** 0.65 **b** 0.44

a $0.65 = \frac{65}{100} = \frac{13}{20}$ (cancel by 5)   **b** $0.44 = \frac{44}{100} = \frac{11}{25}$ (cancel by 4)

Example 4.4 ▷ Convert each of the following fractions to a decimal: **a** $\frac{12}{25}$ **b** $\frac{7}{8}$

a Multiply top and bottom by 4: $\frac{12\ (\times 4)}{25\ (\times 4)} = \frac{48}{100} = 0.48$

b Multiply top and bottom by 12.5: $\frac{7\ (\times 12.5)}{8\ (\times 12.5)} = \frac{87.5}{100} = 0.875$

Example 4.5 ▷ Put the correct sign, < or >, between each pair of fractions **a** $\frac{5}{8} \ldots \frac{3}{5}$ **b** $\frac{16}{25} \ldots \frac{7}{10}$

a Convert to fractions out of 100 (or decimals):

$\frac{5}{8} = \frac{62.5}{100} = 0.625, \frac{3}{5} = \frac{60}{100} = 0.6$, so $\frac{5}{8} > \frac{3}{5}$

b Convert to fractions out of 100 (or decimals):

$\frac{16}{25} = \frac{64}{100} = 0.64, \frac{7}{10} = \frac{70}{100} = 0.7$, so $\frac{16}{25} < \frac{7}{10}$

Exercise 4B

1 Convert each of these top-heavy fractions to a mixed number.

a $\frac{3}{2}$ **b** $\frac{7}{5}$ **c** $\frac{9}{7}$ **d** $\frac{17}{8}$ **e** $\frac{15}{2}$ **f** $\frac{22}{7}$

g $\frac{32}{15}$ **h** $\frac{17}{5}$ **i** $\frac{12}{5}$ **j** $\frac{13}{6}$ **k** $\frac{9}{4}$ **l** $\frac{41}{10}$

2 Convert each of these mixed numbers to a top-heavy fraction.

a $1\frac{1}{4}$ **b** $2\frac{1}{2}$ **c** $3\frac{1}{6}$ **d** $4\frac{2}{7}$ **e** $5\frac{1}{8}$ **f** $2\frac{3}{5}$

g $1\frac{7}{8}$ **h** $3\frac{3}{4}$ **i** $3\frac{2}{5}$ **j** $2\frac{3}{11}$ **k** $4\frac{5}{8}$ **l** $3\frac{2}{9}$

3 Match the top-heavy fractions to improper fractions.

$\frac{5}{2}$ $\frac{7}{4}$ $\frac{7}{5}$ $\frac{11}{5}$

$2\frac{1}{2}$ $1\frac{2}{5}$ $1\frac{3}{4}$ $2\frac{1}{5}$

4 Convert each of the following decimals to a fraction.

a 0.2 **b** 0.28 **c** 0.35 **d** 0.85 **e** 0.9 **f** 0.16

g 0.24 **h** 0.48 **i** 0.95 **j** 0.05 **k** 0.99 **l** 0.27

5 Convert each of the following fractions to a decimal.

a $\frac{3}{10}$	**b** $\frac{4}{25}$	**c** $\frac{3}{20}$	**d** $\frac{3}{8}$	**e** $\frac{23}{100}$	**f** $\frac{6}{25}$
g $\frac{7}{50}$	**h** $\frac{14}{25}$	**i** $\frac{13}{20}$	**j** $\frac{11}{10}$	**k** $\frac{115}{50}$	**l** $\frac{26}{25}$

6 Put the correct sign, < or >, between each pair of fractions.

a $\frac{7}{50} \ldots \frac{2}{20}$ **b** $\frac{27}{50} \ldots \frac{13}{25}$ **c** $\frac{9}{10} \ldots \frac{22}{25}$

7 Put each set of fractions in order of size, smallest first.

a $\frac{7}{25}, \frac{3}{10}, \frac{1}{4}$ **b** $\frac{3}{4}, \frac{37}{50}, \frac{7}{10}$ **c** $1\frac{6}{25}, 1\frac{1}{4}, 1\frac{11}{50}$

8 Which of these fractions is nearer to 1, $\frac{5}{8}$ or $\frac{8}{5}$? Show all your working.

Extension Work

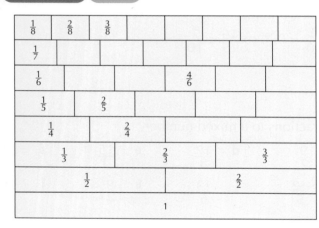

On squared paper outline an 8 × 8 grid.

Mark it off as shown. Then fill in the rest of the values in the boxes.

Use the diagram to put the correct sign (<, > or =) between each pair of fractions.

a $\frac{2}{7} \ldots \frac{1}{5}$ **b** $\frac{3}{8} \ldots \frac{1}{3}$ **c** $\frac{3}{4} \ldots \frac{6}{8}$

d $\frac{1}{2} \ldots \frac{4}{7}$ **e** $\frac{2}{8} \ldots \frac{1}{4}$ **f** $\frac{3}{7} \ldots \frac{1}{3}$

g $\frac{3}{5} \ldots \frac{2}{3}$ **h** $\frac{1}{2} \ldots \frac{5}{8}$ **i** $\frac{5}{8} \ldots \frac{3}{5}$

j $\frac{3}{6} \ldots \frac{1}{2}$ **k** $\frac{5}{7} \ldots \frac{3}{4}$ **l** $\frac{2}{3} \ldots \frac{4}{6}$

Adding and subtracting fractions

Look at the fraction chart and the number line. Explain how you could use the line to show that

$$1\frac{1}{2} + \frac{7}{8} = 2\frac{3}{8} \quad \text{and} \quad 1\frac{1}{2} - \frac{7}{8} = \frac{5}{8}.$$

$\frac{1}{8}$	$\frac{1}{4}$	$\frac{3}{8}$	$\frac{1}{2}$	$\frac{5}{8}$	$\frac{3}{4}$	$\frac{7}{8}$	1
$1\frac{1}{8}$	$1\frac{1}{4}$	$1\frac{3}{8}$	$1\frac{1}{2}$	$1\frac{5}{8}$	$1\frac{3}{4}$	$1\frac{7}{8}$	2
$2\frac{1}{8}$	$2\frac{1}{4}$	$2\frac{3}{8}$	$2\frac{1}{2}$	$2\frac{5}{8}$	$2\frac{3}{4}$	$2\frac{7}{8}$	3
$3\frac{1}{8}$	$3\frac{1}{4}$	$3\frac{3}{8}$	$3\frac{1}{2}$	$3\frac{5}{8}$	$3\frac{3}{4}$	$3\frac{7}{8}$	4

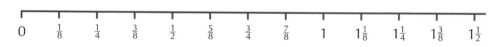

Example 4.6 ▶ Add the following fractions: **a** $2\frac{1}{4} + 1\frac{3}{8}$ **b** $\frac{1}{4} + \frac{5}{8}$

a Start at $2\frac{1}{4}$ on the fraction chart. Add 1 to take you to $3\frac{1}{4}$.
Then count on $\frac{3}{8}$ to $3\frac{5}{8}$.

b Start at $\frac{1}{4}$ on the number line and count on $\frac{5}{8}$ to take you to $\frac{7}{8}$.

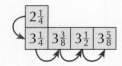

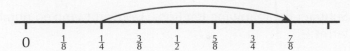

Example 4.7 ▶ Subtract the following fractions: **a** $2\frac{1}{4} - 1\frac{3}{8}$ **b** $1\frac{1}{4} - \frac{5}{8}$

a Start at $2\frac{1}{4}$ on the fraction chart. Subtract 1 to take you to $1\frac{1}{4}$.
Then count back $\frac{3}{8}$ to $\frac{7}{8}$.

b Start at $1\frac{1}{4}$ on the number line and count back $\frac{5}{8}$ to take you to $\frac{5}{8}$.

Example 4.8 ▶ Work out each of the following: **a** $\frac{2}{5} + \frac{1}{5}$ **b** $\frac{3}{7} + \frac{5}{7}$ **c** $\frac{2}{9} + \frac{5}{9} - \frac{1}{9}$

Unless you can use a fraction chart or a number line, fractions must have the same denominator before they can be added or subtracted. The numerator of the answer is just the sum (or difference) of the original numerators. The denominator does not change. Sometimes it is possible to cancel the answer to its lowest terms.

a $\frac{2}{5} + \frac{1}{5} = \frac{3}{5}$ **b** $\frac{3}{7} + \frac{5}{7} = \frac{8}{7} = 1\frac{1}{7}$ **c** $\frac{2}{9} + \frac{5}{9} - \frac{1}{9} = \frac{6}{9} = \frac{2}{3}$

Exercise 4C

1 Work out each of the following.

a $\frac{3}{7} + \frac{2}{7}$ **b** $\frac{3}{11} + \frac{4}{11}$ **c** $\frac{3}{5} + \frac{1}{5}$ **d** $\frac{7}{13} + \frac{3}{13}$

e $\frac{7}{11} - \frac{2}{11}$ **f** $\frac{4}{9} - \frac{2}{9}$ **g** $\frac{3}{7} - \frac{2}{7}$ **h** $\frac{3}{5} - \frac{1}{5}$

2 Work out each of the following. Cancel down to lowest terms.

a $\frac{3}{8} + \frac{1}{8}$ **b** $\frac{1}{12} + \frac{5}{12}$ **c** $\frac{3}{10} + \frac{1}{10}$ **d** $\frac{7}{15} + \frac{2}{15}$

e $\frac{4}{9} - \frac{1}{9}$ **f** $\frac{3}{10} - \frac{1}{10}$ **g** $\frac{5}{6} - \frac{1}{6}$ **h** $\frac{7}{12} - \frac{5}{12}$

3 Add the following fractions. The fraction chart and the number line on page 46 may help.

a $\frac{5}{8} + \frac{1}{2}$ **b** $1\frac{1}{8} + \frac{3}{8}$ **c** $2\frac{2}{8} + 1\frac{5}{8}$ **d** $1\frac{1}{2} + \frac{7}{8}$

e $1\frac{5}{8} + 1\frac{3}{4}$ **f** $2\frac{7}{8} + 1\frac{1}{4}$ **g** $1\frac{3}{8} + 2\frac{3}{8}$ **h** $\frac{3}{8} + 1\frac{1}{2} + 1\frac{3}{4}$

4 Add the following fractions. Convert to mixed numbers or cancel down to lowest terms.

a $\frac{1}{3} + \frac{1}{3}$ **b** $\frac{5}{6} + \frac{5}{6}$ **c** $\frac{3}{10} + \frac{3}{10}$ **d** $\frac{1}{9} + \frac{2}{9}$

e $\frac{4}{15} + \frac{13}{15}$ **f** $\frac{7}{9} + \frac{5}{9}$ **g** $\frac{5}{12} + 1\frac{1}{12}$ **h** $\frac{3}{7} + \frac{5}{7} + \frac{2}{7}$

5 Subtract the following fractions. The fraction chart and the number line on page 46 may help.

a $\frac{5}{8} - \frac{1}{2}$ **b** $2\frac{1}{8} - \frac{5}{8}$ **c** $2\frac{3}{8} - 1\frac{5}{8}$ **d** $1\frac{1}{2} - \frac{7}{8}$

e $2\frac{3}{4} - 1\frac{3}{8}$ **f** $2\frac{7}{8} - 1\frac{1}{4}$ **g** $3\frac{3}{8} - 1\frac{3}{4}$ **h** $1\frac{3}{4} + 1\frac{1}{2} - 1\frac{7}{8}$

6 Subtract the following fractions. Convert to mixed numbers or cancel down to lowest terms.

a $\frac{5}{7} - \frac{2}{7}$ **b** $\frac{5}{6} - \frac{1}{6}$ **c** $\frac{9}{10} - \frac{3}{10}$ **d** $\frac{8}{9} - \frac{2}{9}$

e $\frac{14}{15} - \frac{2}{15}$ **f** $\frac{7}{9} - \frac{4}{9}$ **g** $\frac{11}{12} - \frac{5}{12}$ **h** $\frac{3}{10} + \frac{9}{10} - \frac{5}{10}$

Extension Work

The Ancient Egyptians thought that 360 was a magical number because it had lots of factors.

They also used only fractions with 1 or 2 as the numerator, together with the commonly occurring fractions such as two-thirds, three-quarters, four-fifths and five-sixths.

Write down all the factors of 360 (or use your results from the extension work in Exercise 4A).

Write down the following fractions as equivalent fractions with a denominator of 360.

$$\frac{1}{2}, \frac{1}{3}, \frac{1}{4}, \frac{1}{5}, \frac{1}{6}, \frac{1}{8}, \frac{1}{9}, \frac{1}{10}, \frac{1}{12}$$

Use these results to work out:

a $\frac{1}{2} + \frac{1}{3}$ **b** $\frac{1}{2} + \frac{1}{6}$ **c** $\frac{1}{2} + \frac{1}{5}$ **d** $\frac{1}{3} + \frac{1}{4}$ **e** $\frac{1}{6} + \frac{1}{8}$

f $\frac{1}{3} - \frac{1}{5}$ **g** $\frac{1}{4} - \frac{1}{6}$ **h** $\frac{1}{8} - \frac{1}{10}$ **i** $\frac{1}{3} + \frac{1}{4} + \frac{1}{5}$ **j** $\frac{1}{6} + \frac{1}{12} - \frac{1}{4}$

Cancel down your answers to their simplest form.

Equivalences

Explain why BAG = 70%, HIDE = 2.2 and FED = $1\frac{1}{5}$.

Find the percentage value of CABBAGE. Find the decimal value of BADGE. Find the fraction value of CHIDE. Find the percentage, decimal and fraction value of other words you can make with these letters.

Example 4.9 ▷ Work out each of the following: **a** $\frac{2}{3}$ of 45p **b** $\frac{3}{7}$ of 140 cm **c** $4 \times \frac{3}{5}$

a First find $\frac{1}{3}$ of 45: $45 \div 3 = 15$. So, $\frac{2}{3}$ of 45p = $2 \times 15 = 30$p.

b First find $\frac{1}{7}$ of 140: $140 \div 7 = 20$. So, $\frac{3}{7}$ of 140 cm = $3 \times 20 = 60$ cm.

c $4 \times \frac{3}{5} = \frac{12}{5} = 2\frac{2}{5}$

Example 4.10 ▷ Work out the equivalent fraction, decimal and/or percentage for each of the following.

a 0.14 **b** 0.55 **c** 66% **d** 45% **e** $\frac{9}{25}$ **f** $\frac{3}{8}$

a $0.14 = 14\% = \frac{14}{100} = \frac{7}{50}$ **b** $0.55 = 55\% = \frac{55}{100} = \frac{11}{20}$

c $66\% = 0.66 = \frac{66}{100} = \frac{33}{50}$ **d** $45\% = 0.45 = \frac{45}{100} = \frac{9}{20}$

e $\frac{9}{25} = \frac{36}{100} = 36\% = 0.36$ **f** $\frac{3}{8} = \frac{37.5}{100} = 37\frac{1}{2}\% = 0.375$

Example 4.11 ▷ Work out: **a** 35% of 620 **b** 40% of 56

a 10% of 620 = 62, 5% of 620 = 31. So 35% of 620 = 62 + 62 + 62 + 31 = 217.

b 10% of 56 = 5.6. So, 40% of 56 = 4 × 5.6 = 22.4.

Exercise 4D

1 Work out each of the following.

    a Half of twenty-four   **b** A third of thirty-six   **c** A quarter of forty-four
    d A sixth of eighteen   **e** A fifth of thirty-five   **f** An eighth of forty

2 Work out each of the following.

    a $\frac{2}{3}$ of 36 m   **b** $\frac{3}{4}$ of 44p   **c** $\frac{5}{6}$ of £18   **d** $\frac{4}{5}$ of 35 kg

    e $\frac{3}{8}$ of 40 cm   **f** $\frac{3}{7}$ of 42 km   **g** $\frac{4}{9}$ of 36 mm   **h** $\frac{5}{6}$ of £24

    i $\frac{3}{10}$ of £1   **j** $\frac{7}{8}$ of 84 m   **k** $\frac{7}{12}$ of 48 cm   **l** $\frac{9}{10}$ of 55 km

3 Work out each of these. Convert to mixed numbers or cancel down to lowest terms.

    a $5 \times \frac{2}{3}$ **b** $3 \times \frac{3}{4}$ **c** $4 \times \frac{3}{8}$ **d** $6 \times \frac{2}{9}$

    e $8 \times \frac{5}{6}$ **f** $4 \times \frac{7}{12}$ **g** $5 \times \frac{3}{7}$ **h** $4 \times \frac{3}{10}$

4 Calculate:

    a 10% of 240   **b** 35% of 460   **c** 60% of 150   **d** 40% of 32
    e 15% of 540   **f** 20% of 95   **g** 45% of 320   **h** 5% of 70
    i 75% of 280   **j** 10% of 45   **k** 30% of 45

5 Work out the equivalent percentage and fraction to each of these decimals.

    a 0.3   **b** 0.44   **c** 0.65   **d** 0.8   **e** 0.78
    f 0.27   **g** 0.05   **h** 0.16   **i** 0.96   **j** 0.25

6 Work out the equivalent decimal and fraction to each of these percentages.

    a 35%   **b** 70%   **c** 48%   **d** 40%   **e** 64%
    f 31%   **g** 4%   **h** 75%   **i** 18%   **j** 110%

7 Work out the equivalent percentage and decimal to each of these fractions.

    a $\frac{2}{25}$ **b** $\frac{7}{50}$ **c** $\frac{9}{10}$ **d** $\frac{17}{20}$ **e** $\frac{1}{8}$
    f $\frac{3}{5}$ **g** $\frac{17}{25}$ **h** $1\frac{3}{4}$ **i** $\frac{1}{10}$ **j** $\frac{19}{20}$

6

8 Write down the equivalent decimal and percentage to each of these.

   a $\frac{1}{3}$ **b** $\frac{2}{3}$

Extension **Work**

As a decimal, a fraction and a percentage are all different ways of writing the same thing, we can sometimes make a calculation easier by using an equivalent form instead of the decimal, fraction or percentage given.

Example 1: 20% of 35. As 20% is $\frac{1}{5}$, this is the same as $\frac{1}{5} \times 35 = 7$.

Example 2: 0.3×340. As 0.3 is 30%, this is the same as 30% of 340. 10% of 340 is 34.
           So, 30% of 340 is $3 \times 34 = 102$.

Example 3: $\frac{3}{25}$ of 40. As $\frac{3}{25}$ is 0.12, this is the same as $0.12 \times 40 = 4.8$.

Rewrite the following using an alternative to the percentage, decimal or fraction given. Then work out the answer.

a	20% of 75	**b**	$\frac{2}{25}$ of 60	**c**	25% of 19	**d**	60% of 550
e	$\frac{3}{20}$ of 90	**f**	0.125×64	**g**	$\frac{3}{5}$ of 7	**h**	0.4×270
i	75% of 44	**j**	0.3333×180				

Solving problems

Mrs Bountiful decided to give £10 000 to her grandchildren, nieces and nephews. She gave $\frac{1}{5}$ to her only grandson, $\frac{1}{8}$ to each of her two granddaughters, $\frac{1}{10}$ to each of her three nieces and $\frac{1}{20}$ to each of her four nephews. What was left she gave to charity. How much did they each receive? What **fraction** of the £10 000 did she give to charity?

The best way to do this problem is to work with amounts of money rather than fractions.

The grandson gets $\frac{1}{5} \times £10\,000 = £2000$. Each granddaughter gets $\frac{1}{8} \times £10\,000 = £1250$. Each niece gets $\frac{1}{10} \times £10\,000 = £1000$. Each nephew gets $\frac{1}{20} \times £10\,000 = £500$.

Altogether she gives away $2000 + 2 \times (1250) + 3 \times (1000) + 4 \times (500) = £9500$. This leaves £500. As a fraction of £10 000, this is $\frac{500}{10\,000} = \frac{1}{20}$.

Solve the problems in Exercise 4E. Show all your working and explain what you are doing.

Exercise 4E

FM **1** A shop is taking 10% off all its prices. How much will these items cost after a 10% reduction?

   a Saucepan £16.00   **b** Spoon 60p   **c** Coffee pot £5.80
   d Bread maker £54.00   **e** Cutlery set £27.40   **f** Tea set £20.80

FM **2** A company is offering its workers a 5% pay rise. How much will the salary of each of the following people be after the pay rise?

   a Fred the storeman £12 000   **b** Alice the office manager £25 000
   c Doris the director £40 000   **d** John the driver £15 500

3 Another company is offering its workers a 4% or £700 per annum pay rise, whichever is the greater.

What will the pay of the following people be after the pay rise?
a Alf the storeman £12 000
b Mark the office manager £25 000
c Joe the driver £15 500
d At what salary will a 4% pay rise be the same as a £700 pay rise?

4 Which of these is greater?

a $\frac{3}{5}$ of 45 or $\frac{2}{3}$ of 39? b $\frac{3}{4}$ of 64 or $\frac{7}{9}$ of 63? c $\frac{3}{10}$ of 35 or $\frac{1}{4}$ of 39?

 5 There are 360 passengers on a Jumbo Jet. $\frac{1}{4}$ of them are British, $\frac{2}{5}$ of them are French, $\frac{1}{6}$ of them are German, $\frac{1}{12}$ of them are Italian and the rest are Dutch. How many of each nationality are there? What fraction of the passengers are Dutch?

 6 Which of these dealers is giving the better value?

7 $\frac{4}{15}$ and $\frac{24}{9}$ are examples of three-digit fractions.

a There is only one three-digit fraction equal to $1\frac{1}{2}$. What is it?
b There are three three-digit fractions equal to $2\frac{1}{2}$, $3\frac{1}{2}$ and $4\frac{1}{2}$. Find them and explain why there cannot be more than three equivalent three-digit fractions for these numbers.
c In the series of fractions $2\frac{1}{2}$, $3\frac{1}{2}$, $4\frac{1}{2}$, $5\frac{1}{2}$, ..., the last one that has three equivalent three-digit fractions is $16\frac{1}{2}$. Explain why.

8 There are 54 fractions in the sequence: $\frac{1}{54}$, $\frac{2}{54}$, $\frac{3}{54}$, $\frac{4}{54}$, ..., $\frac{54}{54}$. How many of them will not cancel down to a simpler form?

9 What number is halfway between the two numbers shown on each scale?

a

$\frac{1}{6}$ $\frac{5}{9}$

b

$\frac{1}{10}$ $\frac{9}{20}$

c

$1\frac{1}{4}$ $2\frac{3}{8}$

3   I can recognise and use simple fractions.
I can recognise when two simple fractions are equivalent.

4   I can recognise approximate proportions of a whole.
I can add and subtract simple fractions and those with the same denominator.

5   I can understand equivalent fractions, decimals and percentages.
I can calculate fractions of a quantity.
I can multiply a fraction by an integer.

6   I can convert between fractions, decimals and percentages.
I can add and subtract some mixed fractions.

National Test questions

1   *2005 4–6 Paper 1*

Here are four fractions.

$$\frac{3}{4} \qquad \frac{1}{8} \qquad \frac{1}{3} \qquad \frac{3}{5}$$

Look at the number line below.
Write each fraction in the correct box.

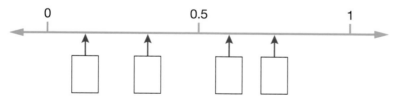

2   *2000 Paper 1*

A pupil recorded how much rain fell on 5 different days.

a   Copy the statements and fill in the gaps with the correct day

The most rain fell on ....

The least rain fell on ....

b   How much more rain fell on Wednesday than on Thursday?

c   How much rain fell altogether on Monday, Tuesday and Wednesday?

Now write your answer in millimetres.

	Amount in cm
Monday	0.2
Tuesday	0.8
Wednesday	0.5
Thursday	0.25
Friday	0.05

3 *2001 Paper 1*

a Look at these fractions: $\frac{1}{2}$ $\frac{1}{3}$ $\frac{5}{6}$

Copy the number line and mark each fraction on it.

The first one has been done for you.

b Copy the fractions and fill in the missing numbers.

$$\frac{2}{12} = \frac{\boxed{}}{6} \qquad \frac{1}{2} = \frac{2}{\boxed{}} \qquad \frac{12}{\boxed{}} = \frac{6}{24}$$

4 *2003 Paper 1*

Fill in the missing numbers.

$\frac{1}{2}$ of 20 = $\frac{1}{4}$ of ...

$\frac{3}{4}$ of 100 = $\frac{1}{2}$ of ...

$\frac{1}{3}$ of 60 = $\frac{2}{3}$ of ...

5 *2001 Paper 1*

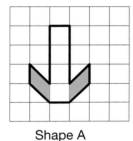
Shape A

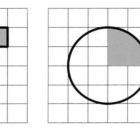
Shape B

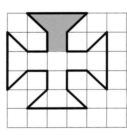
Shape C

Shape D

a What fraction of shape A is shaded?

b What percentage of shape B is shaded?

c Which of shape C or shape D has the greater percentage shaded or are they both the same?

Explain how you know.

Mode, median and range

Statistics is concerned with the collection and organisation of data, the representation of data on diagrams and the interpretation of data.

When interpreting data we often need to find an **average**. For example: the average rainfall in Britain, the average age a mother has her first child, the average weekly wage, the average mark in an examination.

An average is a useful statistic because it represents a whole set of values by just a single or typical value. This section explains how to find two types of average: the **mode** and the **median**. It also explains how to find the **range** of a set of values.

The **mode** is the value that occurs most often in a set of data. It is the only average that can be used for non-numerical data. Sometimes there may be no mode because either all the values are different, or no single value occurs more often than other values. For grouped data, a mode cannot be found, so, instead, we find the **modal class**.

The **median** is the middle value for a set of values when they are put in numerical order. It is often used when one value in the set of data is much larger or much smaller than the rest. This value is called a **rogue value**.

The **range** of a set of values is the largest value minus the smallest value. A small range means that the values in the set of data are similar in size, whereas a large range means that the values differ a lot and therefore are more spread out.

Example 5.1 ▶ Here are the ages of 11 players in a football squad. Find the mode, median and range.

23, 19, 24, 26, 27, 27, 24, 23, 20, 23, 26

First, put the ages in order: 19, 20, 23, 23, 23, 24, 24, 26, 26, 27, 27

The mode is the number which occurs most often. So, the mode is 23.

The median is the number in the middle of the set. So, the median is 24.

The range is the largest number minus the smallest number: 27 − 19 = 8. The range is 8.

Example 5.2 ▷ Below are the marks of ten pupils in a mental arithmetic test. Find the mode, median and range.

     19, 18, 16, 15, 13, 14, 20, 19, 18, 15

First, put the marks in order: 13, 14, 15, 15, 16, 18, 18, 19, 19, 20

There is no mode because no number occurs more often than the others.

There are two numbers in the middle of the set: 16 and 18. The median is the number in the middle of these two numbers. So, the median is 17.

The range is the largest number minus the smallest number: 20 − 13 = 7. The range is 7.

Exercise 5A

1 Find the mode of each of the following sets of data.

   a   red, white, blue, red, white, blue, red, blue, white, red

   b   rain, sun, cloud, fog, rain, sun, snow, cloud, snow, sun, rain, sun

   c   E, A, I, U, E, O, I, E, A, E, A, O, I, U, E, I, E

   d   ♠, ♣, ❤, ♦, ♣, ♠, ❤, ♣, ♦, ❤, ♣, ❤, ♦, ❤

2 Find the mode of each of the following sets of data.

   a   7, 6, 2, 3, 1, 9, 5, 4, 8, 4, 5, 5

   b   36, 34, 45, 28, 37, 40, 24, 27, 33, 31, 41, 34, 40, 34

   c   14, 12, 18, 6, 10, 20, 16, 8, 13, 14, 13

   d   99, 101, 107, 103, 109, 102, 105, 110, 100, 98, 101, 95, 104

3 Find the range of each of the following sets of data.

   a   23, 37, 18, 23, 28, 19, 21, 25, 36

   b   3, 1, 2, 3, 1, 0, 4, 2, 4, 2, 6, 5, 4, 5

   c   51, 54, 27, 28, 38, 45, 39, 50

   d   95, 101, 104, 92, 106, 100, 97, 101, 99

4 Find the mode and range of each set of data.

   a   £2.50 £1.80 £3.65 £3.80 £4.20 £3.25 £1.80

   b   23 kg, 18 kg, 22 kg, 31 kg, 29 kg, 32 kg

   c   132 cm, 145 cm, 151cm, 132 cm, 140 cm, 142 cm

   d   32°, 36°, 32°, 30°, 31°, 31°, 34°, 33°, 32°, 35°

5 A group of nine Year 7 students had their lunch in the school cafeteria. Given below is the amount that each of them spent.

    £2.30 £2.20 £2.00 £2.50 £2.20
    £2.90 £3.60 £2.20 £2.80

   a   Find the mode for the data.

   b   Find the range for the data.

6 Find the median of each of the following sets of data.

    a   8, 7, 3, 4, 2, 10, 6, 5, 9

    b   30, 28, 39, 22, 31, 34, 18, 21, 27, 25, 35

    c   16, 14, 20, 8, 12, 22, 18, 10

    d   100, 101, 108, 104, 110, 103, 106, 111, 101, 99

7 Find the mode, range and median of each set of data.

    a   £3.60, £2.90, £4.75, £4.90, £5.30, £4.35, £2.90

    b   20 kg, 15 kg, 19 kg, 28 kg, 28 kg, 23 kg, 29 kg

    c   121 cm, 134 cm, 140 cm, 121 cm, 129 cm, 131 cm, 121 cm

    d   44°, 48°, 44°, 42°, 43°, 44°, 46°, 45°, 45°, 47°, 46°

8 **a**   Write down a list of seven numbers which has a median of 10 and a mode of 12.

    b   Write down a list of eight numbers which has a median of 10 and a mode of 12.

    c   Write down a list of seven numbers which has a median of 10, a mode of 12 and a range of 8.

Extension **Work**

Surveys

Carry out a survey for any of the following. For each one, collect your data on a survey sheet, find the modal category and draw diagrams to illustrate your data.

1   The most popular mobile phone network in your class.

2   The most common letter in a page of text.

3   The favourite TV soap opera of students in your class.

The mean

The **mean** is the most commonly used average. It is also called the **mean average** or simply the **average**. The mean can be used only with numerical data.

The mean of a set of values is the sum of all the values divided by the number of values in the set. That is:

$$\text{Mean} = \frac{\text{Sum of all values}}{\text{Number of values}}$$

The mean is a useful statistic because it takes all values into account, but it can be distorted by rogue values.

Example 5.3   Find the mean of 2, 7, 9, 10.

$$\text{Mean} = \frac{2 + 7 + 9 + 10}{4} = \frac{28}{4} = 7$$

For more complex data, we can use a calculator. When the answer is not exact, the mean is usually given to one decimal place (1 dp).

Example 5.4 ▷ The ages of seven people are 40, 37, 34, 42, 45, 39, 35. Calculate their mean age.

$$\text{Mean age} = \frac{40 + 37 + 34 + 42 + 45 + 39 + 35}{7} = \frac{272}{7} = 38.9 \text{ (1dp)}$$

Exercise 5B

1 Complete the following.

a Mean of 3, 5, 10 = $\dfrac{3 + 5 + 10}{3} = \dfrac{}{3}$ =

b Mean of 2, 5, 6, 7 = $\dfrac{2 + 5 + 6 + 7}{4} = \dfrac{}{4}$ =

c Mean of 1, 4, 8, 11 = $\dfrac{1 + 4 + 8 + 11}{4} = \dfrac{}{4}$ =

d Mean of 1, 1, 2, 3, 8 = $\dfrac{1 + 1 + 2 + 3 + 8}{5} = \dfrac{}{5}$ =

2 Complete the following.

a Mean of 5, 6, 10 = $\dfrac{5 + 6 + 10}{3} = \text{—} =$

b Mean of 1, 3, 3, 5 = $\dfrac{1 + 3 + 3 + 5}{4} = \text{—} =$

c Mean of 3, 4, 5, 5, 8 = $\dfrac{3 + 4 + 5 + 6 + 8}{5} = \text{—} =$

d Mean of 1, 2, 2, 5, 10 = $\dfrac{1 + 2 + 2 + 5 + 10}{5} = \text{—} =$

3 Complete the following.

a Mean of 1, 5, 6 = $\dfrac{1 + 5 + 6}{} = \text{—} =$

b Mean of 1, 4, 7, 8 = $\dfrac{1 + 4 + 7 + 8}{} = \text{—} =$

c Mean of 2, 2, 3, 6, 7 = $\dfrac{2 + 2 + 3 + 6 + 7}{} = \text{—} =$

d Mean of 4, 6, 10, 20 = $\dfrac{4 + 6 + 10 + 20}{} = \text{—} =$

4 Complete the following.

a Mean of 3, 7, 8 = $\dfrac{}{} = \text{—} =$

b Mean of 5, 8, 10, 17 = $\dfrac{}{} = \text{—} =$

c Mean of 2, 4, 11, 13, 15 = $\dfrac{}{} = \text{—} =$

d Mean of 1, 1, 8, 8 = $\dfrac{}{} = \text{—} =$

5 Find the mean of each of the following sets of data.

a 8, 7, 6, 10, 4

b 23, 32, 40, 37, 29, 25

c 11, 12, 9, 26, 14, 17, 16

d 2.4, 1.6, 3.2, 1.8, 4.2, 2.5, 4.5, 2.2

6 Find the mean of each of the following sets of data, giving your answer to 1 dp.

a 6, 7, 6, 4, 2, 3

b 12, 15, 17, 11, 18, 16, 14

c 78, 72, 82, 95, 47, 67, 77, 80

d 9.1, 7.8, 10.3, 8.5, 11.6, 8.9

7 The heights, in centimetres, of ten children are:

132, 147, 143, 136, 135, 146, 153, 132, 137, 149

a Find the mean height of the children.

b Find the median height of the children.

c Find the modal height of the children.

d Which average do you think is the best one to use? Explain your answer.

8 The numbers of children in the families of a class are:

1,1,1,1,1,1, 2, 2, 2, 2, 3, 3, 3, 3, 4

a Find the mode.

b Find the median.

c Find the mean.

9 The shoe sizes of all the girls in class 7JS are:

3, 3, 3, 3, 3, 4, 4, 4, 5, 6, 6

a Find the mode.

b Find the median.

c Find the mean.

Extension Work

1 **Vital statistics**

Working in groups, calculate the mean for the group's age, height and weight.

2 **Average score**

Throw a dice ten times. Record your results on a survey sheet. What is the mean score?

Repeat the experiment but throw the dice 20 times. What is the mean score now?

Repeat the experiment but throw the dice 50 times. What is the mean score now?

Write down anything you notice as you throw the dice more times.

Statistical diagrams

Once data has been collected from a survey, it can be displayed in various ways to make it easier to understand and interpret.

The most common ways to display data are bar charts, pie charts and line graphs.

Bar charts have several different forms. The questions in Exercise 5C will show you the different types of bar chart that can be used. Notice that data which has single categories gives a bar chart with gaps between the bars. Grouped data gives a bar chart with no gaps between the bars.

Pie charts are used to show data when you do not need to know the number of items in each category of the sample. Pie charts are used to show proportions.

Line graphs are usually used to show trends and patterns in the data.

Exercise 5C

1   The bar chart shows how the pupils in class 7PB travel to school.

  a   How many pupils walk to school?

  b   What is the mode for the way the pupils travel to school?

  c   How many pupils are there in class 7PB?

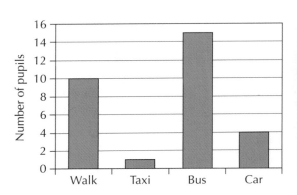

2   The bar chart shows the way the pupils of two Year 7 classes voted for their favourite soap opera.

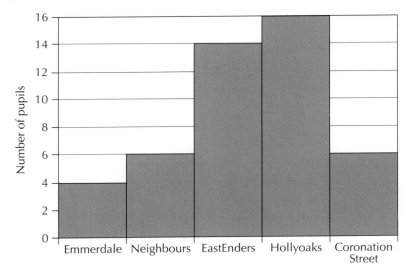

  a   How many voted for *EastEnders*?

  b   Which was the overall favourite of the two classes?

  c   What is the modal choice?

  d   Which of the two soaps had the same number of votes?

3 The pictogram shows the amount of money collected for charity by different year groups in a school.

Year 7   £20 £20 £20 £20 £20

Year 8   £20 £20 £20

Year 9   £20 £20 £20 £20 £20

Year 10 £20 £20 £20 £20

Year 11 £20 £20 £20

Key

£20 represents £20

a How much money was collected by Year 8?

b How much money was collected by Year 10?

c Which year group collected the most money?

d How much money was collected altogether?

4 The pictogram shows how many CDs five pupils have in their collection.

a Who has the most CDs?

b How many CDs does Jessica have?

c How many CDs does Ceri have?

d How many more CDs does Dipesh have than Tania?

e How many CDs do the five pupils have altogether?

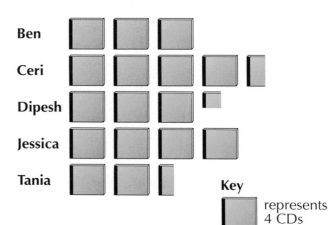

Ben

Ceri

Dipesh

Jessica

Tania

Key

represents 4 CDs

 5 The dual bar chart shows the daily average number of hours of sunshine in London and Edinburgh over a year.

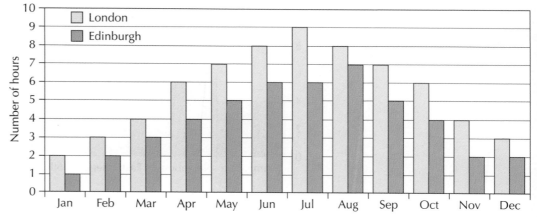

a Which city has the most sunshine?

b Which month is the sunniest for **i** London **ii** Edinburgh?

c What is the range for the number of hours of sunshine over the year for
i London **ii** Edinburgh?

FM **6** The line graph shows the temperature, in °C, in Leeds over a 12-hour period.

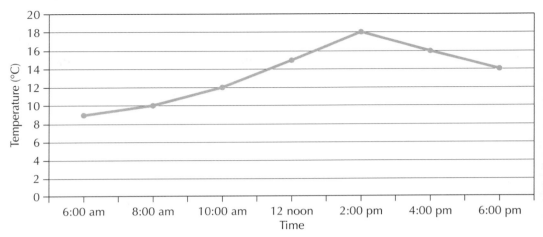

a What is the temperature at midday?

b What is the temperature at 3 pm?

c Write down the range for the temperature over the 12-hour period.

d Explain why the line graph is a useful way of showing the data.

7 The percentage compound bar chart shows the favourite colours for a sample of Year 7 pupils.

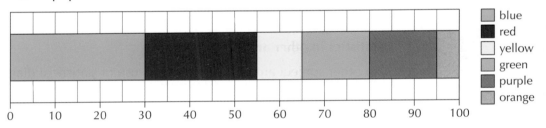

a Which is the colour preferred by most pupils?

b What percentage of the pupils preferred yellow?

c Which two colours were equally preferred by the pupils?

d If there were 40 pupils in the sample, how many of them preferred red?

e Explain why the compound bar chart is a useful way to illustrate the data.

8 The bar chart shows the marks obtained in a mathematics test by the pupils in class 7KG.

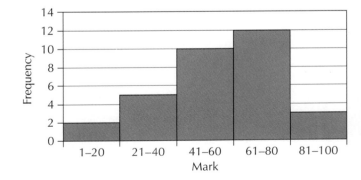

a How many pupils are there in class 7KG?

b What is the modal class for the data?

c How many pupils got a mark over 60?

d Write down the smallest and greatest range of marks possible for the data.

9 The pie chart shows the TV channel that 60 people in a survey most often watched.

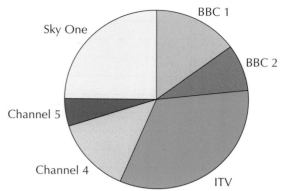

a Which is the most popular channel?
b Which is the least popular channel?

Statistics in the press

Look through newspapers and magazines to find as many statistical diagrams as you can. Make a display to show the variety of diagrams used in the press.

What types of diagram are most common? How effective are the diagrams in showing the information?

Are any of the diagrams misleading? If they are, explain why.

Statistics in other areas

Do other subject areas in school make use of statistical diagrams?

Find examples in textbooks from other subjects to show where statistical diagrams are used most effectively.

Probability

Probability is the way of describing and measuring the chance or likelihood that an **event** will happen.

The chance of an event happening can be shown on a **probability scale**:

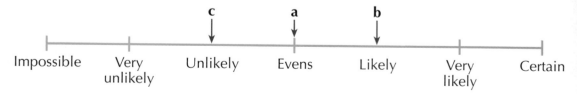

An evens chance is often referred to as 'a 50–50 chance'. Other everyday words used to describe probability are: uncertain, possible, probable, good chance, poor chance.

Example 5.5 ▶ The following events are shown on the probability scale on page 62.

    a   The probability that a new-born baby will be a girl.

    b   The probability that a person is right-handed.

    c   The probability that it will rain tomorrow.

To measure probability, we use a scale from 0 to 1. So probabilities are written as fractions or decimals, and sometimes as percentages, as in the weather forecasts.

The probability scale is now drawn as:

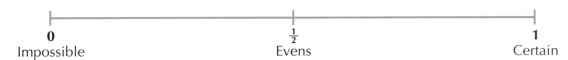

0 $\frac{1}{2}$ **1**
Impossible   Evens   Certain

We define the probability of an event happening as:

$$P(\text{event}) = \frac{\text{Number of outcomes in the event}}{\text{Total number of all possible outcomes}}$$

Example 5.6 ▶ When tossing a fair coin, there are two possible outcomes:
Head (H) or Tail (T)

Each outcome is **equally likely** to happen because it is a fair coin. So:

    $P(H) = \frac{1}{2}$ and $P(T) = \frac{1}{2}$

This is the **probability fraction** for the event.

(Sometimes, people may say a 1 in 2 chance or a 50–50 chance).

Example 5.7 ▶ When throwing a fair dice, there are six equally likely outcomes: 1, 2, 3, 4, 5, 6

So, for example: $P(6) = \frac{1}{6}$ and $P(1 \text{ or } 2) = \frac{2}{6} = \frac{1}{3}$

Probability fractions are *always* cancelled down.

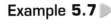
Exercise 5D

  ① Choose one of the following words which best describes the probability for the events listed below.

    impossible, very unlikely, unlikely, evens, likely, very likely, certain

    a   Manchester United will win their next home game.
    b   Someone in your town will win the National Lottery this week.
    c   You have a maths lesson today.
    d   When throwing a dice, the score is an odd number.
    e   You will live to be 200.
    f   You will watch TV this evening.
    g   It will snow on Christmas Day this year.

2 Copy the probability scale shown below:

| Impossible | Very unlikely | Unlikely | Evens | Likely | Very likely | Certain |

Place the following events onto the above probability scale:

A You will be Prime Minister one day.

B You will have some homework this week.

C You can swim to the Moon.

D If you flip a coin, you will get 'heads'.

E You will sit down today.

F It will snow in May.

G If you roll a die, you will get a number bigger than 2.

3 Cards numbered 1 to 10 are placed in a box. A card is drawn at random from the box. Find the probability that the card drawn is:

a 5   **b** an even number   **c** a number in the 3 times table

d 4 or 8   **e** a number less than 12   **f** an odd number

4 Adam picks a card at random from a normal pack of 52 playing cards. Find each of the following probabilities.

a P(a Jack)   **b** P(a Heart)   **c** P(a picture card)

d P(Ace of Spades)   **e** P(a 9 or a 10)   **f** P(Ace)

5 A bag contains five red discs, three blue discs and two green discs. Linda takes out a disc at random. Find the probability that she takes out:

a a red disc   **b** a blue disc   **c** a green disc

d a yellow disc   **e** a red or blue disc

6 Syed is using a fair, eight-sided spinner in a game. Find the probability that the score he gets is:

a 0   **b** 1   **c** 2   **d** 3

7 **a** Write down five events that have a probability of 0.

b Write down five events that have a probability of 1.

8 Sandhu rolls a fair dice. Find each of the following probabilities.

a P(3)   **b** P(odd number)   **c** P(5 or 6)

d P(even number)   **e** P(6)   **f** P(1 or 6)

9 Mr Evans has a box of 25 calculators, but 5 of them do not work very well.

What is the probability that the first calculator taken out of the box at random does not work very well?

Write your fraction as simply as possible.

10 At the start of a tombola, there are 300 tickets inside the drum. There are 60 winning tickets available.

What is the probability that the first ticket taken out of the drum is a winning ticket? Write your fraction as simply as possible.

5

Extension Work

You will need a set of cards numbered 1 to 10 for this experiment.

Line up the cards, face down and in random order.

1 Turn over the first card.

2 Work out the probability that the second card will be higher than the first card.

3 Work out the probability that the second card will be lower than the first card.

4 Turn over the second card.

5 Work out the probability that the third card will be higher than the second card.

6 Work out the probability that the third card will be lower than the second card.

7 Carry on the process. Write down all your results clearly and explain any patterns that you notice.

Repeat the experiment. Are your results the same?

Experimental probability

The probabilities in the previous section were calculated using equally likely outcomes. A probability worked out this way is known as a **theoretical probability**.

Sometimes, a probability can be found only by carrying out a series of experiments and recording the results in a frequency table. The probability of the event can then be estimated from these results. A probability found in this way is known as an **experimental probability**.

To find an experimental probability, the experiment has to be repeated a number of times. Each separate experiment carried out is known as a **trial**.

$$\text{Experimental probability of an event} = \frac{\text{Number of times the event occurs}}{\text{Total number of trials}}$$

It is important to remember that when an experiment is repeated, the experimental probability will be slightly different each time. The experimental probability of an event is an estimate for the theoretical probability. As the number of trials increases, the value of the experimental probability gets closer to the theoretical probability.

Example 5.8

A dice is thrown 50 times. The results of the 50 trials are shown in a frequency table.

Score	1	2	3	4	5	6
Frequency	8	9	8	10	7	8

The experimental probability of getting a 3 $= \frac{8}{50} = \frac{4}{25}$.

Exercise 5E

1 Working in pairs, toss a coin 50 times and record your results in a table such as the following frequency table.

	Tally	Frequency
Head		
Tail		

a Use your results to find the experimental probability of getting a Head.

b What is the experimental probability of getting a Tail?

2 Working in pairs, throw a dice 100 times and record your results in a table such as the following frequency table.

Score	Tally	Frequency
1		
2		
3		
4		
5		
6		

a Find the experimental probability of getting 6.

b Find the experimental probability of getting an even score.

3 Working in pairs, drop a drawing pin 50 times. Copy and record your results in a table such as the following frequency table.

	Tally	Frequency
Point up		
Point down		

a What is the experimental probability that the drawing pin will land point up?

b Is your answer greater or less than an evens chance?

c Explain what would happen if you repeated the experiment.

4 a Working in pairs, take 4 playing cards, one of each suit (♣, ♦, ♥, ♠). Shuffle them. Look at the suit of the top card and complete the following frequency table:

Suit		Tally	Frequency
Clubs	♣		
Diamonds	♦		
Hearts	♥		
Spades	♠		
		Total	

Shuffle after every turn and try to complete about 100 shuffles.

b Find your experimental probability of having the top card a heart.

c Find your experimental probability of having the top card a black suit.

Biased spinners

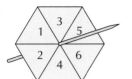

Make a six-sided spinner from card and a cocktail stick.

Weight it by sticking a small piece of Plasticine below one of the numbers on the card. This will make the spinner unfair or biased.

Roll the spinner 60 times and record the scores in a frequency table.

Find the experimental probability for each score.

Compare your results with what you would expect from a fair, six-sided spinner.

Repeat the experiment by making a spinner with a different number of sides.

LEVEL BOOSTER

4
I can collect data using a frequency table.
I can find the mode and range for a set of data.
I can read and interpret statistical diagrams.
I can find simple probability.

5
I can find the mean and median for a set of data.
I can find the mean from a frequency table.
I can interpret pie charts.
I can calculate probabilities using equally likely outcomes.
I can calculate probability from experimental data.

1 *2007 4–6 Paper 2*

These are the names of the twelve people who work for a company.

Ali	Claire	Kiki	Suki
Brian	Claire	Lucy	Tom
Claire	James	Ryan	Tom

a What name is the mode?

b One person leaves the company. A different person joins the company.
Now the name that is the **mode** is **Tom**.

Complete the following sentences, writing in the missing names.

The name of the person who **leaves** is ......

The name of the person who **joins** is ......

2 *2005 4–6 Paper 1*

a There are two children in the Smith family.
The **range** of their ages is **exactly 7 years**.

What could the ages of the two children be?
Give an example.

b There are two children in the Patel family.
They are twins of the **same age**.

What is the **range** of their ages?

 3 *2000 Paper 2*

A newspaper predicts what the ages of secondary school teachers will be in six years' time.

They print this chart.

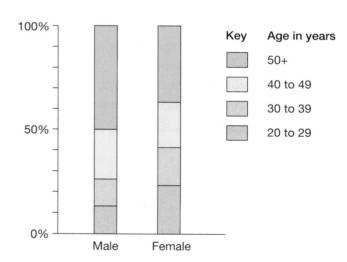

a The chart shows 24% of male teachers will be aged 40 to 49.

About what percentage of female teachers will be aged 40 to 49?

b About what percentage of female teachers will be aged 50+?

c The newspaper predicts there will be about 20 000 male teachers aged 40 to 49.

Estimate the number of male teachers that will be aged 50+.

d Assume that the total number of male teachers will be about the same as the total number of female teachers.

Use the chart to decide which statement is correct.

Generally, male teachers will tend to be younger than female teachers.

Generally, female teachers will tend to be younger than male teachers.

Explain how you used the chart to decide.

4   *2000 Paper 2*

In each box of cereal there is a free gift of a card.

You cannot tell which card will be in a box. Each card is equally likely.

There are four different cards: A, B, C or D

a   Zoe needs card A.

Her brother Paul needs cards C and D.

They buy one box of cereal.

What is the probability that the card is one that Zoe needs?

What is the probability that the card is one that Paul needs?

b   Then their mother opens the box. She tells them the card is not card A.

Now what is the probability the card is one that Zoe needs?

What is the probability that the card is one that Paul needs?

FM School sports day

Teams

1 Ruskin team has seven members with the following ages:

	Age (years)
Joe	14
Kristen	15
Simon	13
Vikas	15
Helen	14
Sarah	13
Quinn	13

a Put these ages into order.

b What is the mode of the ages?

c What is the range of the ages?

d What is the median age?

100 m sprint

2 The girls' 100 m race was run in the following times:

	Time (seconds)
Kate	22
Kerry	25
Maria	21
Oi Yin	25
Sara	23

a Put these times into order.

b What is the mode of the times?

c What is the range of the times?

d What is the median time?

Long jump

3 Alex had ten practice attempts at the long jump. The bar chart illustrates the range of lengths he jumps.

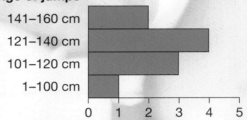

Range of jumps

He is now prepared for his last long jump.

What is the probability that Alex jumps:

a in the 1–100 cm range?

b in the 121–140 cm range?

Rounders competition

4 In the rounders game between Huntsman and Chantry, the following scorecards were produced as tallies. A tally was put next to a player each time they scored a rounder.

Huntsman		Frequency
Afzal	HHT	___
Claire	II	___
Gilbert	III	___
John	HHT II	___
Ali	I	___
Izolda	I	___
Kate	III	___
Joy	HHT HHT I	___
Mari	II	___

Chantry		Frequency
Ellen	IIII	___
Cynthia	II	___
Runuka	HHT I	___
Joanne	II	___
Michael	I	___
Emily	II	___
Julie	HHT II	___
Kay	HHT	___
Sue	III	___

a Which team won the game?

b Which of all the players was the most likely to score a rounder?

This chapter is going to show you

- How to use letters in place of numbers
- How to use the rules (conventions) of algebra
- How to solve puzzles called equations
- How to solve problems using algebra

What you should already know

- Understand and be able to apply the rules of arithmetic
- The meaning of the words term and expression

Algebraic terms and expressions

In algebra, you will keep meeting three words: **variable**, **term** and **expression**.

Variable. This is the letter in a term or an expression whose value can vary. Some of the letters most used for variables are x, y, n and t.

Term. This is an algebraic quantity which contains only a letter (or combination of letters) and may contain a number. For example:

$3n$ means 3 multiplied by the variable n

$\dfrac{n}{2}$ means n divided by 2

n^2 means n multiplied by itself (normally said as 'n squared')

Expression. This is a combination of letters (variables) and signs, often with numbers. For example:

$8 - n$ means subtract n from 8

$n - 3$ means subtract 3 from n

$2n + 7$ means n multiplied by 2 with 7 added on

When you give a particular value to the variable in an expression, the expression takes on a particular value.

For example, if the variable n takes the value of 4, then the terms and expressions which include this variable will have particular values, as shown below:

$3n = 12$ $\dfrac{n}{2} = 2$ $n^2 = 16$ $8 - n = 4$ $n - 3 = 1$ $2n + 7 = 15$

Exercise 6A

1 Write terms, or expressions, to illustrate the following sentences.

a Add four to m.   **b** Multiply t by eight.   **c** Nine minus y.

d Multiply m by itself.   **e** Divide n by five.   **f** Subtract t from seven.

g Multiply n by three, then add five.   **h** Multiply six by t.

i Multiply m by five, then subtract three.   **j** Multiply x by x.

(2) Write down the values of each term for the three values of n.

a $4n$ where **i** $n = 2$ **ii** $n = 5$ **iii** $n = 11$

b $\dfrac{n}{2}$ where **i** $n = 6$ **ii** $n = 14$ **iii** $n = 8$

c n^2 where **i** $n = 3$ **ii** $n = 6$ **iii** $n = 7$

d $3n$ where **i** $n = 7$ **ii** $n = 5$ **iii** $n = 9$

e $\dfrac{n}{5}$ where **i** $n = 10$ **ii** $n = 5$ **iii** $n = 20$

f $9n$ where **i** $n = 2$ **ii** $n = 4$ **iii** $n = 8$

g $\dfrac{n}{10}$ where **i** $n = 20$ **ii** $n = 50$ **iii** $n = 100$

(3) Write down the values of each expression for the three values of n.

a $n + 7$ where **i** $n = 3$ **ii** $n = 4$ **iii** $n = 12$

b $n - 5$ where **i** $n = 8$ **ii** $n = 14$ **iii** $n = 11$

c $10 - n$ where **i** $n = 4$ **ii** $n = 7$ **iii** $n = 1$

d $2n + 3$ where **i** $n = 2$ **ii** $n = 5$ **iii** $n = 7$

e $5n - 1$ where **i** $n = 3$ **ii** $n = 4$ **iii** $n = 8$

f $20 - 2n$ where **i** $n = 1$ **ii** $n = 5$ **iii** $n = 9$

g $4n + 5$ where **i** $n = 4$ **ii** $n = 3$ **iii** $n = 7$

(4) Write down the values of each expression for the three values of n.

a $n^2 - 1$ where **i** $n = 2$ **ii** $n = 3$ **iii** $n = 4$

b $n^2 + 1$ where **i** $n = 5$ **ii** $n = 6$ **iii** $n = 7$

c $5 + n^2$ where **i** $n = 8$ **ii** $n = 9$ **iii** $n = 10$

d $n^2 + 9$ where **i** $n = 5$ **ii** $n = 4$ **iii** $n = 3$

e $25 + n^2$ where **i** $n = 4$ **ii** $n = 5$ **iii** $n = 6$

Extension Work

1 Using the variable n and the operations add, subtract, multiply, divide, square, write down as many different expressions as you can that use:

a two operations **b** three operations

2 Choose any value for n, say 5, and see how many of these expressions have the same value.

Rules of algebra

The rules (conventions) of algebra are the same rules that are used in arithmetic.
For example:

$3 + 4 = 4 + 3$ $a + b = b + a$

$3 \times 4 = 4 \times 3$ $a \times b = b \times a$ or $ab = ba$

But remember, for example, that:

$7 - 5 \neq 5 - 7$ $a - b \neq b - a$

$6 \div 3 \neq 3 \div 6$ $\dfrac{a}{b} \neq \dfrac{b}{a}$

From one fact, other facts can be stated. For example:

$3 + 4 = 7$
gives $7 - 4 = 3$ and $7 - 3 = 4$

$3 \times 4 = 12$
gives $\frac{12}{3} = 4$ and $\frac{12}{4} = 3$

$a + b = 10$
gives $10 - a = b$ and $10 - b = a$

$ab = 10$
gives $\frac{10}{a} = b$ and $\frac{10}{b} = a$

1 In each of the following clouds only two expressions are equal to each other. Write down the equal pair.

a

$3 + 5 \quad 3 - 5$
$3 \times 5 \quad 5 + 3$
$5 \div 3 \quad 5 - 3$

b

$2 + 7 \quad 7 - 2$
$2 \times 7 \quad 7 \div 2 \quad 2 \div 7$
7×2

c

$a + b \quad a - b$
$a \times b \quad b + a$
$b \div a \quad b - a$

d

$m + p \quad m - p$
$m \times p \quad p \div m \quad m \div p$
$p \times m$

2 In each of the following lists, write down all the expressions that equal each other.

a $5 + 6, 5 \times 6, 6 - 5, 6 \times 5, 6 \div 5, 5 - 6, 6 + 5, 5 \div 6$

b $ab, a + b, b - a, ba, a/b, a - b, b/a, b + a, a \div b$

c $k \times t, k + t, k/t, kt, k \div t, tk, t + k, t \times k, k - t$

3 Write down two more facts that are implied by each of the following statements.

a $2 + 8 = 10$ b $a + b = 7$ c $3 \times 5 = 15$ d $ab = 24$

e $3 + k = 9$ f $m + 4 = 5$ g $2n = 6$ h $\frac{8}{a} = 7$

4 Show by the substitution of suitable numbers that:

a $m + n = n + m$ b $ab = ba$ c $p - t \neq t - p$ d $\frac{m}{n} \neq \frac{n}{m}$

5 Show by the substitution of suitable numbers that:

a   If $a + b = 7$, then $7 - a = b$ b   If $ab = 12$, then $a = \frac{12}{b}$

6 Show by the substitution of suitable numbers that:

a $a + b + c = c + b + a$ b $acb = abc = cba$

7 If you know that $a + b + c + d = 180$, write down as many other expressions that equal 180 as you can.

8 It is known that $abcd = 100$. Write down at least ten other expressions that must also equal 100.

1   Write down some values of a and b which make the following statement true.

$a + b = ab$

You will find only one pair of integers. There are lots of decimal numbers to find, but each time try to keep one of the variables an integer.

2   Write down some values of a and b which make the following statement true.

$$a - b = \frac{a}{b}$$

You will find only one pair of integers. There are lots of decimal numbers to find, but each time try to keep one of the variables an integer.

3   Does $(a + b) \times (a - b) = a^2 - b^2$ work for all values of a and b?

Simplifying expressions

If you add 2 cups to 3 cups, you get 5 cups. In algebra, this can be represented as:

$2c + 3c = 5c$

The terms here are called **like terms**, because they are all multiples of c.

Only like terms can be added or subtracted to simplify an expression. Unlike terms cannot be combined.

Check out these two boxes.

Examples of combining like terms

$3p + 4p = 7p$ $5t + 3t = 8t$

$9w - 4w = 5w$ $12q - 5q = 7q$

$a + 3a + 7a = 11a$

$15m - 2m - m = 12m$

Examples of unlike terms

$x + y$ $2m + 3p$

$7 - 3y$ $5g + 2k$

$m - 3p$

Like terms can be combined even when they are mixed together with unlike terms. For example:

2 apples and 1 pear added to 4 apples and 2 kiwis make 6 apples, 1 pear and 2 kiwis, or in algebra

$2a + p + 4a + 2k = 6a + 2k + p$

Examples of different sorts of like terms mixed together

$4t + 5m + 2m + 3t + m = 7t + 8m$

$5k + 4g - 2k - g = 3k + 3g$

Note: You **never** write the one in front of a variable. So,

$g = 1g$ $m = 1m$

There are many situations in algebra where there is a need to use brackets in expressions. They keep things tidy! You can **expand** brackets, as shown in Examples 6.1 and 6.2. This operation is also called **multiplying out**.

Example 6.1 ▷ Expand $3(a + 5)$.

This means that each term in the brackets is multiplied by the number outside the brackets. This gives:

$$3 \times a + 3 \times 5 = 3a + 15$$

Example 6.2 ▷ Expand and simplify $2(3p + 4) + 3(4p + 1)$.

This means that each term in each pair of brackets is multiplied by the number outside the brackets. This gives:

$$2 \times 3p + 2 \times 4 + 3 \times 4p + 3 \times 1$$
$$= 6p + 8 + 12p + 3$$
$$= 18p + 11$$

Exercise 6C

(1) Simplify each of the following expressions.

a $4c + 2c$ 　　b $6d + 4d$ 　　c $7p - 5p$ 　　d $2x + 6x + 3x$

e $4t + 2t - t$ 　　f $7m - 3m$ 　　g $q + 5q - 2q$ 　　h $a + 6a - 3a$

i $4p + p - 2p$ 　　j $2w + 3w - w$ 　　k $4t + 3t - 5t$ 　　l $5g - g - 2g$

(2) Simplify each of the following expressions.

a $2x + 2y + 3x + 6y$ 　　b $4w + 6t - 2w - 2t$ 　　c $4m + 7n + 3m - n$

d $4x + 8y - 2y - 3x$ 　　e $8 + 4x - 3 + 2x$ 　　f $8p + 9 - 3p - 4$

g $2y + 4x - 3 + x - y$ 　　h $5d + 8c - 4c + 7$ 　　i $4f + 2 + 3d - 1 - 3f$

j $8c + 7 - 7c - 4$ 　　k $2p + q + 3p - q$ 　　l $3t + 9 - t$

(3) Expand each of the following expressions.

a $4(x + 5)$ 　　b $2(3t + 4)$ 　　c $5(3m + 1)$ 　　d $4(3w - 2)$

e $6(3m - 4)$ 　　f $7(4q - 3)$ 　　g $2(3x - 4)$ 　　h $3(2t + 7)$

i $7(3k + p - 2)$ 　　j $4(3 - k + 2t)$ 　　k $5(m - 3 + 6p)$ 　　l $4(2 - 5k - 2m)$

(4) Expand and simplify each of the following expressions.

a $4(x + 5) + 3(x + 3)$ 　　　　b $5(p + 7) + 3(p + 3)$

c $3(w + 3) + 4(w - 2)$ 　　　　d $6(d + 3) + 3(d - 5)$

e $3(8p + 2) + 3(5p + 1)$ 　　　　f $4(6m + 5) + 2(5m - 4)$

g $5(3w + 7) + 2(2w - 1)$ 　　　　h $7(3c + 2) + 2(5c - 4)$

i $4(t + 6) + 3(4t - 1)$ 　　　　j $5(3x + 2) + 4(3x - 2)$

When an expression contains brackets within brackets, first simplify the expression within the innermost brackets.

Expand and simplify each of these.

a $2[3x + 5(x + 2)]$ **b** $3[4y + 3(2y - 1)]$

c $4\{m + 2[m + (m - 1)]\}$ **d** $5\{2(t + 1) + 3[4t + 3(2t - 1)]\}$

Formulae

Where you have a **rule** to calculate some quantity, you can write the rule as a **formula**.

Example 6.3 A rule to calculate the cost of hiring a hall for a wedding is £200 plus £6 per person. This rule, written as a formula, is:

$$c = 200 + 6n$$ where c = cost in £
n = number of people

Example 6.4 Use the formula $c = 200 + 6n$ to calculate the cost of a wedding with 70 people.

Cost $= 200 + 6 \times 70 = 200 + 420 = £620$

Exercise 6D

FM **1** Write each of these rules as a formula. Use the first letter of each variable in the formula. (Each letter is printed in red.)

a The **c**ost of hiring a boat is £2 per **h**our.

b **D**ad's age is always **J**oy's age plus 40.

FM **2** A cleaner uses the formula:

$$c = 3 + 2h$$ where c = cost in £
h = number of hours worked

Calculate what the cleaner charges to work for:

a 5 hours   **b** 3 hours   **c** 8 hours

FM **3** A mechanic uses the formula:

$$c = 8 + 5t$$ where c = cost in £
t = time, in hours, to complete the work

Calculate what the mechanic charges to complete the work in:

a 1 hour   **b** 3 hours   **c** 7 hours

FM **4** A singer uses the formula:

$$c = 25 + 15s$$ where c = cost in £
s = number of songs sung

Calculate what the singer charges to sing the following:

a 2 songs   **b** 4 songs   **c** 8 songs

5 The formula for the average speed of a car is:

$$A = D \div T$$

where A = average speed (miles per hour)
D = distance travelled (miles)
T = time taken (hours)

Use the formula to calculate the average speed for the following journeys.

(a) 300 miles in 6 hours

(b) 200 miles in 5 hours

(c) 120 miles in 3 hours

(d) 350 miles in 5 hours

 6 The formula for the cost of a newspaper advert is:

$$C = 5W + 10A$$

where C = charge in £
W = number of words used
A = area of the advert in cm²

Use the formula to calculate the charge for the following adverts.

(a) 10 words with an area of 20 cm²

(b) 8 words with an area of 6 cm²

(c) 12 words with an area of 15 cm²

(d) 17 words with an area of 15 cm²

Extension Work

A three-tier set of number bricks looks like this:

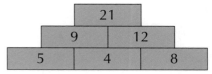

The numbers on two adjacent bricks are added to create the number on the brick above them.

a Find the top brick value when the bottom bricks, in order, are:

    i 6, 7 and 10   **ii** a, b and a **iii** $a + 1$, $a + 2$ and $a + 3$

b If the bottom three bricks are a, b and c, write a formula for the total in the top brick.

c The top number is 10. Each bottom brick is a different positive number. How many different combinations of bottom brick numbers are there?

Equations

An equation states that two things are equal. These can be two expressions or an expression and a quantity.

An equation can be represented by a pair of scales. When the scales balance, both sides are equal.

The left-hand pan has three bags, each containing the same number of marbles.

The right-hand pan has 15 marbles.

How many marbles are there in each bag?

Let the number of marbles in each bag be x, which gives $3x = 15$.

Divide both sides by 3. $\frac{3x}{3} = \frac{15}{3}$

There are 5 marbles in each bag. $x = 5$

Simple equations are solved by adding, subtracting, multiplying and dividing each side to find the value of x.

Example 6.5 ▷ Solve $x + 5 = 9$

Subtract 5 from both sides $\quad x + 5 - 5 = 9 - 5$
$$x = 4$$

Example 6.6 ▷ Solve $\frac{x}{3} = 5$

Multiply both sides by 3 $\quad x = 3 \times 5$
$$x = 15$$

Exercise 6E

1 Solve each of the following equations.

a	$2x = 10$	**b**	$3x = 18$	**c**	$5x = 15$	**d**	$4x = 8$
e	$3m = 12$	**f**	$5m = 30$	**g**	$7m = 14$	**h**	$4m = 20$
i	$6k = 12$	**j**	$5k = 25$	**k**	$3k = 27$	**l**	$2k = 16$
m	$7x = 21$	**n**	$4x = 28$	**o**	$5x = 40$	**p**	$9x = 54$

2 Solve each of the following equations.

a	$x + 2 = 7$	**b**	$x + 3 = 9$	**c**	$x + 8 = 10$	**d**	$x + 1 = 5$
e	$m + 3 = 7$	**f**	$m - 3 = 5$	**g**	$k - 2 = 9$	**h**	$p - 5 = 9$
i	$k + 7 = 15$	**j**	$k - 1 = 3$	**k**	$m + 3 = 9$	**l**	$x - 3 = 7$
m	$x + 8 = 9$	**n**	$n - 2 = 6$	**o**	$m - 5 = 8$	**p**	$x + 12 = 23$

3 Solve each of the following equations.

a	$\frac{x}{2} = 5$	**b**	$\frac{x}{4} = 7$	**c**	$\frac{x}{3} = 11$	**d**	$\frac{x}{5} = 6$
e	$\frac{x}{5} = 8$	**f**	$\frac{x}{2} = 6$	**g**	$\frac{x}{8} = 3$	**h**	$\frac{x}{9} = 10$
i	$\frac{x}{3} = 11$	**j**	$\frac{x}{7} = 3$	**k**	$\frac{x}{5} = 9$	**l**	$\frac{x}{2} = 16$
m	$\frac{x}{10} = 3$	**n**	$\frac{x}{8} = 8$	**o**	$\frac{x}{2} = 20$	**p**	$\frac{x}{9} = 9$

4 Solve each of the following equations.

a	$x + 23 = 35$	**b**	$x + 13 = 21$	**c**	$x + 18 = 30$	**d**	$x + 48 = 54$
e	$m + 44 = 57$	**f**	$m - 13 = 4$	**g**	$k - 12 = 6$	**h**	$p - 15 = -9$
i	$k + 72 = 95$	**j**	$k - 12 = -5$	**k**	$m + 33 = 49$	**l**	$x - 13 = -8$
m	$x + 85 = 112$	**n**	$n - 21 = -10$	**o**	$m - 15 = -9$	**p**	$x + 12 = 37$

Extension **Work**

The solution to each of these equations is a whole number between 1 and 9 inclusive. Try to find the value.

a	$2(3x + 5) = 34$	**b**	$4(2x - 3) = 52$	**c**	$5(3x - 1) = 40$
d	$3(4x - 7) = 15$	**e**	$2(3x - 4) = 16$	**f**	$4(5x - 2) = 52$
g	$5(2x - 1) = 25$	**h**	$3(5x + 2) = 66$	**i**	$2(3x - 2) = 20$

LEVEL BOOSTER

3
I can write a simple algebraic expression for a rule such as 4 more than x, i.e. $x + 4$.
I can recognise equivalent numerical and algebraic expressions such as $4x + 7 = 27$ when $x = 5$.

4
I can substitute numbers into algebraic expressions such as $n^2 + 3$, e.g. when $n = 5$, $n^2 + 3 = 28$.
I can find equivalent algebraic expressions for expressions such as $3x + 2x$ and $7x - 2x$.
I can simplify algebraic expressions such as $2a + 5a$ by collecting like terms, i.e. $7a$.

5
I can find equivalent algebraic expressions for expressions such as $4(x - 2)$ and $2(2x - 4)$.
I can expand a simple expression containing a bracket such as $3(x - 1) = 3x - 3$.
I can find, substitute into and use formulae describing real-life situations such as the cost of a taxi fare as $c = 5 + 2m$, which is £11 when $m = 3$.
I can solve simple equations involving one operation such as $2x = 12$, giving $x = 6$.

6
I can expand and simplify expressions with more than one bracket such as
$3(x + 2) + 4(x - 1) = 3x + 6 + 4x - 4 = 7x + 2$.

National Test questions

1 *2005 4–6 Paper 2*

Look at this algebra grid:

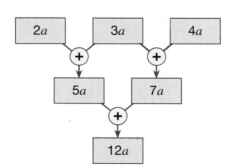

Copy and complete the algebra grids below, simplifying each expression.

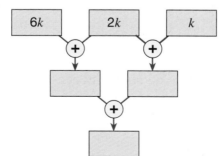

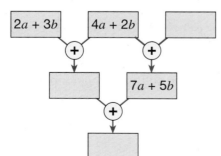

2 *2005 4–6 Paper 1*

Complete the statements below:

When x is 8, $4x$ is ...

When x is ..., $4x$ is 48

When x is 8, ... is 48

3 *2005 5–7 Paper 1*

Solve these equations.

$3y + 1 = 16$ $y = ...$

$18 = 4k + 6$ $k = ...$

Skiing trip

Use the information in the key to answer the following questions.

On-line Ski Hire Prices
- Minimum rental 2 days.
- Prices shown are for 2 days' and 8 days' hire.
- Prices include boots.
- All other days are pro-rata.
- 20% deposit required when ordering.

ADULTS	2 days	8 days
Platinum Saloman Crossmax W12 – or equivalent	€52.32	€192.72
Gold Rossignol Radical 8S ou 8X Oversize – or equivalent	€46.72	€171.94
Silver Saloman Aero RT– or equivalent	€37.60	€138.40
CHILDREN	2 days	8 days
Junior Surf Dynastar Starlett Teen– or equivalent	€26.56	€97.84
Junior Ski Saloman X-wing fury Junior– or equivalent	€16.16	€59.42
Kid Dynastar My First Dynastar– or equivalent	€12.16	€44.74

1 Mr Khan, Mrs Khan, their son Rafiq and their daughter Sufia hire skis for 8 days. Mr Khan hires a pair of Saloman Crossmax W12, Mrs Khan hires a pair of Saloman Aero RT, Rafiq hires a pair of Dynastar Starlett Teen and Sufia hires a pair of Saloman X-wing Fury Junior. What is their total bill?

2 The hire company allows a 25% discount per person for groups of 8 or more people. A party of 12 friends take a skiing trip for 8 days. They all go for the Adult 'Platinum' deal.

   a What is the cost of this deal with the discount?

   b How much will the 12 friends pay altogether?

3 To work out the cost per day subtract the 2-day hire price from the 8-day hire price and divide by 6. For example, for the 'Platinum' deal (192.72 − 52.32) ÷ 6 = 23.40. Work out the cost per day for:

a Adult 'Gold' deal

b Children's 'Junior Ski' deal.

c Explain why 6 days' hire for the Adult 'Gold' deal would cost €130.20.

4 Mr Smith hires some Saloman Crossmax W12 skis for 8 days. He pays £50 as a deposit. The exchange rate is £1 = €1.38. How many more Euros will he have to pay?

5 Colne Valley High School take a party skiing for 6 days. The bill for ski hire is shown below. Complete the bill.

Invoice for Colne Valley

Number of rentals	Type of ski	Rate	Total cost
11	Junior Surf		
9	Junior Ski		
10	Kid		
3	Platinum		
2	Gold	130.20	
	Total hire cost		
	Less 10% discount		
	Less £600 deposit @ 1.42		
Total less discount and deposit			

This chapter is going to show you

- The vocabulary and notation for lines and angles
- How to use angles at a point, angles on a straight line, angles in a triangle and vertically opposite angles
- How to use coordinates in all four quadrants

What you should already know

- The geometric properties of triangles and quadrilaterals
- How to plot coordinates in the first quadrant

Lines and angles

Lines A straight line can be considered to have infinite length.

A **line segment** has finite length.

A ———————————————————————— B

The line segment AB has two end points, one at A and the other at B.

Two lines lie in a **plane**, which is a flat surface.

Two lines are either parallel or intersect.

 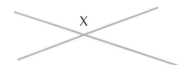 

Parallel lines never meet.   These two lines intersect at a point X.   These two lines intersect at right angles. The lines are said to be **perpendicular**.

Angles When two lines meet at a point, they form an **angle**. An angle is a measure of rotation and is measured in degrees (°).

Types of angle

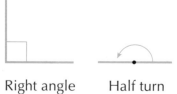    

Right angle
90°

Half turn
180°

Full turn
360°

Acute angle
less than 90°

Obtuse angle
between 90° and 180°

Reflex angle
between 180° and 360°

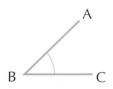

Describing angles

The angle at B can be written as:

∠ B or ∠ ABC or AB̂C

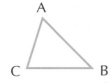

Describing triangles

The triangle can be represented by △ABC. It has three vertices, A, B and C; three angles, ∠A, ∠B and ∠C; three sides, AB, AC and BC.

Example 7.1 ▷ Describe the geometric properties of these two shapes.

a Isosceles triangle ABC

AB = AC
∠ABC = ∠ACB

b Parallelogram ABCD

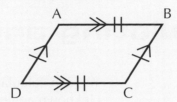

AB = CD and AD = BC
AB is parallel to CD or AB // CD
AD is parallel to BC or AD // BC

Exercise 7A

1 Write down which of the angles below are acute, which are obtuse and which are reflex. Estimate the size of each one.

a 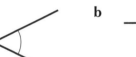 **b**  **c** **d** 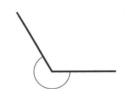 **e** **f**

2 For the shape ABCDE:

a Write down two lines that are equal in length.
b Write down two lines that are parallel.
c Write down two lines that are perpendicular to each other.
d Copy the diagram and draw on the two diagonals BD and CE. What do you notice about the two diagonals?

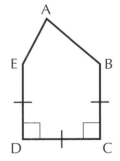

3 Write down the geometric properties of these three shapes.

a Equilateral triangle ABC

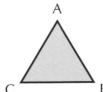

b Square ABCD

c Rhombus ABCD

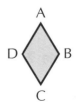

4 Write down four different places in the classroom where you can see:

a parallel lines **b** perpendicular lines

1   For the regular hexagon ABCDEF:

   a   Write down all the pairs of sides that are parallel.

   b   Write down all the diagonals that are perpendicular.

2   Cut the rectangle ABCD into two parts with one straight cut. How many different shapes can you make? Draw a diagram to show each different cut you use.

Calculating angles

You can calculate the **unknown angles** in a diagram from the information given. Unknown angles are usually denoted by letters, such as a, b, c, ...

Remember: usually the diagrams are not to scale.

Angles around a point

Angles around a point add up to 360°.

Example 7.2 ▷

Calculate the size of the angle a.

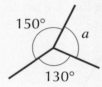

$a = 360° - 150° - 130°$

$a = 80°$

Angles on a straight line

Angles on a straight line add up to 180°.

Example 7.3 ▷

Calculate the size of the angle b.

$b = 180° - 155°$

$b = 25°$

Angles in a triangle   The angles in a triangle add up to 180°.

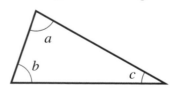

$a + b + c = 180°$

Example 7.4 ▷

Calculate the size of the angle c.

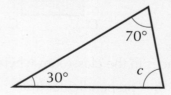

$c = 180° - 70° - 30°$

$c = 80°$

Vertically opposite angles

When two lines intersect, the opposite angles are equal.

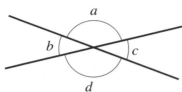

$a = d$ and $b = c$

Example 7.5 ▷

Calculate the sizes of angles d and e.

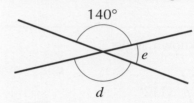

$d = 140°$ (opposite angles)
$e = 40°$ (angles on a straight line)

Exercise 7B

1 Calculate the size of each unknown angle.

a  **b** 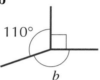 **c** 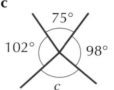 **d**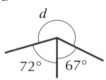

2 Calculate the size of each unknown angle.

a 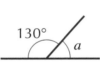 **b** **c** 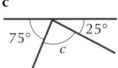 **d**

3 Calculate the size of each unknown angle.

a 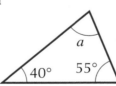 **b** 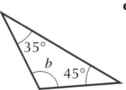 **c** **d**

4 Calculate the size of each unknown angle.

a 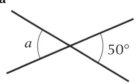 **b**  **c** 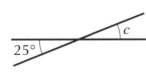 **d**

5 Calculate the size of each unknown angle.

a

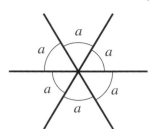

b

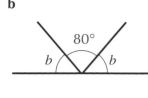

c

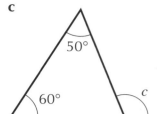

d

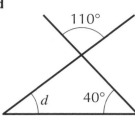

Extension Work

1 Calculate the size of each unknown angle.

a

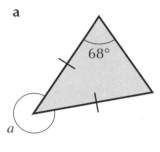

b

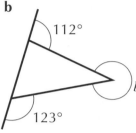

c

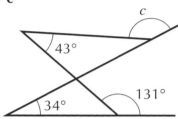

d

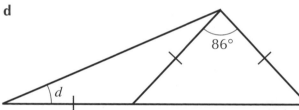

2 One angle in an isosceles triangle is 42°. Calculate the possible sizes of the other two angles.

Coordinates

We use **coordinates** to locate a point on a grid.

The grid consists of two axes, called the **x-axis** and the **y-axis**. They are perpendicular to each other.

The two axes meet at a point called the **origin**, which is labelled O.

The point A on the grid is 4 units across and 3 units up.

We say that the coordinates of A are (4, 3), which is usually written as A(4, 3).

The first number, 4, is the *x*-coordinate of A and the second number, 3, is the *y*-coordinate of A. The *x*-coordinate is *always* written first.

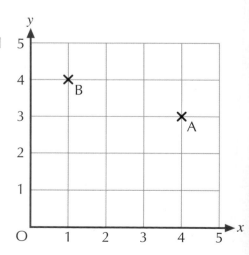

When plotting a point on a grid, a **✗** or a ● is usually used.

The coordinates of the origin are (0, 0) and the coordinates of the point B are (1, 4).

The grid system can be extended to negative numbers and points can be plotted in all **four quadrants**.

Example 7.6 ▶ The coordinates of the points on the grid are:

A(4, 2), B(–2, 3), C(–3, –1), D(1, –4)

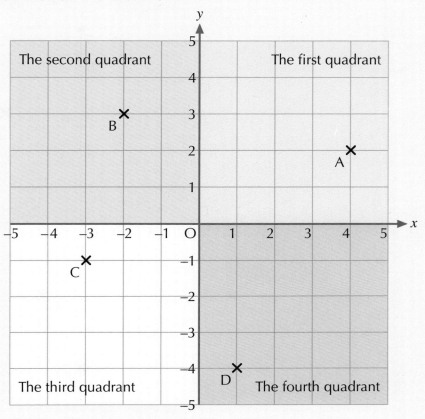

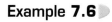

Exercise 7C

(1) Write down the coordinates of the points P, Q, R, S and T.

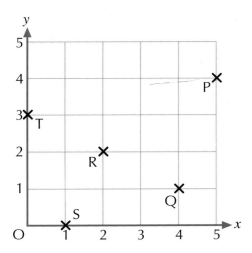

2 **a** Make a copy of the grid in Question 1. Then plot the points A(1, 1), B(1, 5) and C(4, 5).

b The three points are the vertices of a rectangle. Plot point D to complete the rectangle.

c Write down the coordinates of D.

3 Write down the coordinates of the points A, B, C, D, E, F, G and H.

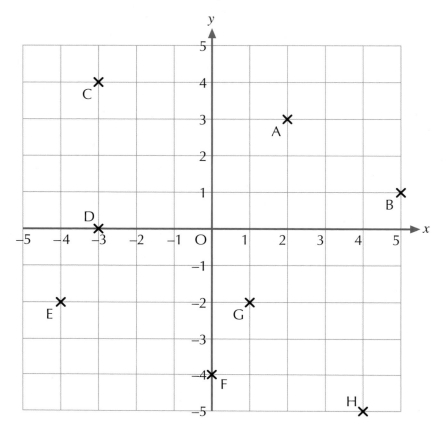

4 **a** Make a copy of the grid in Question 3. Then plot the points A(–4, 3), B(–2, –2), C(0, 1), D(2, –2) and E(4, 3).

b Join the points in the order given. What letter have you drawn?

5 **a** Make a copy of the grid in Question 3. Then plot the points W(3, 4), X(3, –2) and Y(–3, –2).

b The points form three vertices of a square WXYZ. Plot the point Z and draw the square.

c What are the coordinates of the point Z?

d Draw in the diagonals of the square. What are the coordinates of the point of intersection of the diagonals?

Coordinates and lines

- Draw on a grid x-and y-axes from –8 to 8.
- Plot the points (0, 2) and (6, 8) and join them to make a straight line.
- Write down the coordinates of other points that lie on the line.
- Can you spot a rule that connects the x-coordinate and the y-coordinate?
- Extend the line into the third quadrant. Does your rule still work?
- The rule you have found is given by the formula $y = x + 2$.
- Now draw the following lines on different grids using these formulae:

    a $y = x + 3$ **b** $y = x$ **c** $y = x - 2$

LEVEL BOOSTER

4   I can recognise acute, obtuse and reflex angles.
I can use coordinates in the first quadrant.

5   I know the geometrical properties of simple 2-D shapes.
I can find angles on a line and around a point.
I can find the angles in a triangle.
I can use coordinates in all four quadrants.

6   I can find angles in intersecting lines.

National Test questions

1   *2001 Paper 1*

    a   The point K is halfway between points B and C.

       What are the coordinates of point K?

    b   Shape ABCD is a rectangle.

       What are the coordinates of point D?

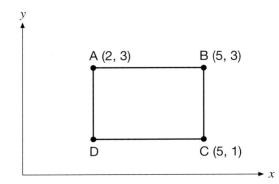

2 *2004 4–6 Paper 2*

I put square tiles on a large grid so that the tiles touch at the corners. The diagram shows part of my diagonal pattern:

a The **bottom right-hand** corner of tile 2 is marked with a •. Write the coordinates of this point.

b **Tile 4** touches two other tiles. Write the coordinates of the points where tile 4 touches two other tiles.

c Write the coordinates of the points where **tile 17** touches two other tiles.

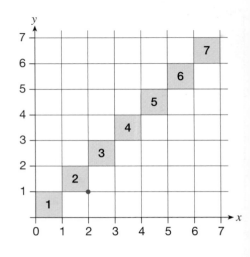

3 *2000 Paper 1*

Look at these angles.

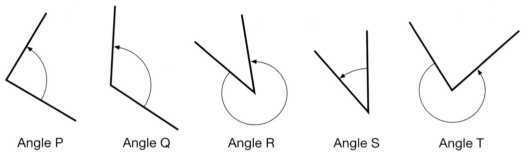

| Angle P | Angle Q | Angle R | Angle S | Angle T |

One of the angles measures 120°. Write its letter.

4 *2005 4–6 Paper 1*

The diagram shows triangle PQR.

Work out the sizes of angles *a*, *b* and *c*.

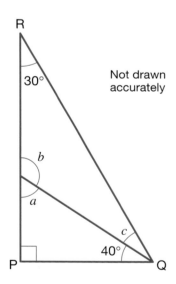

Not drawn accurately

CHAPTER 8 Statistics 2

This chapter is going to show you

- How to collect and organise data
- How to create data collection forms
- How to create questionnaires
- How to use frequency tables to collate data
- How to conduct surveys and experiments
- How to draw simple conclusions from data

What you should already know

- How to create a tally chart
- How to draw bar charts and pictograms

Using a tally chart

What method of transport do pupils use to travel to school – and why?

When pupils are asked this question, they will give different methods of travelling, such as bus, car, bike, walking, train and even some others we don't yet know about!

A good way to collect this data is to fill in a tally chart as each pupil is asked how he or she travels to school. For example:

Type of transport	Tally	Frequency
Bus	⊮⊮⊤ IIII	9
Car	⊮⊮⊤	5
Bike	II	2
Walking	⊮⊮⊤ ⊮⊮⊤ IIII	14
Other		
Total		30

In answering the question 'Why?', the pupils give the sorts of answers listed below.

Bus	Because it's quicker. Because it's too far to walk.
Car	My mum goes that way to work. There's no bus and it's too far. It's easier than the bus.
Bike	It's better than walking.
Walking	It's not too far. It's better than a crowded bus.

After the survey, you look at all the reasons given and pick out those which are common to many pupils. These reasons can be left as a table, or illustrated in different ways.

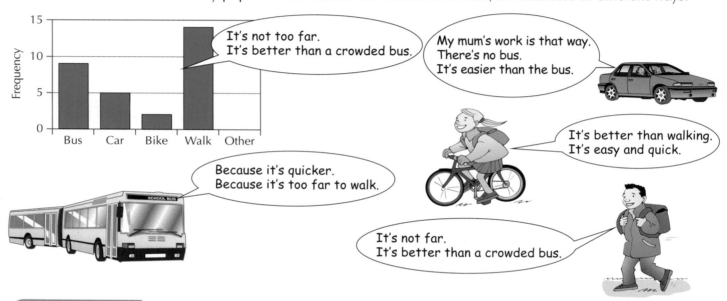

Exercise 8A

4

FM **1** Use your own class tally sheet (or the one on page 93) to draw a chart illustrating the methods of transport used by pupils to get to school, and the reasons why.

FM **2** A class were asked: 'Where would you like to go for our form trip?' They voted as follows:

Place	Tally
Alton Towers	⊞⊞
Camelot	⊞ I
Blackpool	⊞ III
London	III
Bath	IIII

a Draw a chart illustrating the places the students wanted to go to.

b Write suitable reasons why the students might have voted for each place and illustrate these reasons.

Extension Work

Choose five different places to go for a form trip near you and create your own tally sheet. Collect some data for this sheet, then either create a bar chart with some reasons on it, or try using a spreadsheet and creating graphs from that.

Using the correct data

There are many different newspapers about.
Can you list six different national newspapers?

Now consider Ted's question. The strict way to
answer this would be to count, in each
newspaper, all the words and all their letters.
But this would take too long, so we take what is
called a **sample**. We count, say, 100 words from
each newspaper to find the length of each word.

Do certain newspapers
use more long words than
the other newspapers?

Exercise 8B

This whole exercise is a class activity.

1 **a** Select one or two pages from a newspaper.

b Create a data capture form (tally chart) like the one below

Number of letters	Tally	Frequency
1		
2		
3		
4		
5		

c **i** Select at least two different articles.

ii Count the number of letters in each word and complete the tally.

Note: numbers such as 3, 4, 5 count as 1 letter
numbers such as 15, 58 count as 2 letters
numbers such as 156, 897 count as 3 letters etc.
with hyphenated words, e.g. vice-versa, ignore the hyphen

d Fill in the frequency column.

e Create a bar chart for your results.

f You may find it interesting to compare the differences between the different
newspapers.

Look at the following misleading conclusions that arise from not using like data.

Travelling to school Two different classes did a survey of
how pupils travelled to school.

They both made pie charts
to show their results.

Jim's class

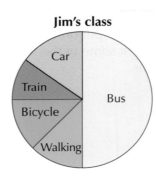

Noriko's class

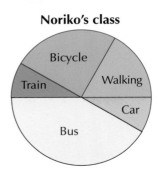

Look at both charts and ask yourself:

Which class had the most pupils using the bus?

Obvious – it's Jim's class!

BUT if you are told:

In Jim's class there were only 24 pupils, and in Noriko's class there were 36 pupils.

Then you will see that:

In Jim's class, half of the 24 used the bus, which is 12.
In Noriko's class, more than one third used the bus, which is about 14.

Clearly, you have to be very careful about interpreting data in its final form.

Here, you can say that a bigger proportion of Jim's class used the bus, but *not* more pupils used the bus than in Noriko's class.

So, it is most important to try to use like numbers of items when you are going to make a comparison of data from different sources.

5

Extension Work

Choose a book or magazine that you like and create a bar chart of the number of letters in each word for selected parts of them (either two paragraphs or two articles).

Grouped frequency

How many times have you walked to school this term?

A class was asked this question and the replies were:

6, 3, 5, 20, 15, 11, 13, 28, 30, 5, 2, 6, 8, 18, 23, 22, 17, 13, 4, 2, 30, 17, 19, 25, 8, 3, 9, 12, 15, 8

There are too many different values here to make a sensible bar chart, so we group them to produce a **grouped frequency table**, as shown below. The different groups the data has been put into are called **classes**. Where possible, classes are kept the same size as each other.

Times	1–5	6–10	11–15	16–20	21–25	26–30
Frequency	7	6	6	5	3	3

A bar chart has been drawn from this data and information put on each bar about some of the reasons.

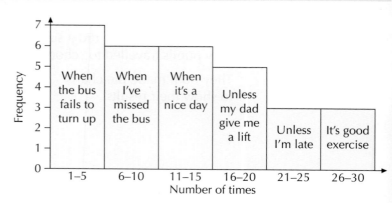

1 A class did a survey on how many text messages each pupil had sent yesterday. The results of this survey are:

4, 7, 2, 18,·1, 16, 19, 15, 13, 0, 9, 17, 4, 6, 10, 12, 15, 8, 3, 14, 2, 14, 15, 18, 5, 16, 3, 6, 5, 18, 12

a Create a grouped frequency table with a class size of 5 as below:

Number of texts	Tally	Frequency
0–4		
5–9		
10–14		
15–19		
	Total:	

b Complete the table using the data above.

c Draw a bar chart of the data.

2 A teacher asked her class, 'Count how many times this week you play games on your computer.'

These were their responses:

3, 6, 9, 2, 23, 18, 6, 8, 29, 27, 2, 1, 0, 5, 19, 23, 13, 21, 7, 4, 23, 8, 7, 1, 0, 25, 24, 8, 13, 18, 15, 16

a Create a grouped frequency table with a class size of 5 as below:

Number of times	Tally	Frequency
0–4		
5–9		
10–14		
15–19		
20–24		
25–29		
	Total:	

b Complete the table using the data above.

c Draw a bar chart of the data.

3 At a youth club, the members were asked, 'How many times have you played table tennis this week?'

Their replies were:

5, 8, 1, 15, 7, 2, 0, 4, 8, 10, 6, 16, 3, 2, 1, 1, 5, 1, 6, 9, 2, 3, 4, 3, 2, 16, 15, 0, 4, 2, 11, 15, 6, 7, 3, 1, 2, 13, 6, 5, 3, 1, 2, 2, 5, 6, 8, 12, 1, 3, 1, 1, 0, 0, 15, 4, 3, 5, 2, 1, 12, 8, 1

a Create a grouped frequency table:
  i with a class size of 3, i.e. 0–2, 3–5, 6–8, 9–11, 12–14, 15–17
  ii with a class size of 5, i.e. 0–4, 5–9, 10–14, 15–19

b Draw a bar chart for each frequency table.

c Which class size seems most appropriate to use?

Design a tally chart, with equal class sizes, to capture data in an experiment to find out how many words there are in sentences in a book.

a Use the tally chart to survey the length of sentences in a book suitable for:
    i a 5-year-old   **ii** an 11-year-old   **iii** an adult

b Draw a bar chart from each frequency table.

c Comment on your results.

Data collection

Let's ask a sample of the pupils in our school these questions. In other words, not everyone, but a few from each group.

You ask each question, then immediately complete your data collection form.

An example of a suitable data collection form is shown below.

Year group	Boy or girl	How much to charge?	Time to start?	Time to finish?	What would you like to eat?
Y7	B	£1	7 pm	11 pm	Crisps, beefburgers, chips
Y7	G	50p	7 pm	9 pm	Chips, crisps, lollies
Y8	G	£2	7:30 pm	10 pm	Crisps, hot dogs
Y11	B	£3	8:30 pm	11:30 pm	Chocolate, pizza

Keep track of the age	Try to ask equal numbers	Once the data is collected, it can be sorted into frequency tables.

There are five stages in running this type of survey:
- Deciding what questions to ask and who to ask.
- Creating a simple, suitable data collection form for all the questions.
- Asking the questions and completing the data collection form.
- After collecting all the data, collating it in frequency tables.
- Analysing the data to draw conclusions from the survey.

The size of your sample will depend on many things. It may be simply the first 50 people you come across. Or you may want 10% of the available people.

In the above example, a good sample would probably be about four from each class, two boys and two girls.

A class did the above survey on a sample of 10 pupils from each of the Key Stage 3 years. Their data collection chart is shown on the next page.

 a   Copy and create the tally chart for the suggested charges from each year group:

Charges	Tallies					
	Y7	Total	Y8	Total	Y9	Total
25p						
50p						
75p						
£1						
£1.25						
£1.50						
£2						
£2.50						
£3						

b   Comment on the differences between the year groups.

 a   Copy and create the tally chart for the suggested starting times from each year group:

Times	Tallies					
	Y7	Total	Y8	Total	Y9	Total
7:00 pm						
7:30 pm						
8:00 pm						
8:30 pm						

b   Comment on the differences between the year groups.

3 a   Copy and create the tally chart for the suggested finishing times from each year group:

Times	Tallies					
	Y7	Total	Y8	Total	Y9	Total
9:00 pm						
9:30 pm						
10:00 pm						
10:30 pm						
11:00 pm						
11:30 pm						

b   Comment on the differences between the year groups.

4 **a** Create and complete a tally chart as before for the food suggestions of each year.

b Comment on the differences between the year groups.

Year group	Boy or girl	How much to charge	Time to start	Time to finish	What would you like to eat?
Y7	B	£1	7 pm	11 pm	Crisps, beefburgers, chips
Y7	G	50p	7 pm	9 pm	Chips, crisps, ice pops
Y8	G	£2	7:30 pm	10 pm	Crisps, hot dogs
Y9	B	£3	8:30 pm	11:30 pm	Chocolate, pizza
Y9	G	£2	8 pm	10 pm	Pizza
Y9	B	£2.50	7:30 pm	9:30 pm	Hot dogs, Chocolate
Y8	G	£1	8 pm	10:30 pm	Crisps
Y7	B	75p	7 pm	9 pm	Crisps, beefburgers
Y7	B	£1	7:30 pm	10:30 pm	Crisps, ice pops
Y8	B	£1.50	7 pm	9 pm	Crisps, chips, hot dogs
Y9	G	£2	8 pm	11 pm	Pizza, chocolate
Y9	G	£1.50	8 pm	10:30 pm	Chips, pizza
Y9	G	£2	8 pm	11 pm	Crisps, pizza
Y7	G	£1.50	7 pm	9 pm	Crisps, ice pops, chocolate
Y8	B	£2	7:30 pm	9:30 pm	Crisps, ice pops, chocolate
Y8	B	£1	8 pm	10 pm	Chips, hot dogs
Y9	B	£1.50	8 pm	11 pm	Pizza
Y7	B	50p	7 pm	9:30 pm	Crisps, hot dogs
Y8	G	75p	8 pm	10:30 pm	Crisps, chips
Y9	B	£2	7:30 pm	10:30 pm	Pizza
Y8	G	£1.50	7:30 pm	10 pm	Chips, hot dogs, chocolate
Y8	B	£1.25	7 pm	9:30 pm	Chips, hot dogs, ice pops
Y9	G	£3	7 pm	9:30 pm	Crisps, pizza
Y9	B	£2.50	8 pm	10:30 pm	Crisps, hot dogs
Y7	G	25p	7:30 pm	10 pm	Crisps, beefburgers, ice pops
Y7	G	50p	7 pm	9 pm	Crisps, pizza
Y7	G	£1	7 pm	9:30 pm	Crisps, pizza
Y8	B	£2	8 pm	10 pm	Crisps, chips, chocolate
Y8	G	£1.50	7:30 pm	9:30 pm	Chips, beefburgers
Y7	B	£1	7:30 pm	10 pm	Crisps, ice pops

Investigate the differences between boys and girls as to the suggested length of time for the disco.

LEVEL BOOSTER

4 I can collect data and record it.
I can represent and interpret collected data in frequency diagrams.

5 I can compare two simple distributions.
I can group data, where appropriate, into equal class intervals.
I can interpret graphs and diagrams, drawing conclusions.

National Test questions

1 *1997 Paper 2*

Some pupils wanted to find out if people liked a new biscuit.

They decided to do a survey and wrote a questionnaire.

a One question was:

How old are you (in years)?

☐   ☐   ☐   ☐   ☐

20 or younger   20 to 30   30 to 40   40 to 50   50 or over

Mary said:

The labels for the middle three boxes need changing.

Explain why Mary was right.

b A different question was:

How much do you usually spend on biscuits each week?

☐ A lot   ☐ A little   ☐ Nothing   ☐ Don't know

Mary said: 'Some of these labels need changing too.'

Write new labels for any boxes that need changing.

You may change as many labels as you want to.

The pupils decide to give their questionnaire to 50 people.

Jon said:

> Let's ask 50 pupils in our school.

c Give one disadvantage of Jon's suggestion.

d Give one advantage of Jon's suggestion.

 2 *2006 5–7 Paper 2*

Wine gums are sweets that are made in different colours.

Pupils tested whether people can taste the difference between black wine gums and other wine gums.

The percentage bar charts show three pupils' results.

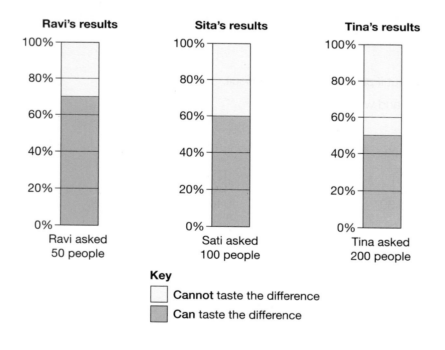

(a) Copy and complete this table.

	Number of people who were tested	Number of people who can taste the difference	Number of people who cannot taste the difference
Ravi	50		
Sita	100		
Tina	200		

(b) Explain why **Tina's** results are likely to be **more reliable** than Ravi's or Sita's.

FM Be a school chef for a day

1 Your class has been asked to transform the school canteen with the help of a professional chef. In order to develop your menu with him, you need to collect certain data before presenting your findings and trialling recipes. The tally chart below shows pupils' choices for food.

	Key Stage 3	Frequency
Pasta	HH1	
Salad	II	
Pizza	HH1 HH1 I	
Jacket potato	HH1	
Curry	HH1 HH1	
Toasties	HH1 I	

	Key Stage 4	Frequency
Pasta	HH1 HH1 III	
Salad	IIII	
Pizza	HH1 I	
Jacket potato	HH1 IIII	
Curry	HH1 HH1 IIII	
Toasties	HH1 HH1 I	

a Explain the differences between the two key stages.

b Combine the two tallies into one and create the single bar chart to illustrate the whole-school choices.

2 You now have to work out how your menu will be priced with the chef. In order to do this you need to know how much pupils will be prepared to pay for lunch each day.

Price	under £1	£1–£2	over £2
Y7	30	45	12
Y8	25	50	18
Y9	18	42	25
Y10	11	52	27
Y11	8	55	22

a Explain the differences between the year groups.

b Combine the table into one and create the single bar chart to illustrate the whole school price choices.`

3 The table below shows the ingredients needed for the chef to create enough of the particular dish for 50 pupils.

Ingredients needed	Tomato & chicken pasta	Spicy Mexican wraps	Chilli jacket potatoes	Pitta pizza
Chopped tomatoes (tins)	20	0	5	0
Mushrooms (punnets)	5	0	2	2
Peppers (×3)	5	10	2	8
Onions (×5)	6	5	5	3
Potatoes (5 kg bags)	0	0	3	0

Chef wanted to create the following dishes on one day:

Tomato & chicken pasta   for 150 pupils
Spicy Mexican wraps   for 25 pupils
Chilli jacket potatoes   for 75 pupils
Pitta pizza   for 350 pupils

Write down the total number required of:

a Tins of chopped tomatoes

b Punnets of mushrooms

c Peppers

d Onions

e 5 kg bags of potatoes

> **This chapter is going to show you**
> - How to round off positive whole numbers and decimals
> - The order of operations
> - How to multiply and divide a three-digit whole number by a two-digit whole number without a calculator
> - How to use a calculator efficiently

> **What you should already know**
> - Tables up to 10 times 10
> - Place value of the digits in a number such as 23.508

Rounding

What is wrong with this picture?

It shows that the woman's weight (60 kg) balances the man's weight (110 kg) when both weights are rounded to the nearest 100 kg!

This example highlights the need to round numbers *sensibly*, depending on the situation in which they occur.

But, we do not always need numbers to be precise, and it is easier to work with numbers that are rounded off.

Example 9.1 ▷ Round off each of these numbers to **i** the nearest 10 **ii** the nearest 100 **iii** the nearest 1000.

a 937 **b** 2363 **c** 3799 **d** 281

a 937 is 940 to the nearest 10, 900 to the nearest 100 and 1000 to the nearest 1000.

b 2363 is 2360 to the nearest 10, 2400 to the nearest 100, and 2000 to the nearest 1000.

c 3799 is 3800 to the nearest 10, 3800 to the nearest 100, and 4000 to the nearest 1000.

d 281 is 280 to the nearest 10, 300 to the nearest 100, and 0 to the nearest 1000.

Example 9.2 ▷ Round off each of these numbers to **i** the nearest whole number **ii** one decimal place (dp).

    a 9.35   **b** 4.323   **c** 5.99

    a 9.35 is 9 to the nearest whole number and 9.4 to 1 dp.

    b 4.323 is 4 to the nearest whole number and 4.3 to 1 dp.

    c 5.99 is 6 to the nearest whole number and 6.0 to 1 dp.

Exercise 9A

(1) Round off each of these numbers to **i** the nearest 10 **ii** the nearest 100 **iii** the nearest 1000.

a	3731	**b**	807	**c**	2111	**d**	4086	**e**	265	**f**	3457
g	4050	**h**	2999	**i**	1039	**j**	192	**k**	3192	**l**	964

(2) i What is the mass being weighed by each scale to the nearest 100 g?

    ii Estimate the mass being weighed to the nearest 10 g.

    a    **b** 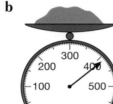   **c**    **d**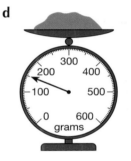

(3) i What is the volume of the liquid in each measuring cylinder to the nearest 10 ml?

    ii Estimate the volume of liquid to the nearest whole number.

    a 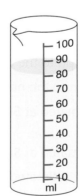   **b** 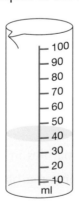   **c** 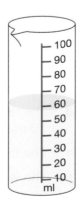   **d**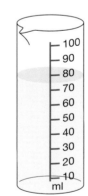

(4) Round off each of these numbers to **i** the nearest whole number **ii** one decimal place.

a	4.72	**b**	3.07	**c**	2.634	**d**	1.932	**e**	0.78	**f**	0.92
g	3.92	**h**	2.64	**i**	3.18	**j**	3.475	**k**	1.45	**l**	1.863

5 How long are each of these ropes to **i** the nearest 100 cm **ii** the nearest 10 cm **iii** the nearest cm **iv** the nearest mm?

a

176   177   178   179 cm

b

62   63   64   65   66 cm

c

278   279   280   281   282 cm

d

3.4   3.5   3.6   3.7   3.8 m

6 a The following are the diameters of the planets in kilometres. Round off each one to the nearest 1000 km. Then place the planets in order of size, starting with the smallest.

Planet	Earth	Jupiter	Mars	Mercury	Neptune	Pluto	Saturn	Uranus	Venus
Diameter (km)	12 800	142 800	6780	5120	49 500	2284	120 660	51 100	12 100

b What would happen if you rounded off the diameters to the nearest 10 000 km?

Extension **Work**

The headteacher says: 'All of our classes have about 30 pupils in them.' Given this number is to the nearest 10, what is the smallest class there could be and what would be the largest?

The deputy head says: 'All of the cars driving past the school are doing about 30 mph.' Given this number is to the nearest 10, what is the lowest speed the cars could be doing and what would be the highest?

Why are these answers different?

Write down the smallest and largest values for each of the following.

a A crowd of people estimated at 80 to the nearest 10 people.

b The speed of a car estimated at 80 mph to the nearest 10 mph.

c The length of a leaf estimated at 8 cm to the nearest centimetre.

d The number of marbles in a bag estimated at 50 to the nearest 10 marbles.

e The number of marbles in a bag estimated at 50 to the nearest marble.

f The weight of some marbles in a bag estimated at 500 grams to the nearest 10 grams.

The four operations

Below are four calculations. Make up problems using the pictures that go with the four calculations.

$70.9 \times 8 = 567.2$

$250 - 198 = 52$

$2.3 + 3.5 + 1.7 = 7.5$

$435 \div 15 = 29$

Example 9.3 ▷   **a** Find the product of 9 and 56.   **b** Find the remainder when 345 is divided by 51.

   a   Product means 'multiply'. So, $9 \times 56 = 9 \times 50 + 9 \times 6 = 450 + 54 = 504$.

   b $345 \div 51 \approx 350 \div 50 = 7$. So, $7 \times 51 = 350 + 7 = 357$ which is too big.
       $6 \times 51 = 306$, which gives $345 - 306 = 39$. The remainder is 39.

Example 9.4 ▷   A box of biscuits costs £1.99. How much will 28 boxes cost?

   The easiest way to do this is: $28 \times £2$ minus $28p = £56 - 28p = £55.72$.

Example 9.5 ▷   Mr Smith travels from Edinburgh (E) to Liverpool (L) and then to Bristol (B). Mr Jones travels directly from Edinburgh to Bristol. Use the distance chart to find out how much further Mr Smith travelled than Mr Jones.

   Mr Smith travels $226 + 237 = 463$ miles. Mr Jones travels 383 miles.
       $463 - 383 = 80$
   So, Mr Smith travels 80 miles further.

	E	L	B
E		226	383
L	226		237
B	383	237	

Exercise 9B

 1 How long does a train journey take if the train leaves at 10:32 am and arrives at 1:12 pm?

2 Which mark is better: 17 out of 20 or 40 out of 50?

 3 How much does it cost to fill a 51-litre petrol tank at 80p per litre?

 4 a A company has 197 boxes to move by van. The van can carry 23 boxes at a time. How many trips must the van make to move all the boxes?

   b The same van does 34 miles to the gallon of petrol. Each trip above is 31 miles. Can the van deliver all the boxes if it has 8 gallons of petrol in the tank?

5 Find the sum and product of   **a** 5, 7 and 20.   **b** 2, 38 and 50.

6 The local video shop is having a sale. Videos are £4.99 each or five for £20.

 a What is the cost of three videos?

 b What is the cost of ten videos?

 c What is the greatest number of videos you can buy with £37?

7 **a** Three consecutive integers have a sum of 90. What are they?

 b Two consecutive integers have a product of 132. What are they?

 c Explain why there is more than one answer to this problem:

 Two consecutive integers have a difference of 1. What are they?

8 Rajid has between 50 and 60 books. He arranged them in piles of four and found that he had one pile of three left over. He then arranged them in piles of five and found that he had one pile of four left over. How many books does Rajid have?

Extension Work

The magic number of this magic square is 50.

That means that the numbers in every row, in every column and in both diagonals add up to 50.

5	18	11	16
12	15	6	17
14	9	20	7
19	8	13	10

However, there are many more ways to make 50 by adding four numbers. For example, each of the following sets of 4 numbers makes 50.

5	18
12	15

5	16
19	10

18	11
8	13

How many more arrangements of four numbers can you find that add up to 50?

BODMAS

The following are instructions for making a cup of tea.

Can you put them in the right order?

Drink tea	Empty teapot	Fill kettle	Put milk in cup	Put teabag in teapot
Switch on kettle	Wait for tea to brew	Rinse teapot with hot water	Pour boiling water in teapot	Pour out tea

It is important that things are done in the right order. In mathematical operations there are rules about this.

The order of operations is called **BODMAS**, which stands for **B** (Brackets), **O** (Order or POwer), **D M** (Division and Multiplication) and **A S** (Addition and Subtraction).

Operations are always done in this order, which means that brackets are done first, followed by powers, then multiplication and division, and finally addition and subtraction.

Example 9.6 ▷

Circle the operation that you do first in each of these calculations. Then work out each one.

a $2 + 6 \div 2$ **b** $32 - 4 \times 5$ **c** $6 \div 3 - 1$ **d** $6 \div (3 - 1)$

a Division is done before addition, so you get $2 + 6 \oplus 2 = 2 + 3 = 5$

b Multiplication is done before subtraction, so you get $32 - 4 \otimes 5 = 32 - 20 = 12$

c Division is done before subtraction, so you get $6 \ominus 3 - 1 = 2 - 1 = 1$

d Brackets are done first, so you get $6 \div (3 - 1) = 6 \div 2 = 3$

Example 9.7 ▷

Work out each of the following, showing each step of the calculation.

a $1 + 3^2 \times 4 - 2$ **b** $(1 + 3)^2 \times (4 - 2)$

a The order will be power, multiplication, addition, subtraction (the last two can be interchanged). This gives:
$$1 + 3^2 \times 4 - 2 = 1 + 9 \times 4 - 2 = 1 + 36 - 2 = 37 - 2 = 35$$

b The order will be brackets (both of them), power, multiplication. This gives:
$$(1 + 3)^2 \times (4 - 2) = 4^2 \times 2 = 16 \times 2 = 32$$

Example 9.8 ▷

Put brackets into each of the following to make the calculation true.

a $5 + 1 \times 4 = 24$ **b** $1 + 3^2 - 4 = 12$ **c** $24 \div 6 - 2 = 6$

Decide which operation is done first.

a $(5 + 1) \times 4 = 24$

b $(1 + 3)^2 - 4 = 12$

c $24 \div (6 - 2) = 6$

Exercise 9C

1 Write down the operation that you do first in each of these calculations. Then work out each one.

a $2 + 3 \times 6$ **b** $12 - 6 \div 3$ **c** $5 \times 5 + 2$ **d** $12 \div 4 - 2$
e $(2 + 3) \times 6$ **f** $(12 - 3) \div 3$ **g** $5 \times (5 + 2)$ **h** $12 \div (4 - 2)$

2 Work out the following showing each step of the calculation.

a $2 \times 3 + 4$ **b** $2 \times (3 + 4)$ **c** $2 + 3 \times 4$ **d** $(2 + 3) \times 4$
e $4 \times 4 - 4$ **f** $5 + 3^2 + 6$ **g** $5 \times (3^2 + 6)$ **h** $3^2 - (5 - 2)$
i $(2 + 3) \times (4 + 5)$ **j** $(2^2 + 3) \times (4 + 5)$ **k** $4 \div 4 + 4 \div 4$
l $44 \div 4 + 4$ **m** $(6 + 2)^2$ **n** $6^2 + 2^2$ **o** $3^2 + 4 \times 6$

3 Put brackets into each of the following to make the calculation true.

a $2 \times 5 + 4 = 18$ **b** $2 + 6 \times 3 = 24$ **c** $2 + 3 \times 1 + 6 = 35$
d $5 + 2^2 \times 1 = 9$ **e** $3 + 2^2 = 25$ **f** $3 \times 4 + 3 + 7 = 28$
g $3 + 4 \times 7 + 1 = 35$ **h** $3 + 4 \times 7 + 1 = 50$ **i** $9 - 5 - 2 = 6$
j $9 - 5 \times 2 = 8$ **k** $4 + 4 + 4 \div 2 = 6$ **l** $1 + 4^2 - 9 - 2 = 18$

4 One of the calculations $2 \times 3^2 = 36$ and $2 \times 3^2 = 18$ is wrong. Which is it and how could you add brackets to make it true?

5 Work out the value of each of these.

a $(4 + 4) \div (4 + 4)$
b $(4 \times 4) \div (4 + 4)$
c $(4 + 4 + 4) \div 4$
d $4 \times (4 - 4) + 4$
e $(4 \times 4 + 4) \div 4$
f $(4 + 4 + 4) \div 2$
g $4 + 4 - 4 \div 4$
h $(4 + 4) \times (4 \div 4)$
i $(4 + 4) + 4 \div 4$

Extension Work

In Question 5, each calculation was made up of four 4s.

Work out the value of: **a** $44 \div 4 - 4$ **b** $4 \times 4 - 4 \div 4$ **c** $4 \times 4 + 4 - 4$

Can you make other calculations using four 4s to give answers that you have not yet obtained in Question 5 or in the three calculations above?

Do as many as you can and see whether you can make all the values up to 20.

Repeat with five 5s. For example:

$(5 + 5) \div 5 - 5 \div 5 = 1$ $(5 \times 5 - 5) \div (5 + 5) = 2$

Long multiplication and long division

Example 9.9

Work out 36×43.

Below are four examples of the ways this calculation can be done. The answer is 1548.

Box method (partitioning)

×	30	6	
40	1200	240	1440
3	90	18	108
			1548

Column method (expanded working)

$$
\begin{array}{r}
36 \\
\times\ 43 \\
\hline
18 \ (3 \times 6) \\
90 \ (3 \times 30) \\
240 \ (40 \times 6) \\
1200 \ (40 \times 30) \\
\hline
1548
\end{array}
$$

Column method (compacted working)

$$
\begin{array}{r}
36 \\
\times\ 43 \\
\hline
108 \ (3 \times 36) \\
1440 \ (40 \times 36) \\
\hline
1548
\end{array}
$$

Chinese method

Example 9.10

Work out $543 \div 31$.

Below are two examples of the ways this can be done. The answer is 17, remainder 16.

Subtracting multiples

$$
\begin{array}{r}
543 \\
-\ 310 \ (10 \times 31) \\
\hline
233 \\
-\ 155 \ (5 \times 31) \\
\hline
78 \\
-\ 62 \ (2 \times 31) \\
\hline
16
\end{array}
$$

Traditional method

$$
\begin{array}{r}
17 \\
31\overline{)543} \\
31 \\
\hline
233 \\
217 \\
\hline
16
\end{array}
$$

1. Work out each of the following long multiplication problems. Use any method you are happy with.

   a 17×23 b 32×42 c 19×45 d 56×46

   e 12×346 f 32×541 g 27×147 h 39×213

2. Work out each of the following long division problems. Use any method you are happy with. Some of the problems will have a remainder.

   a $684 \div 19$ b $966 \div 23$ c $972 \div 36$ d $625 \div 25$

   e $930 \div 38$ f $642 \div 24$ g $950 \div 33$ h $800 \div 42$

Decide whether the following nine problems involve long multiplication or long division. Then do the appropriate calculation, showing your method clearly.

3. Each day 17 Jumbo jets fly from London to San Francisco. Each jet can carry up to 348 passengers. How many people can travel from London to San Francisco each day?

4. A company has 897 boxes to move by van. The van can carry 23 boxes at a time. How many trips must the van make to move all the boxes?

5. The same van does 34 miles to a gallon of petrol. How many miles can it do if the petrol tank holds 18 gallons?

6. The school photocopier can print 82 sheets a minute. If it runs without stopping for 45 minutes, how many sheets will it print?

7. The RE department has printed 525 sheets on Buddhism. These are put into folders in sets of 35. How many folders are there?

8. a To raise money, Wath Running Club are going to do a relay race from Wath to Edinburgh, which is 384 kilometres. Each runner will run 24 kilometres. How many runners will be needed to cover the distance?

   b Sponsorship will bring in £32 per kilometre. How much money will the club raise?

9. Computer floppy disks are 45p each. How much will a box of 35 disks cost? Give your answer in pounds.

10. The daily newspaper sells advertising by the square inch. On Monday, it sells 232 square inches at £15 per square inch. How much money does it get from this advertising?

11. The local library has 13 000 books. Each shelf holds 52 books. How many shelves are there?

Another way of multiplying two two-digit numbers together is the 'Funny Face' method.

This shows how to do 26×57.

$$26 \times 57 = (20 + 6) \times (50 + 7)$$

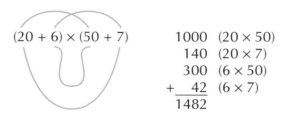

$(20 + 6) \times (50 + 7)$		
	1000	(20×50)
	140	(20×7)
	300	(6×50)
+	42	(6×7)
	1482	

Do a poster showing a calculation using the 'Funny Face' method.

Efficient calculations

You should have your own calculator, so that you can get used to it. Make sure that you understand how to use the basic functions ($\times$, $\div$, $+$, $-$) and the square, square root and brackets keys. They are different even on scientific calculators.

Example 9.11

Use a calculator to work out   **a** $\dfrac{242 + 118}{88 - 72}$ **b** $\dfrac{63 \times 224}{32 \times 36}$

The line that separates the top numbers from the bottom numbers acts both as a divide sign ($\div$) and as brackets.

a   Key the calculation as $(242 + 118) \div (88 - 72) = 22.5$

b   Key the calculation as $(63 \times 224) \div (32 \times 36) = 12.25$

Example 9.12

Use a calculator to work out   **a** $\sqrt{1764}$ **b** 23.4^2 **c** $52.3 - (30.4 - 17.3)$

a   Some calculators need the square root after the number has been keyed, some need it before: $\sqrt{1764} = 42$

b   Most calculators have a special key for squaring: $23.4^2 = 547.56$

c   This can be keyed in exactly as it reads: $52.3 - (30.4 - 17.3) = 39.2$

1   Without using a calculator, work out the value of each of these.

a $\dfrac{17 + 8}{7 - 2}$ **b** $\dfrac{53 - 8}{3.5 - 2}$ **c** $\dfrac{19.2 - 1.7}{5.6 - 3.1}$

2   Use a calculator to do the calculations in Question 1. Do you get the same answers?

For each part, write down the sequence of keys that you pressed to get the answer.

3 Work out the value of each of these. Round off your answers to 1 dp.

a $\dfrac{194 + 866}{122 + 90}$ **b** $\dfrac{213 + 73}{63 - 19}$ **c** $\dfrac{132 + 88}{78 - 28}$ **d** $\dfrac{792 + 88}{54 - 21}$

e $\dfrac{790 \times 84}{24 \times 28}$ **f** $\dfrac{642 \times 24}{87 - 15}$ **g** $\dfrac{107 + 853}{24 \times 16}$ **h** $\dfrac{57 - 23}{18 - 7.8}$

4 Estimate the answer to: $\dfrac{231 + 167}{78 - 32}$

Now use a calculator to work out the answer to 1 dp. Is it about the same?

5 Work out:

a $\sqrt{42.25}$ **b** $\sqrt{68.89}$ **c** 2.6^2 **d** 3.9^2

e $\sqrt{(23.8 + 66.45)}$ **f** $\sqrt{(7 - 5.04)}$ **g** $(5.2 - 1.8)^2$ **h** $(2.5 + 6.1)^2$

6 Work out:

a $8.3 - (4.2 - 1.9)$ **b** $12.3 + (3.2 - 1.7)^2$ **c** $(3.2 + 1.9)^2 - (5.2 - 2.1)^2$

7 Use a calculator to find the quotient and the remainder when:

a 985 is divided by 23   **b** 802 is divided by 36

8 A calculator shows an answer of:

2.33333333333

Write this as a mixed number or a top heavy fraction.

Extension Work

Time calculations are difficult to do on a calculator as there are not 100 minutes in an hour. So, you need to know either the decimal equivalents of all the divisions of an hour or the way to work them out. For example: 15 minutes is 0.25 of an hour.

Copy and complete this table for some of the decimal equivalents to fractions of an hour.

Time (min)	5	6	12	15	20	30	40	45	54	55
Fraction	$\frac{1}{12}$	$\frac{1}{10}$		$\frac{1}{4}$	$\frac{1}{3}$				$\frac{9}{10}$	
Decimal	0.166		0.2	0.25			0.667			0.917

When a time is given as a decimal and it is not one of those in the table above, you need a way to work it out in hours and minutes. For example:

3.4578 hours: subtract 3 to give 0.4578, then multiply by 60 to give 27.468

This is 27 minutes to the nearest minute. So, $3.4578 \approx 3$ hours 27 minutes.

1 Find each of the following decimal times as a time in hours and minutes.

a 2.5 h   **b** 3.25 h   **c** 4.75 h   **d** 3.1 h
e 4.6 h   **f** 3.3333 h   **g** 1.15 h   **h** 4.3 h
i 0.45 h   **j** 0.95 h   **k** 3.666 h

2 Find each of the following times in hours and minutes as a decimal time.

a 2 h 40 min   **b** 1 h 45 min   **c** 2 h 18 min   **d** 1 h 20 min

Calculating with measurements

The following table shows the relationship between the common metric units.

1000	100	10	1	0.1	0.01	0.001
km			m		cm	mm
kg			g			mg
			l		cl	ml

Example 9.13

Add together 1.23 m, 46 cm and 0.034 km.

First convert all the lengths to the same unit.

1000	100	10	1	0.1	0.01	0.001
km			m		cm	mm
			1	2	3	
				4	6	
0	0	3	4			

The answer is 0.035 69 km or 35.69 m or 3569 cm. 35.69 m is the sensible answer.

Example 9.14

A recipe needs 550 grams of flour to make a cake. How many 1 kg bags of flour will be needed to make six cakes?

Six cakes will need $6 \times 550 = 3300$ g, which will need four bags of flour.

Example 9.15

What unit would you use to measure each of these?

a   Width of a football field

b   Length of a pencil

c   Weight of a car

d   Spoonful of medicine

Choose a sensible unit. Sometimes there is more than one answer.

a   Metre   b   Centimetre   c   Kilogram   d   Millilitre

Example 9.16

Convert   a   6 cm to mm   b   1250 g to kg   c   5 l to cl

You need to know the conversion factors.

a   1 cm = 10 mm: $6 \times 10 = 60$ mm

b   1000 g = 1 kg: $1250 \div 1000 = 1.25$ kg

c   1 l = 100 cl: 5 l = $5 \times 100 = 500$ cl

1 Convert each of the following lengths to centimetres.

a 60 mm **b** 2 m **c** 743 mm **d** 0.007 km **e** 12.35 m

2 Convert each of the following lengths to kilometres.

a 456 m **b** 7645 m **c** 6532 cm **d** 21 358 mm **e** 54 m

3 Convert each of the following lengths to millimetres.

a 34 cm **b** 3 m **c** 3 km **d** 35.6 cm **e** 0.7 cm

4 Convert each of the following masses to kilograms.

a 3459 g **b** 215 g **c** 65 120 g **d** 21 g **e** 210 g

5 Convert each of the following masses to grams.

a 4 kg **b** 4.32 kg **c** 0.56 kg **d** 0.007 kg **e** 6.784 kg

6 Convert each of the following capacities to litres.

a 237 cl **b** 3097 ml **c** 1862 cl **d** 48 cl **e** 96 427 ml

7 Convert each of the following times to hours and minutes.

a 70 min **b** 125 min **c** 87 min **d** 200 min **e** 90 min

8 Add together each of the following groups of measurements and give the answer in an appropriate unit.

a 1.78 m, 39 cm, 0.006 km **b** 0.234 kg, 60 g, 0.004 kg

c 2.3 l, 46 cl, 726 ml **d** 0.000 6 km, 23 mm, 3.5 cm

FM **9** Fill in each missing unit.

a A two-storey house is about 7...... high **b** John weighs about 47......

c Mary lives about 2...... from school **d** Ravid ran a marathon in 3......

10 Read the value from each of the following scales.

a  **b** 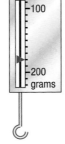 **c**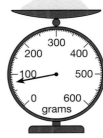

d 0 ↑ 50   **e** 200 ↑ 100   **f** 0 ↑ 20

Area is measured in square millimetres (mm²), square centimetres (cm²), square metres (m²) and square kilometres (km²).

This square shows 1 square centimetre reproduced exactly.

You can fit 100 square millimetres inside this square because a 1 centimetre square is 10 mm by 10 mm.

10 mm
10 mm

How many square centimetres are there in 1 square metre?

How many square metres are there in 1 square kilometre?

1 What unit would you use to measure the area of each of these?

    a Football field   **b** Photograph   **c** Fingernail

    d National park   **e** Pacific Ocean   **f** Stamp

2 Convert **a** 24 cm² to mm²   **b** 6 km² to m²

              c 4000 mm² to cm²   **d** 3 456 000 m² to km²

3 Look up the areas of some countries on the Internet or in an encyclopaedia.

    a Which are the three biggest countries (in terms of area) in the world?

    b Which is the biggest country (in terms of area) in Europe?

Solving problems

MATHEMATICAL MICE

Mrs Farmer is frightened of mice. One day, she finds three mice in her kitchen. A large one, a medium-sized one and a small one.

She tries to scare them out but they are Mathematical Mice who will only leave when a dice is rolled.

When the dice shows 1 or 2, the small mouse goes through the door.

When the dice shows 3 or 4, the medium-sized mouse goes through the door.

When the dice shows 5 or 6, the big mouse goes through the door.

For example: Mrs Farmer rolls the dice. She gets 3, so the medium-sized mouse goes through the door. Next, she rolls 5, so the big mouse goes through the door. Next, she rolls 4, so the medium-sized mouse comes back through the door. Then she rolls 2, so the small mouse leaves. Finally, she rolls 4, so the medium-sized mouse leaves and all three are out of the kitchen.

Can you find a rule for the number of throws that it takes to get out all the mice?

What if there were two mice, or six mice?

Before you start, you should think about how you are going to record your results.

You should make sure that you explain in writing what you are going to do.

If you come up with an idea, you should write it down and explain it or test it.

3   I can remember simple multiplication and division facts.

4   I can read numbers on a range of measuring instruments.

I can round whole numbers to the nearest 10, 100 or 1000.

I know the names and abbreviations of units in everyday use.

5   I can convert between metric units.

I can multiply and divide whole numbers and decimals.

I can round numbers to one decimal place.

I can use brackets appropriately.

I can estimate answers to questions.

National Test questions

1   2006 4–6 paper 1

Work out the missing numbers.
In each part, you can use the first line to help you.

a $16 \times 15 = 240$

$16 \times \boxed{} = 480$

b $46 \times 44 = 2024$

$46 \times 22 = \boxed{}$

c $600 \div 24 = 25$

$600 \div \boxed{} = 50$

2   *2001 Paper 1*

a   Write the answers to $(4 + 2) \times 3 = \ldots\ldots$, $4 + (2 \times 3) = \ldots\ldots$

b   Work out the answer to $(2 + 4) \times (6 + 3 + 1) = \ldots\ldots$

c   Copy and put brackets in the calculation to make the answer 50.

$4 + 5 + 1 \times 5 = 50$

d   Now copy and put brackets in the calculation to make the answer 34.

$4 + 5 + 1 \times 5 = 34$

3 *2006 4–6 Paper 2*

Write down the numbers missing from the boxes.

a 4 × ☐ + 20 = 180   **b** 4 × 20 + ☐ = 180   **c** 4 × ☐ − 20 = 180

FM **4** *2004 4–6 Paper 1*

Steve needs to put **1 litre** of water in a bucket.
He has a **500 ml** jug.

Explain how he can measure 1 litre of water.

FM **5** *2005 4–6 Paper 1*

a I weigh a melon.

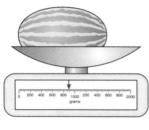

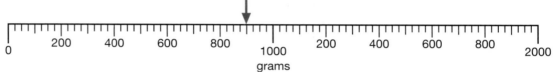

Then I weigh an apple and the melon.

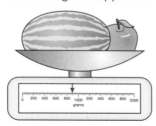

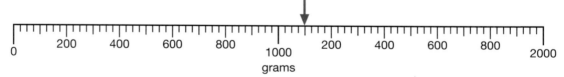

Complete the sentences below, writing in the missing numbers:

The melon weighs ... grams.

The apple weighs ... grams.

b How many **grams** are in one **kilogram**?
Which one of the following numbers is correct?

1   10   100   1000   10 000

a A club wants to take 3000 people on a journey to London using coaches. Each coach can carry 52 people. How many coaches do they need?

b Each coach costs £420. What is the total cost of the coaches?

c How much is each person's share of the cost?

What's your carbon footprint?

Every day we use energy. Scientists can work out our carbon footprint by calculating how much energy we use each year.

Fascinating facts

Our homes use 30% of the total energy used in the UK.

⊜ The average yearly carbon dioxide emissions in the UK are 9.4 tonnes per person.

⊜ A rule for working out the average yearly carbon dioxide emissions of people in the USA is to double the UK figure and add 1. This gives $2 \times 9.4 + 1 = 19.8$ tonnes per person.

⊜ If we turn down the thermostat by one degree we would save 300 kg of carbon dioxide per household per year.

⊜ A family car with a petrol engine uses about 160 grams per kilometre, compared with about 100 grams per kilometre for a small car or 300 grams per kilometre for a large 4×4.

Carbon calculator

1 Carbon dioxide emission (kg) = Distance (km) $\times$ 0.17

a Work out the carbon dioxide emission for a distance of 8 kilometres. Give your answer in grams.

b A school bus holds 75 passengers. Work out the carbon dioxide emissions per person.

c Work out the carbon dioxide emissions for a person travelling 8 kilometres by family car.

Food miles

2 The food you eat may have travelled across the globe to reach your plate.

For example:

Strawberries from Turkey: 1760 miles

Peas from Egypt: 2181 miles

Tomatoes from Mexico: 5551 miles

● How many miles is this altogether?

Round your answer to the nearest thousand.

Carbon dioxide emissions per person

3 **a** Work out the difference between the average yearly carbon dioxide emissions of people in the UK and the USA.

b A rule for working out the average yearly carbon dioxide emissions of people in China is to add 0.2 to the UK figure and divide by 3. Use this rule to work out the figure for China.

Save energy

4 If 5000 households turn down their thermostat by one degree for a year, how much carbon dioxide would be saved?

Give your answer in tonnes.

This chapter is going to show you	What you should already know
● What square numbers and triangle numbers are ● How to draw graphs from functions ● How to use algebra to solve problems ● How to use a calculator to find square roots	● How to find the term-to-term rule in a sequence ● How to plot coordinates ● How to solve simple equations

Square numbers and square roots

When we multiply any number by itself, the answer is called the **square of the number** or the **number squared**. We call this operation **squaring**. We show it by putting a small 2 at the top right-hand corner of the number being squared. For example:

$$4 \times 4 = 4^2 = 16$$

The result of squaring a number is also called a **square number**. The first ten square numbers are shown below.

1×1	2×2	3×3	4×4	5×5	6×6	7×7	8×8	9×9	10×10
1^2	2^2	3^2	4^2	5^2	6^2	7^2	8^2	9^2	10^2
1	4	9	16	25	36	49	64	81	100

You need to learn all of these.

The **square root** of a number is that number which, when squared, gives the starting number. It is the opposite of finding the square of a number. We represent a square root by the symbol $\sqrt{}$. For example:

$$\sqrt{1} = 1 \qquad \sqrt{4} = 2 \qquad \sqrt{9} = 3 \qquad \sqrt{16} = 4 \qquad \sqrt{25} = 5$$

Only the square root of a square number will give an integer (whole number) as the answer.

Exercise 10A

1 Look at the pattern on the right.

    a Copy this pattern and draw the next two shapes in the pattern.

    b What is special about the total number of dots in each pattern number?

Pattern 1   Pattern 2   Pattern 3

  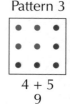

1   1 + 3   4 + 5
         4   9

c What is special about the number of blue dots in each pattern number?

d What is special about the number of red dots in each pattern number?

e Write down a connection between square numbers and odd numbers.

② $45 = 9 + 36 = 3^2 + 6^2$

Give each of the following numbers as the sum of two square numbers, as above.

a 29	**b** 34	**c** 65	**d** 100	**e** 82
f 25	**g** 85	**h** 73	**i** 106	**j** 58

③ You should have noticed from Question 2f above that $3^2 + 4^2 = 5^2$.

This is a *special square sum* (made up of only square numbers). There are many to be found. See which of the following pairs of squares will give you a special square sum.

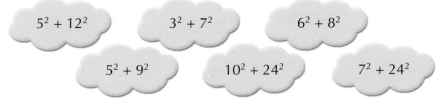

$5^2 + 12^2$ $3^2 + 7^2$ $6^2 + 8^2$

$5^2 + 9^2$ $10^2 + 24^2$ $7^2 + 24^2$

④ Write down the value represented by each of the following. Do not use a calculator.

a $\sqrt{16}$	**b** $\sqrt{36}$	**c** $\sqrt{4}$	**d** $\sqrt{49}$	**e** $\sqrt{1}$
f $\sqrt{9}$	**g** $\sqrt{100}$	**h** $\sqrt{81}$	**i** $\sqrt{25}$	**j** $\sqrt{64}$

⑤ With the aid of a calculator, write down the value represented by each of the following.

a $\sqrt{289}$	**b** $\sqrt{961}$	**c** $\sqrt{529}$	**d** $\sqrt{2500}$	**e** $\sqrt{1296}$
f $\sqrt{729}$	**g** $\sqrt{3249}$	**h** $\sqrt{361}$	**i** $\sqrt{3969}$	**j** $\sqrt{1764}$

⑥ Make an estimate of each of the following square roots. Then use your calculator to see how many you got right.

a $\sqrt{256}$	**b** $\sqrt{1089}$	**c** $\sqrt{625}$	**d** $\sqrt{2704}$	**e** $\sqrt{1444}$
f $\sqrt{841}$	**g** $\sqrt{3481}$	**h** $\sqrt{441}$	**i** $\sqrt{4096}$	**j** $\sqrt{2025}$

Extension **Work**

1 **a** Choose any two square numbers: for example, m and n.

b Multiply them together: $m \times n = R$.

c What is the square root of this result, $\sqrt{R}$?

d Can you find a connection between this square root and the two starting numbers?

e Try this again for more square numbers.

f Is the connection the same no matter what two square numbers you choose?

2 See if you can find any more sets of the special square sums.

Triangle numbers

The number of dots used to make each triangle in this pattern form the sequence of **triangle numbers**.

The first few triangle numbers are   1   3   6

1, 3, 6, 10, 15, 21, 28, 36, 45, ...

You need to remember how to generate the sequence of triangle numbers.

Exercise 10B

1   Look at the following sequence.

Pattern number	1	2	3	4	5	6	7
Number of blue dots	1	3	6				
Number of yellow dots	0	1	3				
Total number of dots	1	4	9				

a   Continue the sequence for the next three shapes.

b   Complete the table to show the number of dots in each shape.

c   What is special about the number of **blue** dots?

d   What is special about the number of **yellow** dots?

e   What is special about the **total number** of dots in each pattern number?

f   Write down a connection between triangle numbers and square numbers.

2   Look at the numbers in the box on the right.

Write down the numbers that are:

a   square numbers   **d**   multiples of 5

b   triangle numbers   **e**   factors of 100

c   even numbers   **f**   prime numbers

1	2	3	5	6	9
10	13	15	18	21	
25	26	28	29	36	
38	64	75	93	100	

3   Each of the following numbers can be given as the sum of two triangle numbers. Write each sum in full.

a   7   **b**   24   **c**   16   **d**   31

e   21   **f**   25   **g**   36   **h**   42

4 a   Write down the first 12 triangular numbers.

b   How many of these numbers are **i** even **ii** odd.

c   How many of these numbers are multiples of 3?

d   Look at the numbers that are not multiples of 3. What is special about them all?

e   Test parts **b** to **d** with the next 12 triangle numbers.

f   What do you notice about your answers to part **e**?

1 and 36 are both square numbers and triangular numbers. Which are the next two numbers to be both square and triangular? You will need to use a spreadsheet as the numbers are quite large. Hint: the first is between the 40th and 50th square number and the next is a few below the 300th triangular number.

From mappings to graphs

Think about the function →[+ 1]→.

We can show this function in a diagram (right).

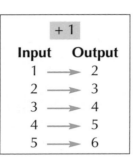

If we put the numbers together to form ordered pairs, we get:

(1, 2), (2, 3), (3, 4), (4, 5), (5, 6)

We have chosen just five starting points, but we could have chosen many more.

We can use these ordered pairs as coordinates, and plot them on a pair of axes, as shown on the right.

Notice how we use the first number to go along to the right, and the second number to go up. We can join up all the points with a straight line.

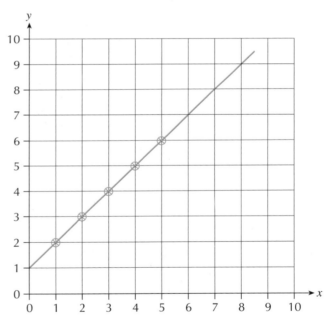

① For each of the following:

i Complete the input/output diagram.

ii Complete the coordinates alongside.

iii Plot the coordinates and draw the graph.

a

The same		Coordinates
0 → 0		(0, 0)
1 → 1		(1, 1)
2 →		(2,)
3 →		(3,)
4 →		(4,)
5 →		(5,)

b

+ 2		Coordinates
0 → 2		(0, 2)
1 → 3		(1, 3)
2 →		(2,)
3 →		(3,)
4 →		(4,)
5 →		(5,)

c

×2		Coordinates
0 → 0		(0, 0)
1 → 2		(1, 2)
2 →		(2,)
3 →		(3,)
4 →		(4,)
5 →		(5,)

d

×2 → −1		Coordinates
1 → 1		(1, 1)
2 → 3		(2, 3)
3 →		(3,)
4 →		(4,)
5 →		(5,)
6 →		(6,)

e

×2 → +3		Coordinates
0 → 3		(0, 3)
1 → 5		(1, 5)
2 →		(2,)
3 →		(3,)
4 →		(4,)
5 →		(5,)

f

×3 → −2		Coordinates
1 → 1		(1, 1)
2 → 4		(2, 4)
3 →		(3,)
4 →		(4,)
5 →		(5,)
6 →		(6,)

2 Choose some of your own starting points and create a graph from each of the following functions.

a → + 3 →

b → × 3 → + 2 →

c → × 2 → − 3 →

d → × 4 → − 3 →

Extension Work

a Draw a mapping diagram for the function → square →

b Use the mapping to help you find some coordinates. Then draw the graph.

Naming graphs

When we use coordinates, we call the left-hand number the **x-coordinate** and the right-hand number the **y-coordinate**.

This means we can write a *general* coordinate pair as (x, y).

What do you notice about the coordinates $(0, 3), (1, 3), (2, 3), (3, 3), (4, 3)$?

The second number, the y-coordinate, is always 3. In other words, $y = 3$.

Look what happens when we plot it.

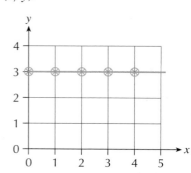

See also the graphs of $y = 2$ and $y = 5$, shown below.

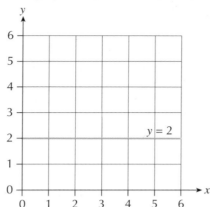 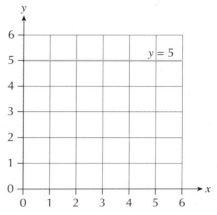

Note: The graphs are always horizontal lines for $y = A$, where A is any fixed number.

When we repeat this for an x-value, say $x = 2$, we get a vertical line, as shown.

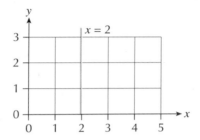

1. Write down the name of the straight line that goes through each of these pairs of points on the diagram.

   a A and B   **b** C and D
   c E and F   **d** G and H
   e I and D   **f** J and D
   g K and A   **h** G and F

2. Draw each of the following graphs on the same grid, and label them.

   a $y = 1$ **b** $y = 4$
   c $y = 6$ **d** $x = 1$
   e $x = 3$ **f** $x = 5$

   Axes
   x-axis from 0 to 7
   y-axis from 0 to 7

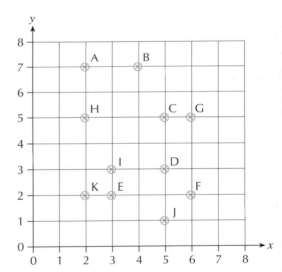

129

3 Write down the letters that are on each of the following lines.

a	$x = 1$	**b**	$y = 1$
c	$y = 6$	**d**	$y = 2$
e	$x = 3$	**f**	$x = 2$
g	$y = 4$	**h**	$x = 5$
i	$x = 6$	**j**	$y = 3$

4 Draw each of the following pairs of lines on the same grid. Write down the coordinates of the point where they cross.

a $y = 1$ and $x = 3$

b $y = 4$ and $x = 1$

c $x = 5$ and $y = 6$

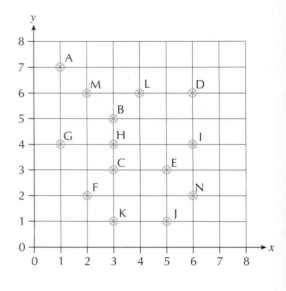

Extension Work

Here are eight pairs of coordinates:

$A(2, 3)$ $B(3, 5)$ $C(7, 3)$ $D(2, 5)$ $E(3, 7)$ $F(7, 4)$ $G(3, 4)$ $H(7, 7)$

Try to write down the names of the straight lines that the following points are on. Then plot the points on the graphs to check your answers.

a	A and C	**b**	B and D	**c**	C and F	**d**	A and D
e	E and H	**f**	F and G	**g**	B and G	**h**	C and H

Naming sloping lines

Here is the input/output diagram which uses the function 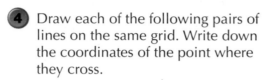, and the graph it produces.

The same		Coordinates
0 → 0		(0, 0)
1 → 1		(1, 1)
2 → 2		(2, 2)
3 → 3		(3, 3)
4 → 4		(4, 4)
5 → 5		(5, 5)

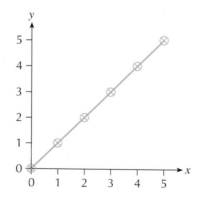

We give this straight-line graph the name $y = x$, because the x-coordinate is *always the same* as the y-coordinate.

1 Copy and complete the following input/output diagram for each of the given functions.

→ function →	**Coordinates**
0 ——→ ?	(0,)
1 ——→ ?	(1,)
2 ——→ ?	(2,)
3 ——→ ?	(3,)
4 ——→ ?	(4,)
5 ——→ ?	(5,)

a ——→ [+ 1] ——→

b ——→ [+ 2] ——→

c ——→ [+ 3] ——→

d ——→ [+ 4] ——→

e ——→ [+ 5] ——→

2 Plot each set of coordinates from Question 1 on the same grid and match the following names to each straight line. Write the name on the line.

$$y = x + 1 \qquad y = x + 3 \qquad y = x + 5 \qquad y = x + 2 \qquad y = x + 4$$

Extension Work

Write down pairs of values for x and y that are true for these equations (they do not have to be pairs of whole numbers).

a $x + y = 6$ **b** $x + y = 8$ **c** $x + y = 3$

Plot the values on a graph.

Describe anything you notice.

LEVEL BOOSTER

4 I can recognise the square numbers 1, 4, 9, 16, 25, etc.
I know all the square numbers from 1^2 to 15^2.
I know the square roots of square numbers from 1 to 225.
I can work out square numbers with a calculator.
I can find square roots using a calculator.
I can estimate square roots of numbers up to 200.
I can recognise the triangular number pattern and the triangle numbers, 1, 3, 6, 10, 15, 21, …
I can continue the triangular number pattern for at least ten terms up to the triangle number 55.

5 I can work out and plot coordinates using a mapping diagram of an algebraic relationship such as $y = x + 2$, i.e.
$$2 \rightarrow 4$$
$$3 \rightarrow 5$$
$$4 \rightarrow 6$$
I can test if a coordinate such as (3, 4) obeys an algebraic relationship such as $y = x - 1$, i.e. $4 \neq 3 - 1$.

6 I can draw the graph of a simple algebraic relationship such as $y = 2x$ by working out coordinate points, i.e. (3, 6), (4, 8), etc.

5

1 *2000 Paper 2*

   a Write down the next two numbers in the sequence below.

| 1 | 4 | 9 | 16 | 25 | | |

   b Describe the pattern in part **a** in your own words.

2 *2000 Paper 1*

   These straight line graphs all pass through the point (10, 10).

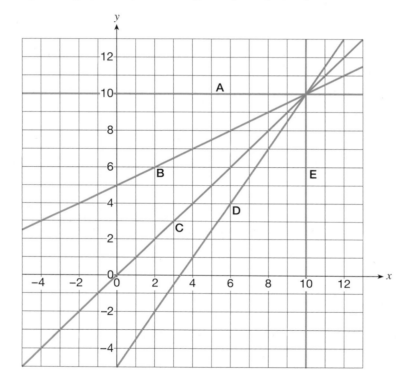

   a Which line has the equation $x = 10$?

   b Which line has the equation $y = 10$?

   c Which line has the equation $y = x$?

   d Which line has the equation $y = 1.5x - 5$?

   e Which line has the equation $y = 0.5x + 5$?

3 *2003 Paper 2*

The diagram shows a square drawn on a square grid.

The points A, B, C and D are at the vertices of the square.

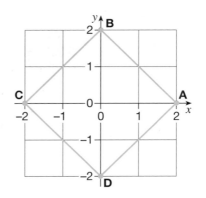

Match the correct line to each equation.
One is done for you.

| $y = 0$ |

| $x = 0$ |

| $x + y = 2$ |

| $x + y = -2$ |

| Line through C and D |

| Line through A and C |

| Line through A and D |

| Line through B and D |

| Line through B and C |

| Line through A and B |

<table>
<tr>
<td>

This chapter is going to show you

- How to measure and draw angles
- How to construct triangles and other shapes
- The geometrical properties of triangles and quadrilaterals

</td>
<td>

What you should already know

- How to use a protractor to measure and draw angles
- How to calculate angles on a straight line and around a point
- How to calculate angles in a triangle

</td>
</tr>
</table>

Measuring and drawing angles

Notice that on a semicircular protractor there are two scales. The outer scale goes from 0° to 180°, and the inner one goes from 180° to 0°. It is important that you use the correct scale.

When measuring or drawing an angle, always decide first whether it is an acute angle or an obtuse angle.

Example 11.1 ▷

First, decide whether the angle to be measured is acute or obtuse. This is an acute angle (less than 90°).

Place the centre of the protractor at the corner of the angle, as in the diagram.

The two angles shown on the protractor scales are 60° and 120°. Since you are measuring an acute angle, the angle is 60° (to the nearest degree).

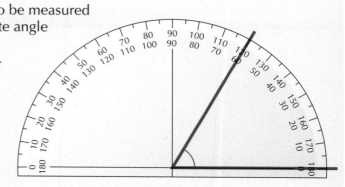

Example 11.2 ▷

Measure the size of this reflex angle.

First, measure the inside or interior angle. This is an obtuse angle.

The two angles shown on the protractor scales are 30° and 150°. Since you are measuring an obtuse angle, the angle is 150°.

The size of the reflex angle is found by subtracting this angle from 360°. The reflex angle is therefore 360° − 150°, which is 210° (to the nearest degree).

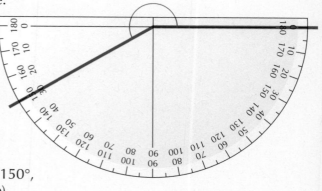

Exercise 11A

1 Measure the size of each of the following angles, giving your answer to the nearest degree.

a

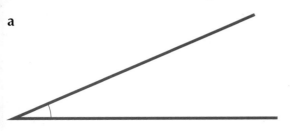

b

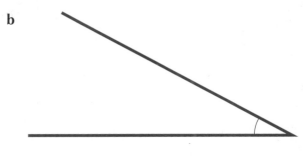

c

d

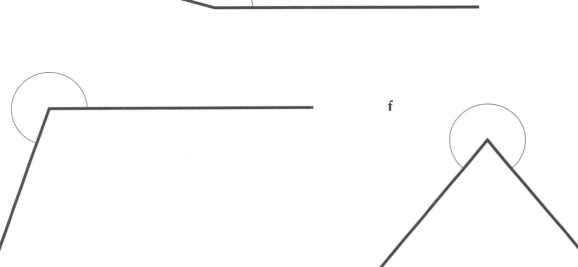

e

f

2 Draw and label each of the following angles.

| **a** 20° | **b** 35° | **c** 72° | **d** 100° | **e** 145° |
| **f** 168° | **g** 220° | **h** 258° | **i** 300° | **j** 347° |

3 **a** Measure the three angles in triangle ABC.
b Add the three angles together.
c Comment on your answer.

Estimating angles

- Copy the table below.

Angle	Estimate	Actual	Difference
1			
2			
3			
4			

- Estimate the size of each of the four angles below and complete the Estimate column in the table.

1  2 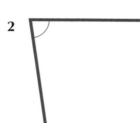 3  4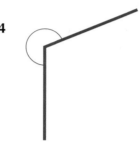

- Now measure the size of each angle to the nearest degree and complete the Actual column.
- Work out the difference between your estimate and the actual measurement for each angle and complete the Difference column.

Constructions

You need to be able to draw a shape exactly from information given on a diagram, using a ruler and a protractor. This is known as **constructing a shape**.

When constructing a shape you need to draw lines to the nearest millimetre and the angles to the nearest degree.

Example 11.3

Construct the triangle ABC.
- Draw line BC 7.5 cm long.
- Draw an angle of 50° at B.
- Draw line AB 4.1 cm long.
- Join AC to complete the triangle.

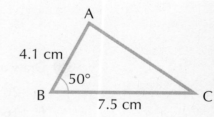

The completed, full-sized triangle is given below.

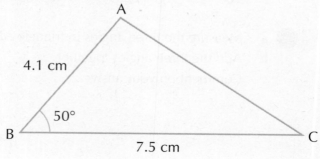

Example 11.4 ▶ Construct the triangle XYZ.
- Draw line YZ 8.3 cm long.
- Draw an angle of 42° at Y.
- Draw an angle of 51° at Z.
- Extend both angle lines to intersect at X to complete the triangle.

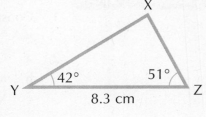

The completed, full-sized triangle is given below.

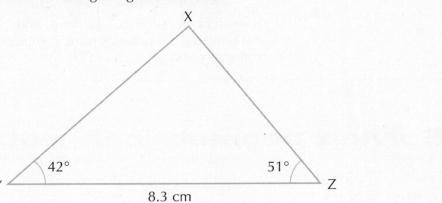

Exercise 11B

1 Construct each of the following triangles. Remember to label all lines and angles.

a

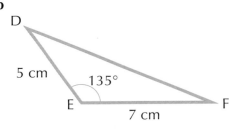

A, 6 cm, 60°, B, 5 cm, C

b

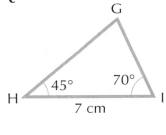

D, 5 cm, 135°, E, 7 cm, F

c

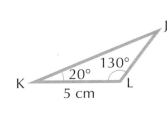

G, 45°, 70°, H, 7 cm, I

d

J, 20°, 130°, K, 5 cm, L

2 a Construct the triangle PQR.
   b Measure the size of ∠P and ∠R to the nearest degree.
   c Measure the length of the line PR to the nearest millimetre.

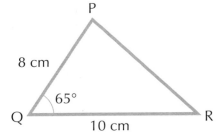

P, 8 cm, 65°, Q, 10 cm, R

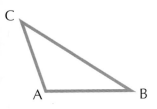

C, A, B

3 Construct the triangle ABC with ∠A = 100°, ∠B = 40° and AB = 8 cm.

4 a Construct the trapezium ABCD.
   b Measure the size of ∠B to the nearest degree.
   c Measure the length of the lines AB and BC to the nearest millimetre.

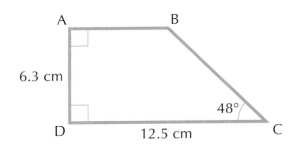

A, B, 6.3 cm, D, 12.5 cm, 48°, C

1 Construct the parallelogram ABCD with AB = 7.4 cm, AD = 6.4 cm, ∠A = 50° and ∠B = 130°.

2 a Construct the quadrilateral PQRS.
   b Measure ∠P and ∠Q to the nearest degree.
   c Measure the length of the line PQ to the nearest millimetre.

3 If you have access to ICT facilities, find out how to draw triangles using computer software packages such as LOGO.

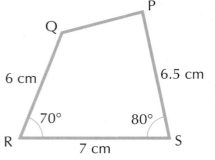

Solving geometrical problems

Types of triangle

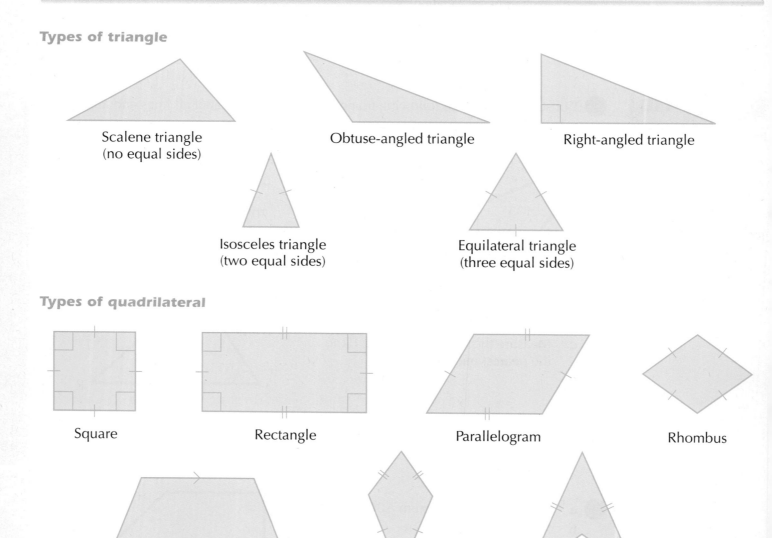

Scalene triangle
(no equal sides)

Obtuse-angled triangle

Right-angled triangle

Isosceles triangle
(two equal sides)

Equilateral triangle
(three equal sides)

Types of quadrilateral

Square

Rectangle

Parallelogram

Rhombus

Trapezium

Kite

Arrowhead or delta

Exercise 11C

1 Which quadrilaterals have the following properties?

  a Four equal sides

  b Two different pairs of equal sides

  c Two pairs of parallel sides

  d Only one pair of parallel sides

  e Adjacent sides equal

2 Explain the difference between:

  a a square and a rhombus.

  b a rhombus and a parallelogram.

  c a trapezium and a parallelogram.

3 How many distinct triangles can be constructed on this 3 by 3 pin-board?

Use square dotted paper to record your triangles. Below each one, write down what type of triangle it is.

Here are two examples:

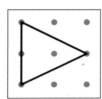

4 Copy this square on a piece of card. Then draw in the two diagonals and cut out the four triangles.

How many different triangles or quadrilaterals can you make with the following?

  a Four of the triangles

  b Three of the triangles

  c Two of the triangles

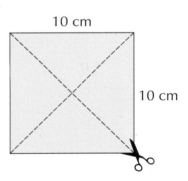

10 cm

10 cm

Extension Work

How many distinct quadrilaterals can be constructed on this 3 by 3 pin-board?

Use square dotted paper to record your quadrilaterals. Below each one, write down what type of quadrilateral it is.

Here are two examples:

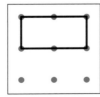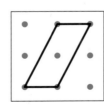

4 I can recognise the different types of angle.
I know the names of the different types of triangles and quadrilaterals.

5 I can draw and measure angles.
I can draw triangles from given information.

6 I know all the properties of different quadrilaterals.

National Test questions

1 *2001 Paper 1*

a I start with a rectangle of paper. I fold it in half, then I cut out three shapes.

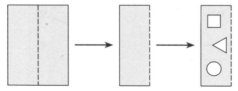

Then I unfold my paper. Which diagram below shows what my paper looks like now?

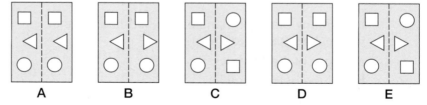

A   B   C   D   E

b I start again with a different rectangle of paper. I fold it in half, then in half again, then I cut out two shapes.

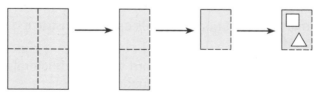

Then I unfold my paper. Which diagram below shows what my paper looks like now?

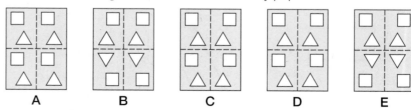

A   B   C   D   E

c   I start with a square of paper. I fold it in half, then in half again, then I cut out one shape.

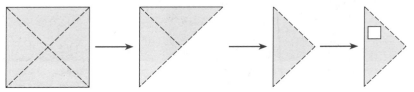

Then I unfold my paper. Which diagram below shows what my paper looks like now?

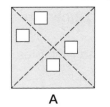
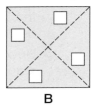
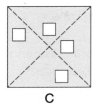
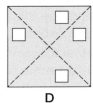
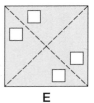

A   B   C   D   E

2   *2000 Paper 1*

Look at these angles.

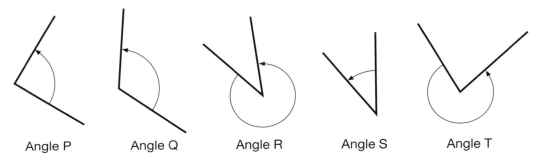

Angle P   Angle Q   Angle R   Angle S   Angle T

a   One of the angles measures **120°**

Write its letter.

b   Complete the drawing below to show an angle of **157°**

Label the angle 157°

This chapter is going to show you	What you should already know
• How to find simple percentages and use them to compare proportions • How to work out ratio, leading into simple direct proportion • How to solve problems using ratio	• How to find equivalent fractions, percentages and decimals • How to find multiples of 10% of a quantity • Division facts from tables up to 10×10

Percentages

One of these labels is from a packet of porridge oats. The other is from a toffee cake.

Compare the percentages of protein, carbohydrates, fat and fibre.

PORRIDGE OATS	
Typical values	**per 100 g**
Energy	1555 kJ/ 372 kcal
Protein	7.5 g
Carbohydrates	71 g
Fat	6.0 g
Fibre	6.0 g
Sodium	0.3 g

TOFFEE CAKE	
Typical values	**per 100 g**
Energy	1421 kJ/ 340 kcal
Protein	2.9 g
Carbohydrates	39.1 g
Fat	19.1 g
Fibre	0.3 g
Sodium	0.2 g

Example 12.1 ▷ Without using a calculator find: **a** 12% of £260   **b** 39% of 32

a 12% = 10% + 1% + 1% = 26 + 2.6 + 2.6 = £31.20

b 39% = 10% + 10% + 10% + 10% − 1% = 4 × 3.2 − 0.32 = 12.8 − 0.32 = 12.48

Example 12.2 ▷ Work out: **a** 6% of £190   **b** 63% of 75 eggs

a (6 ÷ 100) × 190 = £11.40

b (63 ÷ 100) × 75 = 47.25 = 47 eggs

Example 12.3 ▷ Which is greater, 42% of 560 or 62% of 390?

(42 ÷ 100) × 560 = 235.2   (62 ÷ 100) × 390 = 241.8

62% of 390 is greater.

1 Write each percentage as a combination of simple percentages. The first two have been done for you.

    a 12% = 10% + 1% + 1%   **b** 49% = 50% − 1%

    c 31%   **d** 18%

    e 11%   **f** 28%

    g 52%   **h** 99%

2 Use your answers to question 1 to work out each of the following.

    a 12% of 320   **b** 49% of 45   **c** 31% of 260   **d** 18% of 68

    e 11% of 12   **f** 28% of 280   **g** 52% of 36   **h** 99% of 206

3 Work out each of these.

    a 13% of £560   **b** 46% of 64 books   **c** 73% of 190 chairs

    d 34% of £212   **e** 64% of 996 pupils   **f** 57% of 120 buses

    g 37% of 109 plants   **h** 78% of 345 bottles   **i** 62% of 365 days

    j 93% of 2564 people   **k** 54% of 456 fish   **l** 45% of £45

    m 65% of 366 eggs   **n** 7% of £684   **o** 9% of 568 chickens

4 Which is bigger:

    a 45% of 68 or 34% of 92?   **b** 22% of £86 or 82% of £26?

    c 28% of 79 or 69% of 31?   **d** 32% of 435 or 43% of 325?

5 Write down or work out the equivalent percentage and decimal to each of these fractions.

    a $\frac{1}{5}$ **b** $\frac{2}{5}$ **c** $\frac{1}{4}$ **d** $\frac{3}{4}$ **e** $\frac{1}{8}$

    f $\frac{3}{8}$ **g** $\frac{1}{20}$ **h** $\frac{3}{20}$ **i** $\frac{1}{25}$ **j** $\frac{21}{25}$

6 Write down or work out the equivalent percentage and fraction to each of these decimals.

    a 0.1   **b** 0.3   **c** 0.8   **d** 0.75

    e 0.34   **f** 0.85   **g** 0.31

7 Write down or work out the equivalent fraction and decimal to each of these percentages.

    a 5%   **b** 15%   **c** 62%   **d** 62.55%

    e 80%   **f** 8%   **g** 66.6%

8 Javid scores 17 out of 25 on a maths test, 14 out of 20 on a science test and 33 out of 50 on an English test. Work out each score as a percentage.

9 Arrange these numbers in order of increasing size.

    a 21%, $\frac{6}{25}$, 0.2   **b** 0.39, 38%, $\frac{3}{8}$ **c** $\frac{11}{20}$, 54%, 0.53

The pie chart shows the percentage of each constituent of the toffee cake given in the label on page 142.

Draw a pie chart to show the percentage of each constituent of the porridge oats given on the same page.

Obtain labels from a variety of cereals and other food items. Draw a pie chart for each of them.

What types of food have the most fat? What types of food have the most energy?

Is there a connection between the energy of food and the fat and carbohydrate content?

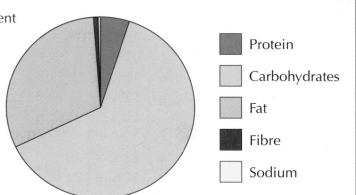

- ■ Protein
- ■ Carbohydrates
- ■ Fat
- ■ Fibre
- □ Sodium

Ratio and proportion

Look at the fish tank. There are three types of fish – plain, striped and spotted.

What proportion of the fish are plain? What proportion are striped? What proportion are spotted?

What is the ratio of plain fish to striped fish?

What is the ratio of striped fish to spotted fish?

What is the ratio of plain fish to striped fish?

Proportion is a way of comparing the parts of a quantity to the whole quantity.

Example 12.4 ▷ What proportion of this metre rule is shaded? What is the ratio of the shaded part to the unshaded part?

40 cm out of 100 cm are shaded. This is 40% (or 0.4 or $\frac{2}{5}$). The ratio of shaded to unshaded is $40:60 = 2:3$.

Example 12.5 ▷ A fruit drink is made by mixing 20 cl of orange juice with 60 cl of pineapple juice. What is the proportion of orange juice in the drink?

Total volume of drink is $20 + 60 = 80$ cl.

The proportion of orange is 20 out of $80 = \frac{20}{80} = \frac{1}{4}$.

Example 12.6 ▷ Another fruit drink is made by mixing orange juice and grapefruit juice. The proportion of orange is 40%. 60 cl of orange juice is used. What proportion of grapefruit is used? How much grapefruit juice is used?

The proportion of grapefruit is $100\% - 40\% = 60\%$. Now 40% = 60 cl, so 10% = 15 cl. Hence, 60% = 90 cl of grapefruit juice.

Example 12.7 ▷ Five pens cost £3.25. How much do 8 pens cost?

First, work out the cost of 1 pen: £3.25 ÷ 5 = £0.65
Hence, 8 pens cost 8 × £0.65 = £5.20

Exercise 12B

 1 Three bars of soap cost £1.80. How much would:

    a 1 bar cost?   **b** 12 bars cost?   **c** 30 bars cost?

 2 One euro is worth £0.62. How many pounds will I get for each of the following numbers of euros?

    a 5 euros   **b** 8 euros   **c** 600 euros

 3 These are the ingredients to make four pancakes.

    a How much of each ingredient will be needed to make 12 pancakes?

    b How much of each ingredient will be needed to make six pancakes?

> 1 egg
> 3 ounces of plain flour
> 5 fluid ounces of milk

4 For each of these metre rules:

    i What proportion of the rule is shaded?

    ii What is the ratio of the shaded part to the unshaded part?

5 For each bag of black and white balls:

    i What proportion of the balls are black?

    ii What is the ratio of black to white balls?

    a   **b**   **c**   **d**

6 Tom and Jerry have some coins. This table shows the coins they have.

	1p	2p	5p	10p	20p	50p
Tom	15	45	50	80	20	40
Jerry	18	36	72	24	20	30

    a How much do they each have altogether?

    b How many coins do they each have?

c Copy and complete the table below, which shows the proportion of each coin that they have.

	1p	2p	5p	10p	20p	50p
Tom	6%	18%				
Jerry						

d Add up the proportions for Tom and for Jerry. Explain your answer.

(FM) (7) One litre of fruit squash contains 24 cl of fruit concentrate and the rest is water.

a What proportion of the drink is fruit concentrate?

b What proportion of the drink is water?

(8) The ratio of British cars to foreign cars in the staff car park is 1 : 4. Explain why the proportion of British cars is 20% and not 25%.

(9) Steve wears only red or black socks. The ratio of red to black pairs that he owns is 1 : 3. If he doesn't favour any particular colour, what proportion of days will he wear red socks?

Extension Work

Direct proportion can be used to solve problems such as: In 6 hours, a woman earns £42. How much would she earn in 5 hours?

First, you have to work out how much she earns in 1 hour: 42 ÷ 6 = £7. Then multiply this by 5 to get how much she earns in 5 hours: 5 × £7 = £35.

(FM) Answer the following questions but be careful! Two of them are trick questions.

(1) 3 kg of sugar cost £1.80. How much do 4 kg of sugar cost?

(2) A man can run 10 km in 40 minutes. How long does he take to run 12 km?

(3) In two days my watch loses 20 seconds. How much time does it lose in a week?

(4) It takes me 5 seconds to dial the 10 digit number of a friend who lives 100 km away. How long does it take me to dial the 10 digit number of a friend who lives 200 miles away?

(5) A jet aircraft with 240 people on board takes 2 h 30 min to fly 1000 km. How long would the same aircraft take to fly 1500 km when it had only 120 people on board?

Calculating ratios and proportions

The fish have been breeding!

What is the ratio of striped fish to spotted fish?

What is the ratio of plain fish to spotted fish?

What is the ratio of plain fish to striped fish?

If five more plain fish are added to the tank, how many more striped fish would have to be added to keep the ratio of plain to striped the same?

Example 12.8 ▷ Reduce the following ratios to their simplest form: **a** 4:6   **b** 5:25

    a   The highest common factor of 4 and 6 is 2. So, divide 2 into both values, giving 4:6 = 2:3.

    b   The highest common factor of 5 and 25 is 5. So, divide 5 into both values, giving 5:25 = 1:5.

Example 12.9 ▷ A fruit drink is made by mixing 20 cl of orange juice with 60 cl of pineapple juice. What is the ratio of orange juice to pineapple juice?

Orange:pineapple = 20:60 = 1:3 (cancel by 20).

Example 12.10 ▷ Another fruit drink is made by mixing orange juice and grapefruit juice in the ratio 2:5. 60 cl of orange juice are used. How much grapefruit juice is needed?

The problem is 60:? = 2:5. You will see that, instead of cancelling, your need to multiply by 30. So, 2:5 = 60:150.

Hence, 150 cl of grapefruit juice will be needed.

Exercise 12C

1 Reduce each of the following ratios to its simplest form.

    a 4:8   **b** 3:9   **c** 2:10   **d** 9:12   **e** 5:20   **f** 8:10
    g 4:6   **h** 10:15   **i** 2:14   **j** 4:14   **k** 6:10   **l** 25:30

2 Write down the ratio of black:white from each of these metre rules.

    a

    b

    c

3 There are 300 lights on a Christmas tree. 120 are white, 60 are blue, 45 are green and the rest are yellow.

    a   Write down the percentage of each colour.

    b   Write down each of the following ratios in its simplest form.
        i   white:blue   **ii**   blue:green
        iii green:yellow   **iv** white:blue:green:yellow

FM **4** To make jam, Josh uses strawberries to preserving sugar in the ratio 3 cups : 1 cup.

    a   How many cups of each will he need to make 20 cups of jam altogether?

    b   If he has 12 cups of strawberries, how many cups of sugar will he need?

    c   If he has $2\frac{1}{2}$ cups of sugar, how many cups of strawberries will he need?

Proportion can be used to solve 'best buy' problems.

For example: A large tin of dog food costs 96p and contains 500 grams.
A small tin costs 64p and contains 300 grams. Which tin is the better value?
For each tin, work out how much 1 gram costs.

Large tin: 500 ÷ 96 = 5.2 grams per penny.
Small tin: 300 ÷ 64 = 4.7 grams per penny. So, the large tin is the better buy.

1 A bottle of shampoo costs £2.62 and contains 30 cl. A different bottle of the same shampoo costs £1.50 and contains 20 cl. Which is the better buy?

2 A large roll of Sellotape has 25 metres of tape and costs 75p. A small roll of Sellotape has 15 metres of tape and costs 55p. Which roll is better value?

3 A pad of A4 paper costs £1.10 and has 120 sheets. A thicker pad of A4 paper costs £1.50 and has 150 sheets. Which pad is the better buy?

4 A small tin of peas contains 250 grams and costs 34p. A large tin costs 70p and contains 454 grams. Which tin is the better buy?

Solving problems

A painter has a 5-litre can of blue paint and 3 litres of yellow paint in a 5-litre can (Picture 1).

Picture 1

Picture 2

Picture 3

He pours 2 litres of blue paint into the other can (Picture 2) and mixes it thoroughly.

He then pours 1 litre from the second can back into the first can (Picture 3) and mixes it thoroughly.

How much blue paint is in the first can now?

Example 12.11 ▶ Divide £150 in the ratio 1 : 5.

There are 1 + 5 = 6 portions. This gives £150 ÷ 6 = £25 per portion. So one share of the £150 is 1 × 25 = £25, and the other share is 5 × £25 = £125.

Example 12.12 ▶ Two-fifths of a packet of bulbs are daffodils. The rest are tulips. What is the ratio of daffodils to tulips?

Ratio is $\frac{2}{5} : \frac{3}{5} = 2 : 3$.

1 Divide £100 in the ratio:

    a   2 : 3   **b**   1 : 9   **c**   3 : 7

    d   1 : 3   **e**   9 : 11

2 There are 350 pupils in a primary school. The ratio of girls to boys is 3 : 2. How many boys and girls are there in the school?

3 Freda has 120 CDs. The ratio of pop CDs to dance CDs is 5 : 7. How many of each type of CD are there?

4 James is saving 50p coins and £1 coins. He has 75 coins. The ratio of 50p coins to £1 coins is 7 : 8. How much money does he have altogether?

5 Mr Smith has 24 calculators in a box. The ratio of ordinary calculators to scientific calculators is 5 : 1. How many of each type of calculator does he have?

6 An exam consists of three parts. A mental test, a non-calculator paper and a calculator paper. The ratio of marks for each is 1 : 3 : 4. The whole exam is worth 120 marks. How many marks does each part of the exam get?

7 **a**   There are 15 bottles on the wall. The ratio of green bottles to brown bottles is 1 : 4. How many green bottles are there on the wall?

    b   One green bottle accidentally falls. What is the ratio of green to brown bottles now?

8 **a**   Forty-nine trains pass through Barnsley station each day. They go to Huddersfield or Leeds in the ratio 3 : 4. How many trains go to Huddersfield?

    b   One day, due to driver shortages, six of the Huddersfield trains are cancelled and three of the Leeds trains are cancelled. What is the ratio of Huddersfield trains to Leeds trains that day?

Extension Work

Uncle Fred has decided to give his nephew and niece, Jack and Jill, £100 between them. He decides to split the £100 in the ratio of their ages. Jack is 4 and Jill is 6.

a   How much do each get?

b   The following year he does the same thing with another £100. How much do each get now?

c   He continues to give them £100 shared in the ratio of their ages for another 8 years. How much will each get each year?

d   After the 10 years, how much of the £1000 given in total will Jack have? How much will Jill have?

4 I can recognise simple proportions of a whole and describe them using fractions or percentages.
I can work out simple percentages.

5 I can write down and simplify ratios.
I can calculate a percentage of a quantity.

6 I can divide a quantity in a given ratio.

National Test questions

1 *2004 4–6 Paper 2*

Here are the ingredients for a cordial used to make a drink.

> 50 g ginger
> 1 lemon
> 1.5 litres of water
> 900 g sugar

a Jenny is going to make this cordial with **25 g** of ginger.
How much lemon, water and sugar should she use?

> 25 g ginger
> ... lemon
> ... litres of water
> ... g sugar

b The finished drink should be $\frac{1}{3}$ cordial and $\frac{2}{3}$ water.
Jenny puts **100 ml** of cordial in a glass.
How much water should she put with it?

2 *2005 4–6 Paper 1*

a Complete the sentences:

... **out of ten** is the same as **70%**

10 out of 20 is the same as ... %

b Complete the sentence:

... **out of** ... is the same as **5%**

Now complete the sentence using **different** numbers.

... **out of** ... is the same as **5%**

3 *2006 4–6 Paper 1*

a Work out the missing values.

10% of 84 = …   5% of 84 = … $2\frac{1}{2}$% of 84 = …

b The cost of a CD player is £84 plus $17\frac{1}{2}$% tax.

What is the **total** cost of the CD player?
You can use part **a** to help you.

4 *2000 Paper 1*

The table shows some percentages of amounts of money.

Use the table to work out:

	£10	£30	£45
5%	50p	£1.50	£2.25
10%	£1	£3	£4.50

a 15% of £30 = ……

b £6.75 = 15% of ……

c £3.50 = …… % of £10

d 25p = 5% of ……

5 *2000 Paper 2*

Calculate: **a** 8% of £26.50   **b** $12\frac{1}{2}$% of £98

FM Smoothie bar

Small	300 ml	£2.50
Medium	400 ml	£3
Large	600 ml	£4

Fruity Surprise
100 g mango
50 g strawberries
75 g bananas
250 ml orange juice

Tropical Fruit
250 g tropical fru[...]
100 ml yoghurt
85 g raspberries
$\frac{1}{2}$ lime juice
1 tsp honey

To make a small smoothie:
Use 75% of the ingredients in the medium recipe.

To make a large smoothie:
Just add 200 ml of fruit juice or milk.

1 Work out the recipe for a small Fruity Surprise.

2 Work out the recipe for a large Chocolate.

3 How much milk would be needed to make 50 small Breakfast Boost Smoothies? Give the answer in litres.

6 What proportion of a medium Fruity Surprise is orange juice?

7 I am buying 15 small smoothies. They are Tropical Fruit and Breakfast Boost in the ratio 2 : 3. How many of each type am I buying?

8 If I buy one smoothie of each size, how much will I save using the offer?

This chapter is going to show you

- How to solve different types of problem using algebra

What you should already know

- Understand the conventions of algebra
- How to use letters in place of numbers
- How to solve equations

Solving 'brick wall' problems

Example 13.1 ▷ The numbers in two 'bricks' which are side by side (adjacent) are added together. The answer is written in the 'brick' above. Find the number missing from the 'brick' in the bottom layer.

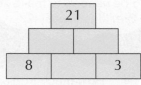

Let the missing number be x. This gives:

Adding the terms in adjacent 'bricks' gives:

$$(x + 8) + (x + 3) = 21$$
$$x + 8 + x + 3 = 21$$
$$2x + 11 = 21$$
$$2x + 11 - 11 = 21 - 11 \text{ (Take 11 from both sides)}$$
$$2x = 10$$
$$\frac{2x}{2} = \frac{10}{2} \text{ (Divide both sides by 2)}$$
$$x = 5$$

So, the missing number is 5.

Exercise 13A Find the unknown number x in each of these 'brick wall' problems.

1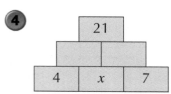

2

3

4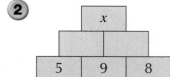

5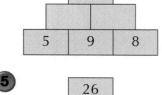

6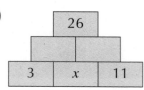

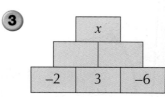

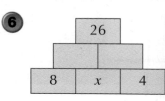

7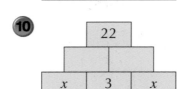

8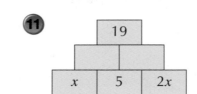

9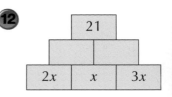

10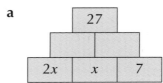

11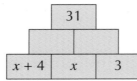

12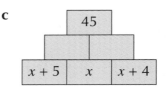

Extension Work

1 Find the value of x in each of these:

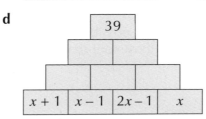

a 27 / $2x$ | x | 7

b 31 / $x + 4$ | x | 3

c 45 / $x + 5$ | x | $x + 4$

d 39 / $x + 1$ | $x - 1$ | $2x - 1$ | x

2 Make up some of your own 'brick wall' problems.

Solving square-and-circle problems

The number in each square is the sum of the numbers in the two circles on either side of the square.

Example 13.2

The values of A, B, C and D are to be positive. Can you work out all possible values of A, B, C and D?

First, write down four equations from this diagram:

$A + B = 10$
$B + C = 12$
$C + D = 13$
$D + A = 11$

There may be more than one solution to this problem. So, continue by asking yourself: 'What if I let $A = 1$?'

$A = 1$ gives $B = 10 - 1 = 9$
$B = 9$ gives $C = 12 - 9 = 3$
$C = 3$ gives $D = 13 - 3 = 10$
$D = 10$ gives $A = 11 - 10 = 1$, which is the starting value, $A = 1$

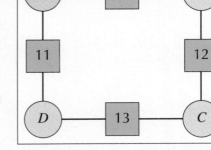

Example 13.2

continued

This gives one of a series of possible solutions to this problem. So, set up a table to calculate and display these solutions, which are called the **solution set**.

A	B	C	D	A (check)
1	9	3	10	1
2	8	4	9	2
3	7	5	8	3
4	6	6	7	4
5	5	7	6	5
6	4	8	5	6
7	3	9	4	7
8	2	10	3	8
9	1	11	2	9

Note: The last column is used as a check.

Such a table allows you to look at all possible solutions. If all the answers had to be different, you would choose only those four that were different.

Example 13.3

Again, the values of A, B, C and D are to be positive.

Starting with $A = 1$, gives $B = 8$, which makes C negative. Since you are looking only for positive solutions, you cannot have $A = 1$. So try $A = 2$. This will give $C = 0$, so you cannot use $A = 2$.

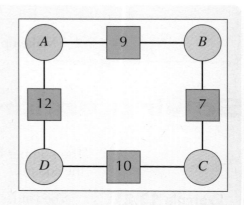

This will lead to the following solution set.

A	B	C	D	A (check)
3	6	1	9	3
4	5	2	8	4
5	4	3	7	5
6	3	4	6	6
7	2	5	5	7
8	1	6	4	8

Some of these would have to be rejected if all the solutions had to be different.

Exercise 13B

1 Find the solution set to each of the following square and circle puzzles for the value of A stated.

a

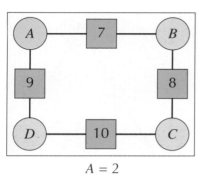

A = 2

b

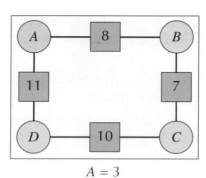

A = 3

c

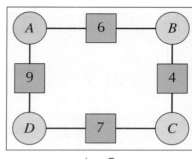

A = 5

6

2 Find the solution set to each of the following square-and-circle puzzles. All solutions must use positive numbers.

a

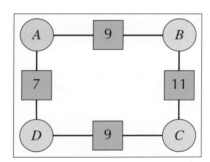

b

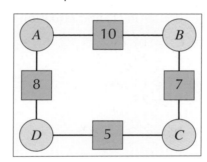

c

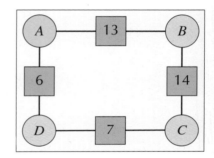

Extension **Work**

1 Triangular square and circle problems only have one solution.

Find the values that fit in the circle for these triangles.

Hint: Start with a value for A then work out B and C and make sure A works.

a

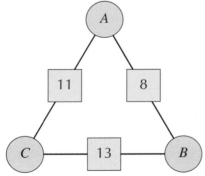

b

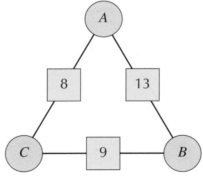

c

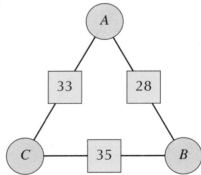

2 Make up some triangular square and circle problems. Try them out on your friends.

3 What is the connection between the sum of the squares and the sum of the circles?

Triangle-and-circle problems

Look at the diagram on the right. The number in each box is the sum of the two numbers in the circles on each side of the box.

The values of A, B and C are positive integers and no two are the same. What are they?

The values of A, B and C can be found by using algebraic equations, as shown below.

Three equations can be written down from the diagram. They are:

$$A + B = 14 \quad (1)$$
$$B + C = 11 \quad (2)$$
$$A + C = 13 \quad (3)$$

First, add together equation (1) and equation (2). This gives:

$$A + B + B + C = 14 + 11$$
$$A + C + 2B = 25$$

We know that $A + C = 13$, so:

$$13 + 2B = 25$$
$$2B = 12$$
$$B = 6$$

If $B = 6$, then $A = 8$ and $C = 5$.

Check that these values work.

Exercise 13C

1 Use algebra to solve each of these triangle-and-circle problems. All the solutions are positive integers.

a

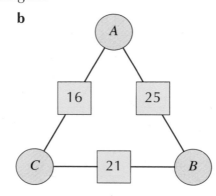

b

c

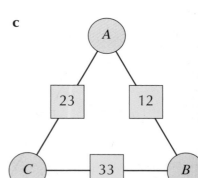

2 Use algebra to solve each of these triangle-and-circle problems. The solutions are positive and negative integers.

a
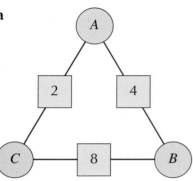

b
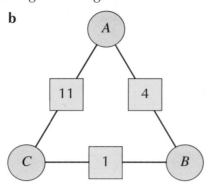

c
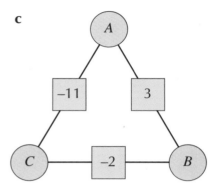

Extension **Work**

Use algebra to solve this triangle-and-circle problem.
The solutions are positive and negative numbers.

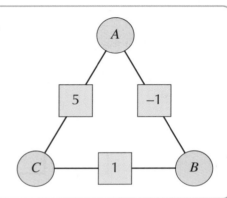

LEVEL BOOSTER

5 I can solve a simple problem using simple algebra such as finding the value of *a* in the given brick wall problem.

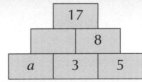

I can solve a mathematical problem such as the triangle and circle problem on the right using trial and improvement.

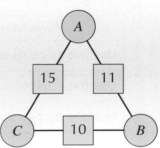

6 I can use algebra to set up and solve mathematical problems, e.g. 4 friends each have *m* sweets. Ann eats 5, Ben eats 3, Chas eats 4 and Denny eats 2. They then have 46 sweets left between them. What is the value of *m*?

4

1 *2000 Paper 1*

Here is a number triangle.

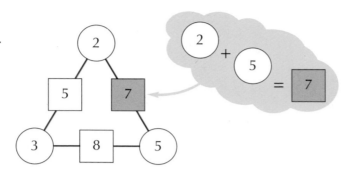

You will find the number in a square by adding the numbers in the two circles on either side of it.

Look at the following number triangles.

Copy the triangles and fill in the missing numbers.

a

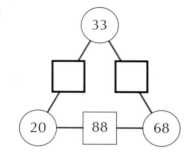

b

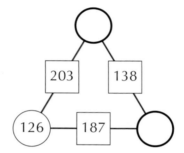

2 *2004 4–6 Paper 2*

I have some **5p** coins and some **2p** coins.

I can use some of my coins to make **27p**.

a The table shows different ways to make 27p from 5p and 2p coins.

The first way is done for you. What are the numbers missing from the second and third ways?

5p coins   2p coins

Ways to make 27p
Use **five** 5p coins and **one** 2p coin.
Use **three** 5p coins and ☐ 2p coins.
Use **one** 5p coin and ☐ 2p coins.

b I cannot make 27p from 5p coins and 2p coins using an **even** number of **5p coins**.

Explain why not.

3 *2005 4–6 Paper 2*

Arrange **all** the numbers **1**, **2**, **3**, **4** and **5** into two groups so that **doubling** the **sum** of the first group gives the **sum** of the second group.

There are three different ways the numbers can be arranged. The first one is done for you. Write down the other two ways.

First group	**Second group**
5	1 , 2 , 3 , 4

FM Child trust fund

Use the information in the child trust funds key to answer the following questions

Child trust fund

- Children born on or after 1 September 2002 get a £250 voucher from the government to start their child trust fund account.
- They get a further payment of £250 from the government on their seventh birthday.
- If the household income is below the Child Tax Credit income threshold they get an additional £250 with each payment.
- Parents, relatives and friends can contribute a maximum of £1200 a year between them to the fund.
- All interest or earnings on the account is tax-free.
- The child (and no-one else) can withdraw the money in the fund when they are 18.
- Money cannot be taken out of the account until the child is 18.

Average annual growth 3%										
		Average annual investment								
		0	150	300	450	600	750	900	1050	1200
Potential amount in account after years shown	1	258	408	558	708	858	1008	1158	1308	1458
	7	565	1714	2864	4013	5162	6312	7461	8611	9760
	13	675	3017	5360	7703	10045	12388	14731	17073	19416
	18	782	4294	7806	11319	14831	18343	21855	25367	28879

Average annual growth 6%										
		Average annual investment								
		0	150	300	450	600	750	900	1050	1200
Potential amount in account after years shown	1	265	415	565	715	865	1015	1165	1315	1465
	7	641	1900	3159	4418	5677	6936	8195	9454	10714
	13	909	3741	6574	9406	12238	15071	17903	20735	23568
	18	1217	5852	10488	15124	19760	24396	29032	33668	38303

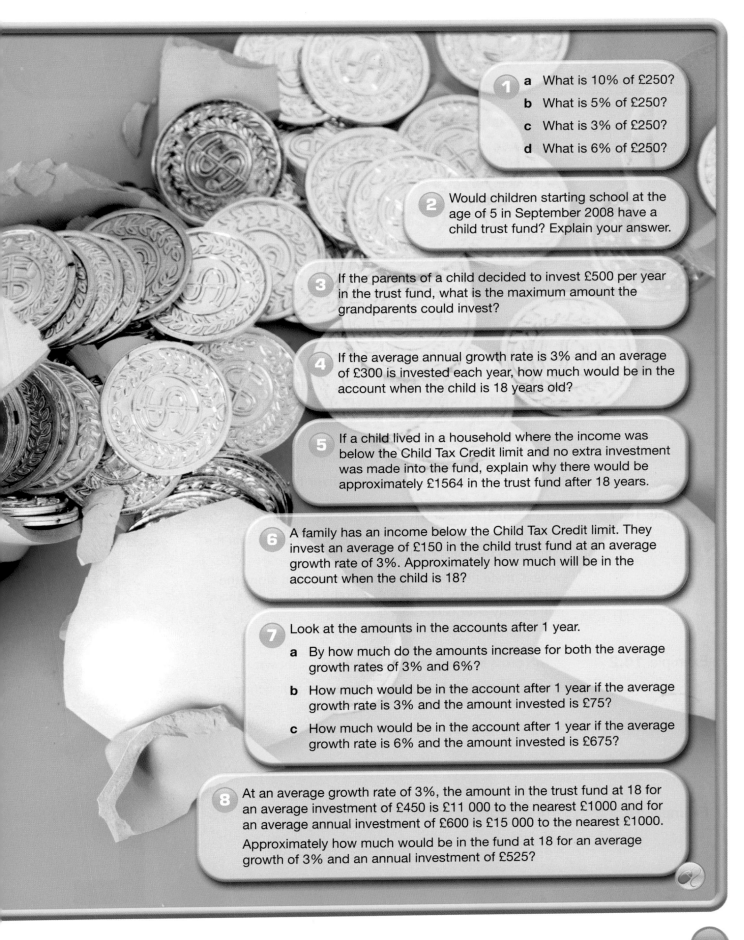

1
  a What is 10% of £250?
  b What is 5% of £250?
  c What is 3% of £250?
  d What is 6% of £250?

2 Would children starting school at the age of 5 in September 2008 have a child trust fund? Explain your answer.

3 If the parents of a child decided to invest £500 per year in the trust fund, what is the maximum amount the grandparents could invest?

4 If the average annual growth rate is 3% and an average of £300 is invested each year, how much would be in the account when the child is 18 years old?

5 If a child lived in a household where the income was below the Child Tax Credit limit and no extra investment was made into the fund, explain why there would be approximately £1564 in the trust fund after 18 years.

6 A family has an income below the Child Tax Credit limit. They invest an average of £150 in the child trust fund at an average growth rate of 3%. Approximately how much will be in the account when the child is 18?

7 Look at the amounts in the accounts after 1 year.
  a By how much do the amounts increase for both the average growth rates of 3% and 6%?
  b How much would be in the account after 1 year if the average growth rate is 3% and the amount invested is £75?
  c How much would be in the account after 1 year if the average growth rate is 6% and the amount invested is £675?

8 At an average growth rate of 3%, the amount in the trust fund at 18 for an average investment of £450 is £11 000 to the nearest £1000 and for an average annual investment of £600 is £15 000 to the nearest £1000.

Approximately how much would be in the fund at 18 for an average growth of 3% and an annual investment of £525?

This chapter is going to show you

- How to use line and rotation symmetry
- How to reflect shapes in a mirror line
- How to rotate shapes about a point
- How to translate shapes

What you should already know

- Be able to recognise shapes that have reflective symmetry
- Be able to recognise shapes that have been translated

Line symmetry

A 2-D shape has a **line of symmetry** when one half of the shape fits exactly over the other half when the shape is folded along that line.

A mirror or tracing paper can be used to check whether a shape has a line of symmetry. Some shapes have no lines of symmetry while others have more than one.

A line of symmetry is also called a **mirror line** or an **axis of reflection**.

Example 14.1 ▷

This T-shape has one line of symmetry, as shown.

Put a mirror on the line of symmetry and check that the image in the mirror is half the T-shape.

Next, trace the T-shape and fold the tracing along the line of symmetry to check that both halves of the shape fit exactly over each other.

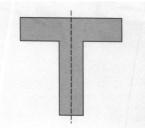

Example 14.2 ▷

This cross has four lines of symmetry, as shown.

Check that each line drawn here is a line of symmetry. Use either a mirror or tracing paper.

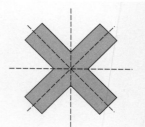

Example 14.3 ▷

This L-shape has no lines of symmetry.

1 Copy each of these shapes and draw its lines of symmetry. Write below each shape the number of lines of symmetry it has.

a   b   c   d   e    f

Isosceles   Equilateral   Square   Rectangle   Parallelogram   Kite
triangle   triangle

2 Write down the number of lines of symmetry for each of the following shapes.

a   b 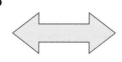   c   d

e   f   g   h

3 Write down the number of lines of symmetry for each of these road signs.

a   b   c   d    e    f

Extension Work

1 Symmetry squares

Two squares can be put together along their sides to make a shape that has line symmetry.

Three squares can be put together along their sides to make 2 different shapes that have line symmetry.

Investigate how many different symmetrical arrangements there are for four squares. What about five squares?

One symmetrical
arrangement for two squares

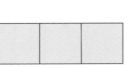

Two symmetrical arrangement
for three squares

2 Sports logo

Design a logo for a new sports and leisure centre that is due to open soon. Your logo should have four lines of symmetry.

Rotational symmetry

A 2-D shape has **rotational symmetry** when it can be rotated about a point to look exactly the same in a new position.

The **order of rotational symmetry** is the number of different positions in which the shape looks the same when it is rotated about the point through one complete turn (360°).

A shape has no rotational symmetry when it has to be rotated through one complete turn to look exactly the same. So it is said to have rotational symmetry of order 1.

To find the order of rotational symmetry of a shape, use tracing paper.

- First, trace the shape.
- Then rotate the tracing paper until the tracing again fits exactly over the shape.
- Count the number of times that the tracing fits exactly over the shape until you return to the starting position.
- The number of times that the tracing fits is the order of rotational symmetry.

Example 14.4 ▷   This shape has rotational symmetry of order 3.

Example 14.5 ▷   This shape has rotational symmetry of order 4.

Example 14.6 ▷   This shape has no rotational symmetry.
Therefore, it has rotational symmetry of order 1.

Exercise 14B

1 Copy each of these capital letters and write below its order of rotational symmetry.

a H   b M   c N   d S   e W   f X

2 Write down the order of rotational symmetry for each of the shapes below.

a   b   c   d   e   f

3 Copy and complete the table for each of the following regular polygons.

a 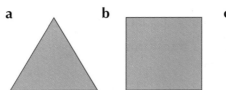 b  c 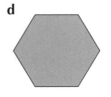 d e

	Shape	Number of lines of symmetry	Order of rotational symmetry
a	Equilateral triangle		
b	Square		
c	Regular pentagon		
d	Regular hexagon		
e	Regular octagon		

What do you notice?

Extension Work

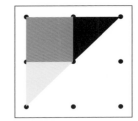

a Make eight copies of this shape on square dotty paper.

b Cut them out and arrange them to make a pattern with rotational symmetry of order 8.

c Design your own pattern which has rotational symmetry of order 8.

Reflections

The picture shows an L-shape reflected in a mirror.

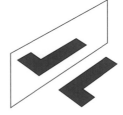

You can draw the picture without the mirror, as follows:

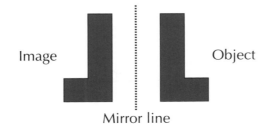

Image   Object

Mirror line

The **object** is reflected in the mirror line to give the **image**. The mirror line becomes a line of symmetry. So, if the paper is folded along the mirror line, the object will fit exactly over the image. The image is the same distance from the mirror line as the object.

A reflection is an example of a **transformation**. A transformation is a way of changing the position or the size of a shape.

Example 14.7 ▷

Reflect this shape in the given mirror line.

Notice that the image is the same size as the object, and that the mirror line becomes a line of symmetry.

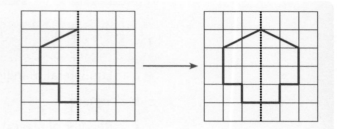

Example 14.8 ▷

Triangle A′B′C′ is the reflection of triangle ABC in the given mirror line.

When we change the position of a shape, we sometimes use the term **map**. Here we could write:

△ABC is mapped onto △A′B′C′ by a reflection in the mirror line.

Notice that the line joining A to A′ is perpendicular to the mirror line. This is true for all corresponding points on the object and the image. Also, all corresponding points on the object and image are at the same perpendicular distance from the mirror line.

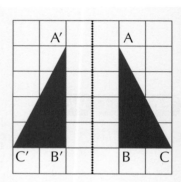

Example 14.9 ▷

Reflect this rectangle in the mirror line shown.

Use tracing paper to check the reflection.

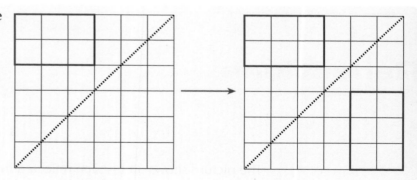

Exercise 14C

1 Copy each of these diagrams onto squared paper and draw its reflection in the given mirror line.

a

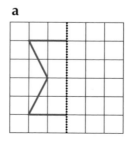

b

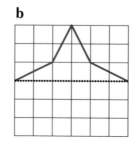

c

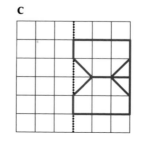

d

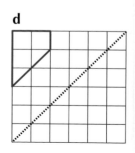

2 Copy each of these shapes onto squared paper and draw its reflection in the given mirror line.

a 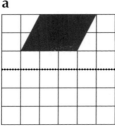 **b** 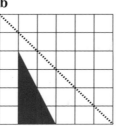 **c** 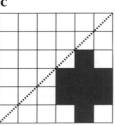 **d**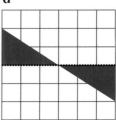

3 The points A(1, 2), B(2, 5), C(4, 4) and D(6, 1) are shown on the grid.

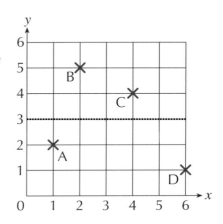

  a Copy the grid onto squared paper and plot the points A, B, C and D. Draw the mirror line.

  b Reflect the points in the mirror line and label them A′, B′, C′ and D′.

  c Write down the coordinates of the image points.

  d The point E(12, 6) is mapped onto E′ by a reflection in the mirror line. What are the coordinates of E′?

Extension Work

1 a Copy the diagram onto squared paper and reflect the triangle in the series of parallel mirrors.

  b Make up your own patterns using a series of parallel mirrors.

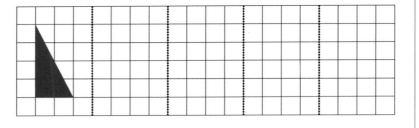

2 a Copy the grid onto squared paper and draw the triangle ABC. Write down the coordinates of A, B and C.

  b Reflect the triangle in the x-axis. Label the vertices of the image A′, B′ and C′. What are the coordinates of A′, B′ and C′?

  c Reflect triangle A′B′C′ in the y-axis. Label the vertices of this image A″, B″ and C″. What are the coordinates of A″, B″ and C″?

  d Reflect triangle A″B″C″ in the x-axis. Label the vertices A‴, B‴ and C‴. What are the coordinates of A‴B‴C‴?

  e Describe the reflection that maps triangle A‴B‴C‴ onto triangle ABC.

3 Use ICT software, such as Logo, to reflect shapes in mirror lines.

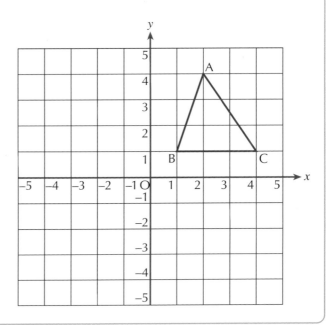

Rotations

Another type of transformation in geometry is **rotation**.

To describe the rotation of a 2-D shape, three facts must be known:
- **Centre of rotation** – the point about which the shape rotates.
- **Angle of rotation** – this is usually 90° ($\frac{1}{4}$ turn), 180° ($\frac{1}{2}$ turn) or 270° ($\frac{3}{4}$ turn).
- **Direction of rotation** – clockwise or anticlockwise.

When you rotate a shape, it is a good idea to use tracing paper.

As with reflections, the original shape is called the object, and the rotated shape is called the image.

Example 14.10 ▷ The flag is rotated through 90° clockwise about the point X.

Notice that this is the same as rotating the flag through 270° anticlockwise about the point X.

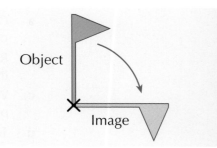

Example 14.11 ▷ This right-angled triangle is rotated through 180° clockwise about the point X.

Notice that this triangle can be rotated either clockwise or anticlockwise when turning through 180°.

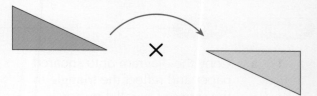

Example 14.12 ▷ △ABC has been mapped onto △A′B′C′ by a rotation of 90° anticlockwise about the point X.

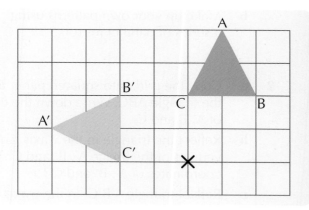

Exercise 14D

① Copy each of the flags below and draw the image after each one has been rotated about the point marked X through the angle indicated. Use tracing paper to help.

a

b

c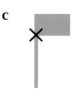

d

90° anticlockwise   180° clockwise   90° clockwise   270° anticlockwise

2 Copy each of the shapes below onto a square grid. Draw the image after each one has been rotated about the point marked X through the angle indicated. Use tracing paper to help.

a

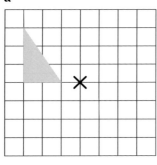

180° clockwise

b

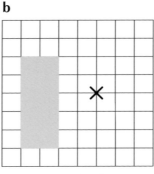

90° anticlockwise

c

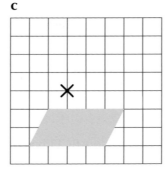

180° anticlockwise

d

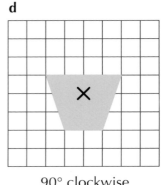

90° clockwise

3 **a** Rotate the rectangle ABCD through 90° clockwise about the point $(1, 2)$ to give the image A′B′C′D′.

b Write down the coordinates of A′, B′, C′ and D′.

c Which coordinate point remains fixed throughout the rotation?

d What rotation will map the rectangle A′B′C′D′ onto the rectangle ABCD?

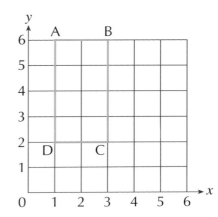

Extension Work

1 **Inverse rotations**

The **inverse** of a rotation is that rotation required to map the image back onto the object, using the same centre of rotation. Investigate inverse rotations by drawing your own shapes and using different rotations.

Write down any properties you discover about inverse rotations.

2 Use ICT software, such as Logo, to rotate shapes about different centres of rotation.

Translations

A translation is the movement of a 2-D shape from one position to another without reflecting it or rotating it.

The distance and direction of the translation are given by the number of unit squares moved to the right or left, followed by the number of unit squares moved up or down.

As with reflections and rotations, the original shape is called the object, and the translated shape is called the image.

Example 14.13 ▷

Triangle A has been mapped onto triangle B by a translation 3 units right, followed by 2 units up.

Points on triangle A are mapped by the same translation onto triangle B, as shown by the arrows.

When an object is translated onto its image, every point on the object moves the same distance.

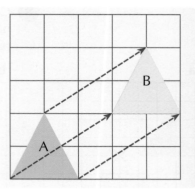

Example 14.14 ▷

The rectangle ABCD has been mapped onto rectangle A′B′C′D′ by a translation 3 units left, followed by 3 units down.

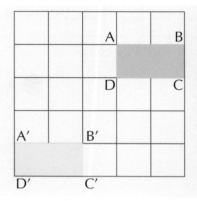

Exercise 14E

1 Describe each of the following translations:

   a   from A to B

   b   from A to C

   c   from A to D

   d   from A to E

   e   from B to D

   f   from C to E

   g   from D to E

   h   from E to A

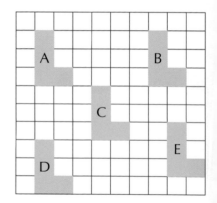

2 Copy the triangle ABC onto squared paper. Label it P.

   a   Write down the coordinates of the vertices of triangle P.

   b   Translate triangle P 6 units left and 2 units down. Label the new triangle Q.

   c   Write down the coordinates of the vertices of triangle Q.

   d   Translate triangle Q 5 units right and 4 units down. Label the new triangle R.

   e   Write down the coordinates of the vertices of triangle R.

   f   Describe the translation which maps triangle R onto triangle P.

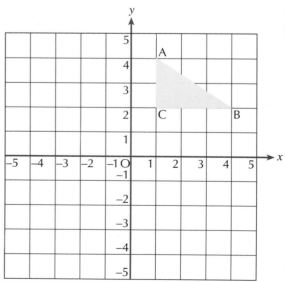

Extension Work

Use squared dotty paper or a pin-board for this investigation.

a How many different translations of the triangle are possible on this 3 by 3 grid?

b How many different translations of this triangle are possible on a 4 by 4 grid?

c Investigate the number of translations that are possible on any size grid.

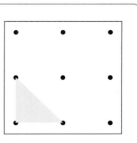

LEVEL BOOSTER

4 I can reflect simple shapes in a mirror line.

5 I can find the order of rotational symmetry of a 2-D shape.
I can rotate 2-D shapes about a centre of rotation.
I can translate 2-D shapes.

National Test questions

1 *1998 Paper 1*

These patterns are from Islamic designs. Write down the number of lines of symmetry for each pattern.

a    **b**    **c**

4

2   *2006 4–6 Paper 2*

The square grid shows a rectangle reflected in **two mirror lines.**

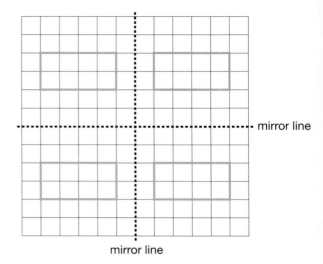

On a copy of the square grid below, show the **triangle** reflected in the two mirror lines.

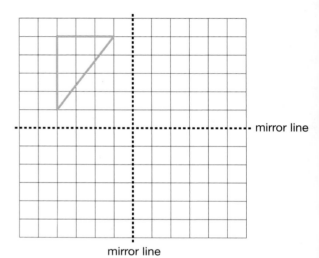

3   *2005 4–6 Paper 1*

The shapes below are drawn on square grids.
The diagrams show a rectangle that is rotated, then rotated again,
The centre of rotation is marked •.

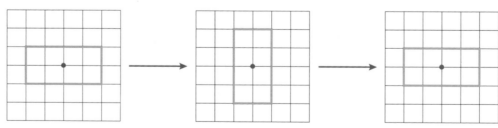

Rotate
90° clockwise

Rotate another
90° clockwise

Copy and complete the diagrams below to show the triangle when it is rotated, then rotated again. The centre of rotation is marked •.

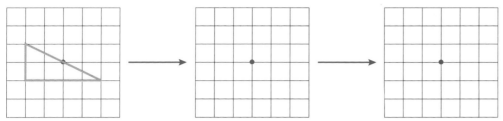

Rotate
90° clockwise

Rotate another
90° clockwise

4 *2003 4–6 Paper 1*

I have a square grid and two rectangles.

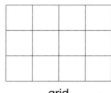

grid

two rectangles

I make a pattern with the grid and the two rectangles:

The pattern has **no** lines of symmetry.

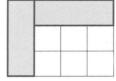

a Put both rectangles on the grid to make a pattern with **two** lines of symmetry.

You must **shade** the rectangles.

b Put both rectangles on the grid to make a pattern with **only one** line of symmetry.

You must **shade** the rectangles.

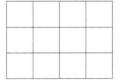

c Put both rectangles on the grid to make a pattern with **rotation** symmetry of **order 2**.

You must **shade** the rectangles.

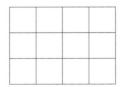

FM Landmark spotting

Look at the symmetry of these famous landmarks

d The Angel of the North

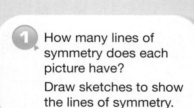

1 How many lines of symmetry does each picture have?

Draw sketches to show the lines of symmetry.

2 The picture for some of the buildings will have a different number of lines if the picture was taken directly from above. We call this the aerial view.

How many lines of symmetry would a picture of the Eiffel Tower have from an aerial view?

Draw a sketch to show the lines of symmetry.

Explain why it may not be possible to do this for the aerial views of the other buildings.

a Notre Dame Cathedral

3 The window on the picture of Notre Dame Cathedral also has rotational symmetry.

Design a window of your own that has rotational symmetry.

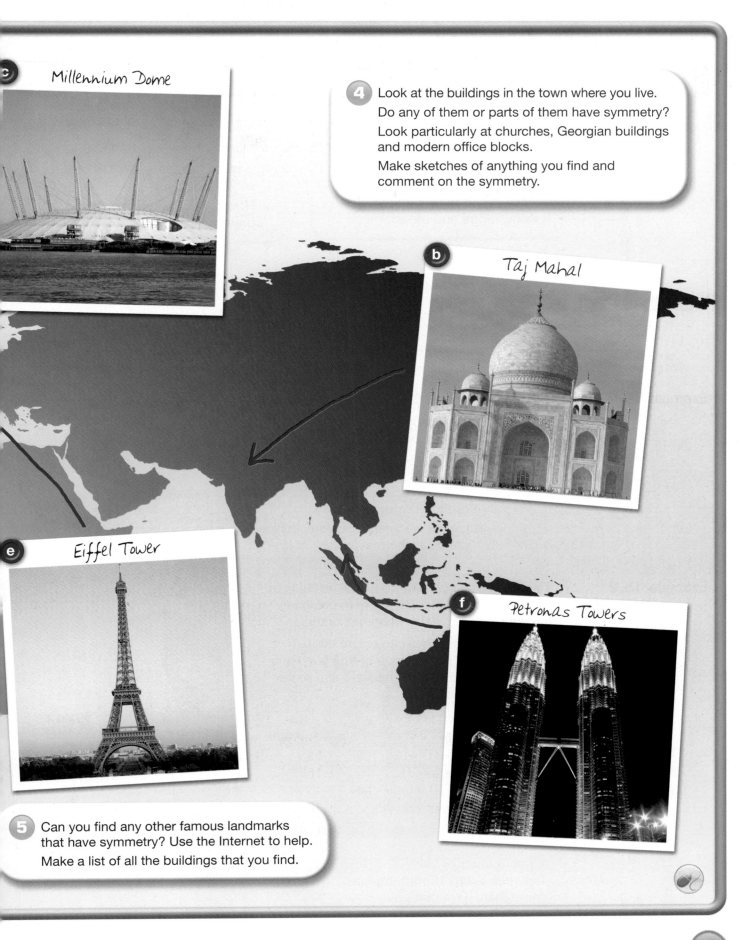

Millennium Dome

4 Look at the buildings in the town where you live.

Do any of them or parts of them have symmetry?

Look particularly at churches, Georgian buildings and modern office blocks.

Make sketches of anything you find and comment on the symmetry.

b Taj Mahal

e Eiffel Tower

f Petronas Towers

5 Can you find any other famous landmarks that have symmetry? Use the Internet to help.

Make a list of all the buildings that you find.

Pie charts

Sometimes we are presented with pie charts showing percentages. The simplest of these are split into 10 sections each section representing 10%, like the ones shown below.

Example 15.1 ▷ The pie chart shows the favourite drink of some Year 7 pupils.

We see that: Tea occupies 1 sector, hence 10% have tea as their favourite.

Milk occupies 3 sectors, hence 30% have milk as their favourite.

Coke occupies 4 sectors, hence 40% have coke as their favourite.

Coffee occupies 2 sectors, hence 20% have coffee as their favourite.

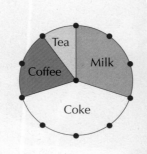

Example 15.2 ▷ The two pie charts show how late the trains of Britain and Spain are. Use them to compare the punctuality of trains in both countries.

From the pie charts we can create tables interpreting the data, remembering that each division represents 10% (hence half a sector will be 5%).

The tables we can create are:

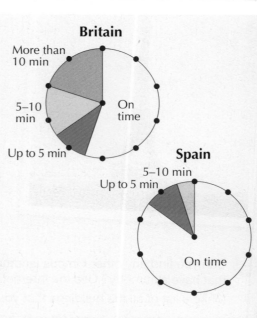

Lateness: Britain	Percentage
On time	55
Up to 5 minutes late	10
Between 5 and 10 minutes late	15
More than 10 minutes late	20

Lateness: Spain	Percentage
On time	85
Up to 5 minutes late	10
Between 5 and 10 minutes late	5
More than 10 minutes late	0

We can see that:

- a higher percentage of trains in Spain are on time.
- the same percentage of trains are up to 5 minutes late in both countries.
- a higher percentage of trains in Britain are over 5 minutes late.

Exercise 15A

For each of the pie charts, start with a copy of the circle that is divided into ten sectors. Remember to label your pie chart.

1. The pie chart on the right shows the percentage of cars in a car park of different colours.

   What percentage of the cars were:
   a red   b blue   c green
   d yellow   e black?

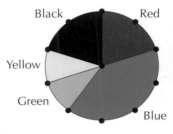

2. The pie chart on the right shows the percentage of pets of pupils in a Y7 group.

   What percentage of the pets were:
   a dogs   b cats   c birds
   d fish   e gerbils?

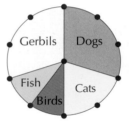

3. The pie chart on the right shows the percentage of various school subjects that pupils chose as their favourite.

   What percentage of the pupils said their favourite subject was:
   a maths   b English   c geography
   d history   e PE?

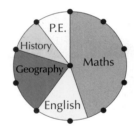

4. The pie chart on the right shows the percentage of various television soap operas that pupils chose as their favourite.

   What percentage of the pupils said their favourite soap opera was:
   a EastEnders   b Hollyoaks
   c Coronation Street   d Neighbours?

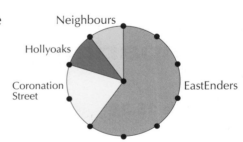

5. The pie chart on the right shows the percentage of various age groups living in Rotherham.

   What percentage of the people in Rotherham were aged:
   a under 16   b 16–25   c 26–40
   d 41–60   e over 60?

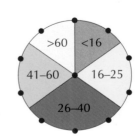

6 The pie chart on the right shows the percentage of various age groups living in Eastbourne.

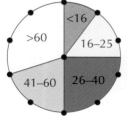

What percentage of the people in Eastbourne were aged:

  a under 16   **b** 16–25   **c** 26–40

  d 41–60   **e** over 60?

7 The chart on the right is the distribution of ages in an Indian village. What percentage of the people in the Indian village were aged:

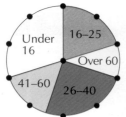

  a under 16   **b** 16–25   **c** 26–40

  d 41–60   **e** over 60?

FM **8** Use the information in questions 5, 6 and 7 to decide which of the following statements are TRUE or FALSE:

  a There is a greater percentage of under 16s in Rotherham than Eastbourne.

  b There is a greater percentage of over 60s in Rotherham than Eastbourne.

  c There is a greater percentage of people aged 16–40 in Rotherham than Eastbourne.

  d There is an equal percentage of people aged 41–60 in Rotherham and Eastbourne.

  e There is a smaller percentage of under 16s in Rotherham than the village in India.

  f There is a smaller percentage of over 60s in the village in India than Eastbourne.

  g There is a smaller percentage of people aged 41–60 in the village in India than Eastbourne.

Extension **Work**

Find data that is given as percentages. For example, the table of constituents on the side of a cereal packet.

Draw pie charts to compare these and display them as a poster.

Comparing data

Example 15.3

You are organising a ten-pin bowling match. You have one team place to fill.

These are the last five scores for Carol and Doris.

Carol	122	131	114	162	146
Doris	210	91	135	99	151

Who would you pick to be in the team and why?

The mean for Carol is 135 and the range is 48.
The mean for Doris is 137.2 and the range is 119.

You could pick Doris as she has the greater mean, or you could pick Carol as she is more consistent.

Example 15.4 ▷ Your teacher thinks that the girls in the class are absent more often than the boys.

There are 10 boys in your class. Their days absent over last term were:

    5   0   3   4   6   3   0   8   6   5

There are 12 girls in the class. Their days absent over last term were:

    2   1   0   0   5   3   1   2   3   50   2   3

Is your teacher correct? Explain your answer.

The mean for the boys is 4 and the range is 8.
The mean for the girls is 6 and the range is 50.

It looks as though your teacher is correct. But if you take out the girl who was absent 50 times because she was in hospital, the mean for the girls becomes 2 and the range 5. In that case, your teacher would be wrong.

Exercise 15B

 1 You have to choose someone to play darts for your team. You ask Bill and Ben to throw ten times each. These are their scores.

| **Ryan** | 32 | 16 | 25 | 65 | 12 | 24 | 63 | 121 | 31 | 11 |
| **Ali** | 43 | 56 | 40 | 31 | 37 | 49 | 49 | 30 | 31 | 24 |

  a Work out the mean for Ryan.   **b** Work out the range for Ryan.
  c Work out the mean for Ali.   **d** Work out the range for Ali.
  e Who would you choose and why?

2 You have to catch a bus regularly. You can catch bus A or bus B. On the last ten times you caught these buses. You noted down, in minutes, how late they were.

| **Bus A** | 1 | 2 | 4 | 12 | 1 | 3 | 5 | 6 | 2 | 9 |
| **Bus B** | 6 | 5 | 5 | 6 | 2 | 4 | 4 | 5 | 6 | 7 |

  a Work out the mean for bus A.   **b** Work out the range for bus A.
  c Work out the mean for bus B.   **d** Work out the range for bus B.

3 Each day at break I buy a bag of biscuits from the school canteen. I can buy them from canteen A or canteen B. I made a note of how many biscuits were in each bag I got from each canteen.

| **Canteen A** | 12 | 11 | 14 | 10 | 13 | 12 | 9 | 12 | 15 | 12 |
| **Canteen B** | 5 | 18 | 13 | 15 | 10 | 15 | 17 | 8 | 11 | 13 |

  a Work out the mean for Canteen A.   **b** Work out the range for Canteen A.
  c Work out the mean for Canteen B.   **d** Work out the range for Canteen B.

 4 You have to choose someone for a quiz team. The last ten quiz scores (out of 20) for Bryan and Ryan are:

| **Bryan** | 1 | 19 | 2 | 12 | 20 | 13 | 2 | 6 | 5 | 10 |
| **Adeel** | 8 | 7 | 9 | 12 | 13 | 8 | 7 | 11 | 7 | 8 |

  a Work out the mean for Bryan.   **b** Work out the range for Bryan.
  c Work out the mean for Adeel.   **d** Work out the range for Adeel.
  e Who would you choose for the quiz team and why?

Work in pairs.

a Measure the length of the fingers on each hand with a ruler as accurately as you can.

b Repeat this for both of you.

c Calculate the mean and the range of the lengths of the fingers for each of you.

d Comment on your results.

e Try to compare your results with others in your class.

f Compare the results for boys and girls. What do you notice?

Statistical surveys

You are about to carry out some statistical surveys and create charts to display your results.

Your data may be obtained in one of the following ways:

● A survey of a sample of people. Your sample size should be more than 30. To collect data from your chosen sample, you will need to use a data collection sheet or a questionnaire.

● Carry out experiments. You will need to keep a record of your observations on a data collection sheet.

Exercise 15C

1 **a** Find a sample of 30 people or more and ask them the following question, keeping a tally of the answers.

Approximately how many hours do you watch TV over a typical weekend?

Time (hours)	Tally	Frequency
2 hours or less		
Over 2 but less than 4 hours		
Between 4 and 8 hours		
Over 8 hours		

b Create a chart illustrating your collected data.

2 For this question, change some of the named sports if you wish.

a Find a sample of 30 Year 7 boys and ask them the following question, keeping a tally of the answers.

Which of the following sports do you play outside school?

Sport	Tally	Frequency
Football		
Cricket		
Tennis		
Badminton		
Something else		

b Now find a sample of 30 Year 7 girls and ask them the same question, keeping a tally of the results.

c Create charts illustrating your data and also illustrating any differences between the two groups.

3 For this question, change some of the bands if you wish.

a Find a sample of 30 Year 7 pupils and ask them the following question, keeping a tally of the answers

Which of the following bands would you most want to go and listen to at a concert?

Band	Tally	Frequency
Red Hot Chili Peppers		
Mika		
Ordinary Boys		
Kaiser Chiefs		
Arctic Monkeys		

b Create charts illustrating your data.

4 a Ask the following sequence of questions to 30 people or more:

i Before this year, have you normally gone abroad for your holiday?   Yes/No
ii Are you intending to go abroad on holiday this year?   Yes/No

b Use your results to complete the following two way table:

	Going abroad this year	Not going abroad this year
Normally go abroad		
Do not normally go abroad		

c From your results, is it true to say 'More people are taking holidays abroad this year'?

Extension Work

By choosing a suitable sample of people, investigate the young woman's statement.

Taller people have a larger head circumference.

Probabilities from two way tables

In the media you will often see two way tables that show information. From these tables we can determine probabilities of events.

Example 15.5 ▷

Vicky did a survey of the time spent on homework the previous night of all the pupils in her class. This table shows her results:

	Number of boys	Number of girls
under 1 hour	13	9
1 hour or more	3	5

What is the probability that at random, we select from this class a pupil who:

a is a boy who spent an hour or more on his homework?

b is someone who spent under an hour on their homework?

Each person in the class can only be in one section of the table, so by adding up all the four sections we can tell how many are in the class altogether. This is 13 + 9 + 3 + 5, which equals 30.

a We see from the table that 3 boys spent one hour or more doing their homework, and, as there are 30 pupils in the class, the probability of selecting at random a boy that spent one hour or more doing his homework will be $\frac{3}{30}$, which cancels down to $\frac{1}{10}$.

b We see from the table that there are 13 + 9 pupils who spent less than 1 hour on their homework, which is 22. So, the probability of selecting someone who spent under an hour on their homework is $\frac{22}{30}$, which cancels down to $\frac{11}{15}$.

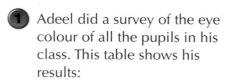

Exercise 15D

1 Adeel did a survey of the eye colour of all the pupils in his class. This table shows his results:

	Number of boys	Number of girls
Blue eyes	9	11
Brown eyes	4	6

a How many pupils are in Adeel's class?

b How many boys in Adeel's class have blue eyes?

c How many boys are there in Adeel's class?

d What is the probability of selecting a pupil at random that:
  i is a boy with blue eyes?
  ii is a boy?

2 Shauna did a survey of how all the pupils in her class travelled to school. This table shows her results:

	Number of boys	Number of girls
Walked	10	4
Bus	6	9

a How many pupils are in Shauna's class?

b How many boys in Shauna's class walked to school?

c How many girls are there in Shauna's class?

d What is the probability of selecting a pupil at random that:
  i is a boy who walks to school?
  ii is a girl?

3 Chi did a survey of hair colour of all the pupils in her class. This table shows her results:

	Number of boys	Number of girls
Dark hair	12	6
Light hair	4	9

a How many pupils are in Chi's class?

b How many girls in Chi's class had dark hair?

c How many pupils in Chi's class had dark hair?

d What is the probability of selecting a pupil at random that:
  i is a girl with dark hair?
  ii is a dark-haired pupil?

4 There are 17 boys and 12 girls in Padmini's class. 8 boys and 4 girls have dark hair.

The others all have light hair.

a Copy and complete this table for Padmini's class.

	Number of boys	Number of girls
Dark hair		
Light hair		

b What is the probability of selecting a pupil at random that:
  i is a light-haired boy?
  ii is a girl with light hair?

Extension Work

Find the necessary data to find the following probabilities, selecting at random a pupil from your class that is:

a a blue-eyed boy

b a girl that can swim

c a dark-haired boy

d a girl that has been abroad for her holiday

e a girl that can ride a bike

LEVEL BOOSTER

4
I can collect and record data in a frequency table.
I can use the range to describe a set of data.

5
I can compare two distributions using mean and range, then draw conclusions.
I can interpret pie charts.
I can calculate probabilities based on experimental evidence.

4

1 *2006 4–6 Paper 1*

Red kites are large birds that were very rare in England.

Scientists set free some red kites in 1989 and hoped that they would build nests.

The diagrams show how many nests the birds built from 1991 to 1996.

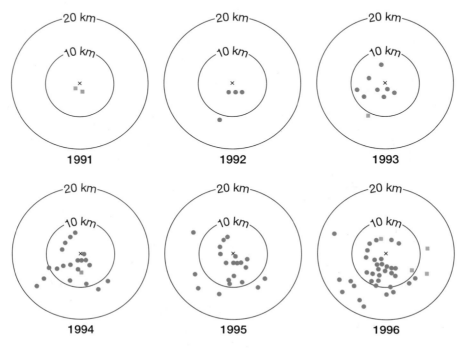

Key:

× shows where the birds were set free

▪ represents a nest without eggs

● represents a nest with eggs

Use the diagrams to answer these questions:

a Which was the first year there were nests **with eggs**?

b In **1993**, how many nests were **without eggs**?

c In **1995**, how many nests were **more than 10 km** from where the birds were set free?

d Explain what happened to the **number** of nests over the years.

e Now explain what happened to the **distances** of the nests from where the birds were set free, over the years.

5

2 *2005 4–6 Paper 2*

Look at this information:

> **In 1976, a man earned £16.00 each week.**

The pie chart shows how this man spent his money:

a How much did the man spend on **food** each week?

b Now look at this information:

> **In 2002, a man earned £500.00 each week.**

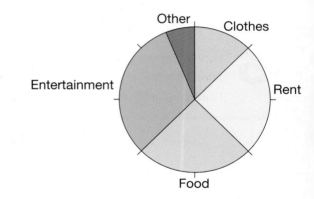

This table shows how he spent his money:

Draw a pie chart to show how this man spent his money.

Remember to **label** each sector of the pie chart.

Rent	£200
Food	£100
Entertainment	£150
Other	£50

3 *2007 3–5 Paper 2*

The diagram shows five fair spinners with grey and white sectors.

Each spinner is divided into equal sectors.

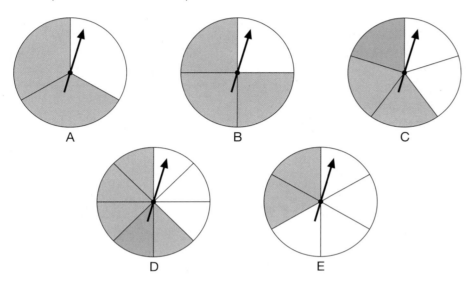

I am going to spin all the pointers.

a For one of the spinners, the probability of spinning **grey** is $\frac{3}{4}$.

Which spinner is this? Write its letter.

b For two of the spinners, the probability of spinning **grey** is **more than 60%** but **less than 70%**.

Which two spinners are these? Write their letters.

4 *2000 Paper 2*

A school has a new canteen. A special person will be chosen to perform the opening ceremony.

The names of all the pupils, all the teachers and all the canteen staff are put into a box. One name is taken out at random.

A pupil says:

'There are only three choices. It could be a pupil, a teacher or one of the canteen staff. The probability of it being a pupil is $\frac{1}{3}$.'

The pupil is wrong. Explain why.

<table>
<tr><td>

This chapter is going to show you

- How to multiply and divide decimals by whole numbers
- How to use the memory keys on a calculator
- How to use the square root and sign change keys on a calculator
- How to calculate fractions and percentages of quantities

</td><td>

What you should already know

- How to do long and short multiplication and division
- Equivalence of fractions, decimals and percentages
- How to use a calculator efficiently, including the use of brackets

</td></tr>
</table>

Adding and subtracting decimals

You have already met addition and subtraction of decimals in Chapter 2. In this section, you will be doing problems involving whole numbers, decimals and metric units.

Example 16.1 ▷ Work out: **a** $4 + 0.86 + 0.07$ **b** $6 - 1.45$

a Whole numbers have a decimal point after the units digit. So, put in zeros for the missing place values, and line up the decimal points:

$$\begin{array}{r} 4.00 \\ 0.86 \\ + \underline{0.07} \\ \underline{4.93} \\ {\scriptstyle 1} \end{array}$$

b As in the previous sum, put in zeros to make up the missing place values, and line up the decimal points:

$$\begin{array}{r} {\scriptstyle 5\ 9\ 1} \\ \cancel{6}.\cancel{0}0 \\ - \underline{1.45} \\ \underline{4.55} \end{array}$$

Example 16.2 ▷ Nazia has done 4.3 km of a 20 km bike ride. How far does Nazia still have to go?

The units are the same, so

$$\begin{array}{r} {\scriptstyle 1\ 9\ 1} \\ 2\cancel{0}.0 \\ - \underline{\ \ 4.3} \\ \underline{15.7} \end{array}$$

Nazia still has to go 15.7 km.

Example 16.3 ▷

Mary wants to lose 3 kg in weight. So far she has lost 650 grams. How much more does she need to lose?

The units need to made the same. So change 650 grams into 0.65 kg. This gives:

$$\begin{array}{r} {}^{2}\cancel{3}.{}^{9}\cancel{0}{}^{1}0 \\ -\ 0.65 \\ \hline 2.35 \end{array}$$

Mary still has to lose 2.35 kg.

Exercise 16A

1 Without using a calculator, work out each of these.

a	3.5 + 4.7	**b**	6.1 + 2.8
c	3.4 + 1.7	**d**	12.41 + 8.69
e	9.3 − 6.1	**f**	3.5 − 2.7
g	17.5 − 13.7	**h**	27.65 − 16.47

2 Without using a calculator, work out each of these.

a	4 − 2.38	**b**	5 − 1.29	**c**	8 − 3.14	**d**	12 − 2.38
e	7 − 1.08	**f**	10 − 2.66	**g**	24 − 12.3	**h**	15 − 6.09

3 The diagram shows the lengths of the paths in a park.

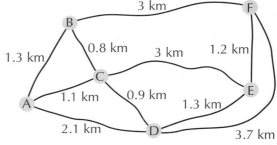

a   How long are the paths altogether?

b   John wants to visit all the points A, B, C, D, E and F in this order. He wants to start and finish at A and go along each and every path. Explain why he cannot do this in the distance you worked out for part **a**.

c   Work out the shortest distance John could walk if he wanted to visit each point, starting and finishing at A.

4 A Christmas cake weighs 2 kg. Arthur takes a slice weighing 235 grams. How much is left?

5 23 cl of water is poured from a jug containing 3 litres. How much is left?

6 1560 millimetres of ribbon is cut from a roll that is 5 metres long. How much ribbon is left?

7 The three legs of a relay are 3 km, 4.8 km and 1800 m. How far is the race altogether?

8 Three packages weigh 4 kg, 750 grams and 0.08 kg. How much do they weigh altogether?

Write down all the pairs of single-digit numbers that add up to 9: for example, 2 + 7.

By looking at your answers to Question 2 in Exercise 16A and working out the following:

a 1 – 0.435   **b** 6 – 2.561   **c** 12 – 3.6754

explain how you can just write down the answers when you are taking away a decimal from a whole number.

Make a poster to explain this to a Year 6 pupil.

Multiplying and dividing decimals

When you add together 1.2 + 1.2 + 1.2 + 1.2, you get 4.8.

This sum can be written as $4 \times 1.2 = 4.8$. It can also be written as $4.8 \div 4 = 1.2$.

You are now going to look at how to multiply and divide decimals by whole numbers.

These two operations are just like any type of division and multiplication but you need to be sure where to put the decimal point. As a general rule, there will be the same number of decimal places in the answer as there were in the original problem.

Example 16.4 ▷

Work out: **a** 5×3.7 **b** 8×4.3 **c** 9×1.08 **d** 6×3.5

Each of these can be set out in a column:

a   3.7
  × 5
  ‾‾‾‾
  18.5
   3

b   4.3
  × 8
  ‾‾‾‾
  34.4
   2

c   1.08
  × 9
  ‾‾‾‾
  9.72
   7

d   3.5
  × 6
  ‾‾‾‾
  21.0
   3

You see that the decimal point stays in the *same* place. You would give the answer to part **d** as 21.

Example 16.5 ▷

Work out: **a** $22.8 \div 6$ **b** $33.6 \div 7$ **c** $9.59 \div 7$ **d** $26.2 \div 5$

These can be set out as short division:

a   3.8
  6)22.⁴8

b   4.8
  7)33.⁵6

c   1.37
  7)9.⁵⁴9

d   5.24
  5)26.¹2⁰

Once again, the decimal point stays in the same place. Notice that a zero had to be put in part **d**.

1 Without using a calculator, work out each of these.

a 3.14×5 **b** 1.73×8 **c** 1.41×6 **d** 2.26×9

e 6×3.35 **f** 9×5.67 **g** 5×6.17 **h** 9×9.12

2 Without using a calculator, work out each of these.

    a   17.04 ÷ 8   **b**   39.2 ÷ 7   **c**   27.2 ÷ 8   **d**   30.6 ÷ 5

    e   25.88 ÷ 4   **f**   4.44 ÷ 3   **g**   27.72 ÷ 9   **h**   22.4 ÷ 5

 3 A piece of wood, 2.8 metres long, is cut into five equal pieces. How long is each piece?

 4 Five bars of metal each weigh 2.35 kg. How much do they weigh together?

 5 A cake weighing 1.74 kg is cut into six equal pieces. How much does each piece weigh?

 6 Eight bottles of pop cost £6.24. How much is one bottle?

 7 One floppy disk holds 1.44 Mb of information. How much information will six floppy disks hold?

Extension **Work**

Use a calculator to work out each of the following.

a   46 × 34   **b**   4.6 × 34   **c**   4.6 × 3.4   **d**   0.46 × 0.34

Try some examples of your own.

You will notice that the digits of all the answers are the same but that the decimal point is in different places. Can you see the rule for placing the decimal point?

Using a calculator

Your calculator is broken. Only the keys shown are working. Using just these keys, can you make all the numbers up to 25? For example:

     1 = 4 − 3   12 = 3 × 4   15 = 4 + 4 + 7

You have already met brackets on a calculator in Chapter 9 (page 114). With the most recent calculators, using brackets is probably the best way to do lengthy calculations. The problem with keying in a calculation using brackets is that there is no intermediate working to check where you made mistakes. One way round this is to use the memory keys, or to write down the intermediate values. (This is what examiners call 'working'.)

The memory is a location inside the calculator where a number can be stored.

The memory keys are not exactly the same on different makes of calculators, but they all do the same things. Let us look at the four main keys:

Min   This key puts the value in the display into the memory and the contents of the memory are lost. This is STO on some calculators.

M+   This key adds the contents of the display to the contents of the memory.

M–   This key subtracts the contents of the display from the contents of the memory. This is SHIFT M+ on some calculators.

MR   This key recalls the contents of the memory and puts it in the display. The contents of the display will disappear but may still be involved in the calculation.

Example 16.6 ▷   Calculate: **a** $\dfrac{16.8 + 28.8}{23.8 - 16.2}$ **b** $60.3 \div (16.3 - 9.6)$

a   Type in 23.8 – 16.2 =, which gives an answer of 7.6. Store this in the memory with Min.

Type in 16.8 + 28.8 =, which gives 45.6 in the display. Type ÷ MR =. This should give an answer of 6.

b   Type in 16.3 – 9.6 =, which gives an answer of 6.7. Store this with Min.

Type in 60.3 ÷ MR =, which should give an answer of 9.

Two other very useful keys are the square root key √ and the sign change key **+/–** .

Note that not all calculators have a sign change key. Some have **(–)** . Also, the square root key has to be pressed before the number on some calculators and after the number on others.

The best thing to do is to get your own calculator and learn how to use it.

Example 16.7 ▷   Calculate: **a** $\sqrt{432}$ **b** $180 - (32 + 65)$

a   Either √ 432 = or 432 √ = should give 20.78460969. Round this off to 20.78.

b   Type in 32 + 65 =, which should give 97. Press the sign change key and the display should change to –97. Type in +180 =, which should give 83.

The sign change key is also used to input a negative number. For example, on some calculators, 2 **+/–** will give a display of –2.

Exercise 16C

1   Use the memory keys to work out each of the following. Write down any values that you store in the memory.

   a $\dfrac{17.8 + 25.6}{14.5 - 8.3}$ **b** $\dfrac{35.7 - 19.2}{34.9 - 19.9}$ **c** $\dfrac{16.9 + 23.6}{16.8 - 14.1}$ **d** $\dfrac{47.2 - 19.6}{11.1 - 8.8}$

   e $45.6 - (23.4 - 6.9)$ **f** $44.8 \div (12.8 - 7.2)$ **g** $(4 \times 28.8) \div (9.5 - 3.1)$

2   Use the sign change key to enter the first negative number. Then use the calculator to work out the value of each of these.

   a $-2 + 3 - 7$ **b** $-4 - 6 + 8$ **c** $-6 + 7 - 8 + 2$ **d** $-5 + 3 - 8 + 9$

3   Use the square root key to work out:

   a $\sqrt{400}$ **b** $\sqrt{300}$ **c** $\sqrt{150}$ **d** $\sqrt{10}$

4   What happens if you press the sign key twice in succession?

5 Calculate each of the following **i** using the brackets keys, and **ii** using the memory keys.

Write out the key presses for each. Which method uses fewer key presses?

a $\dfrac{12.9 + 42.9}{23.7 - 14.4}$ **b** $\dfrac{72.4 - 30.8}{16.85 - 13.6}$ **c** $25.6 \div (6.7 - 3.5)$

6 If you start with 16 and press the square root key twice in succession, the display shows 2. If you start with 81 and press the square root key twice in succession, the display shows 3.

Explain what numbers are shown in the display.

Extension Work

It helps to understand how a calculator works if you can think like a calculator. So, do the following without using a calculator.

You are told what the number in the memory and the number in the display are.

After each series of operations shown below, what number will be in the display and what number will be in the memory? The first one has been done as an example.

	Starting number in display	Starting number in memory	Operations	Final number in display	Final number in memory
	6	10	M+, M+, M+	6	28
a	6	10	Min, M+, M+		
b	6	10	M−, MR		
c	12	5	M+, MR, M+		
d	10	6	M+, M+, M+, MR		
e	10	6	MR, M+, M+		
f	8	8	M−, M+, MR, M+		
g	15	20	M−, M−, MR, M+		

Fractions of quantities

This section is going to help you to revise the rules for working with fractions.

Example 16.8 Find: **a** $\frac{2}{7}$ of £28   **b** $\frac{3}{5}$ of 45 sweets   **c** $1\frac{2}{3}$ of 15 m

a First, find $\frac{1}{7}$ of £28: $28 \div 7 = 4$. So, $\frac{2}{7}$ of £28 $= 2 \times 4 = £8$.

b First, find $\frac{1}{5}$ of 45 sweets: $45 \div 5 = 9$. So, $\frac{3}{5}$ of 45 sweets $= 3 \times 9 = 27$ sweets.

c Either calculate $\frac{2}{3}$ of 15 and add it to 15, or make $1\frac{2}{3}$ into a top-heavy fraction and work out $\frac{5}{3}$ of 15.

$15 \div 3 = 5$, so $\frac{2}{3}$ of 15 $= 10$. Hence, $1\frac{2}{3}$ of 15 m $= 15 + 10 = 25$ m.

$15 \div 3 = 5$, so $\frac{5}{3}$ of 15 $= 25$ m.

Example 16.9 ▷ Find: **a** $7 \times \frac{3}{4}$ **b** $8 \times \frac{2}{3}$ **c** $5 \times 1\frac{3}{5}$

    a $7 \times \frac{3}{4} = \frac{21}{4} = 5\frac{1}{4}$

    b $8 \times \frac{2}{3} = \frac{16}{3} = 5\frac{1}{3}$

    c $5 \times 1\frac{3}{5} = 5 \times \frac{8}{5} = \frac{40}{5} = 8$

Example 16.10 ▷ A magazine has 96 pages. $\frac{5}{12}$ of the pages have adverts on them. How many pages have adverts on them?

    $\frac{1}{12}$ of 96 = 8. So, $\frac{5}{12}$ of 96 = 5 × 8 = 40 pages.

Exercise 16D

1 Find each of these.

   a $\frac{2}{3}$ of £27   **b** $\frac{3}{5}$ of 75 kg   **c** $1\frac{2}{3}$ of 18 metres   **d** $\frac{4}{9}$ of £18

   e $\frac{3}{10}$ of £46   **f** $\frac{5}{8}$ of 840 houses   **g** $\frac{3}{7}$ of 21 litres   **h** $1\frac{2}{5}$ of 45 minutes

   i $\frac{5}{6}$ of £63   **j** $\frac{3}{8}$ of 1600 loaves   **k** $1\frac{4}{7}$ of 35 km   **l** $\frac{7}{10}$ of 600 crows

   m $\frac{2}{9}$ of £1.26   **n** $\frac{4}{9}$ of 540 children   **o** $\frac{7}{12}$ of 144 miles   **p** $3\frac{3}{11}$ of £22

2 Find each of these as a mixed number.

   a $5 \times \frac{3}{4}$ **b** $8 \times \frac{2}{7}$ **c** $6 \times 1\frac{2}{3}$ **d** $4 \times \frac{3}{8}$

   e $9 \times \frac{1}{4}$ **f** $5 \times 1\frac{5}{6}$ **g** $9 \times \frac{4}{5}$ **h** $7 \times 2\frac{3}{4}$

   i $3 \times 3\frac{3}{7}$ **j** $8 \times \frac{2}{11}$ **k** $4 \times 1\frac{2}{7}$ **l** $6 \times \frac{7}{9}$

   m $2 \times 3\frac{3}{4}$ **n** $3 \times \frac{7}{10}$ **o** $5 \times 1\frac{3}{10}$ **p** $2 \times 10\frac{5}{8}$

 3 A bag of rice weighed 1300 g. $\frac{2}{5}$ of it was used to make a meal. How much was left?

 4 Mrs Smith weighed 96 kg. She lost $\frac{3}{8}$ of her weight due to a diet. How much did she weigh after the diet?

 5 A petrol tank holds 52 litres. $\frac{3}{4}$ is used on a journey. How many litres are left?

 6 A GCSE textbook has 448 pages. $\frac{3}{28}$ of the pages are the answers. How many pages of answers are there?

 7 A bar of chocolate weighs $\frac{5}{8}$ of a kilogram. How much do seven bars weigh?

 8 A Smartie machine produces 1400 Smarties a minute. $\frac{2}{7}$ of them are red. How many red Smarties will the machine produce in an hour?

 9 A farmer has nine cows. Each cow eats $1\frac{2}{3}$ bales of silage a week. How much do they eat altogether?

10 A cake recipe requires $\frac{2}{3}$ of a cup of walnuts. How many cups of walnuts will be needed for five cakes?

This is about dividing fractions by a whole number.

Dividing a fraction by 2 has the same effect as halving the fraction. For example:

$\frac{2}{7} \div 2 = \frac{2}{7} \times \frac{1}{2} = \frac{1}{7}$

Work out each of the following.

a $\frac{2}{3} \div 2$ b $\frac{3}{4} \div 2$ c $\frac{4}{5} \div 2$ d $\frac{7}{8} \div 2$

e $\frac{4}{7} \div 3$ f $\frac{2}{5} \div 5$ g $\frac{3}{8} \div 4$ h $\frac{3}{10} \div 5$

Percentages of quantities

This section will show you how to calculate simple percentages of quantities. This section will also revise the equivalence between fractions, percentages and decimals.

Example 16.11

Calculate: a   15% of £670   b   40% of £34

Calculate 10%, then use multiples of this.

a   10% of £670 = £67, 5% = 33.50. So, 15% of £670 = 67 + 33.5 = £100.50.

b   10% of £34 = £3.40. So, 40% of £34 = 4 × 3.40 = £13.60.

Example 16.12

Write down the equivalent percentage and fraction for each of these decimals.

a   0.6   b   0.28

To change a decimal to a percentage, multiply by 100. This gives: a   60%   b   28%

To change a decimal to a fraction, multiply and divide by 10, 100, 1000 as appropriate and cancel if possible. This gives:

a $0.6 = \frac{6}{10} = \frac{3}{5}$ b $0.28 = \frac{28}{100} = \frac{7}{25}$

Example 16.13

Write down the equivalent percentage and decimal for each of these fractions.

a $\frac{7}{20}$ b $\frac{9}{25}$

To change a fraction into a percentage, make the denominator 100. This gives:

a $\frac{7}{20} = \frac{35}{100} = 35\%$ b $\frac{9}{25} = \frac{36}{100} = 36\%$

To change a fraction into a decimal, divide the top by the bottom, or make into a percentage, then divide by 100. This gives:

a   0.35   b   0.36

Example 16.14 ▷ Write down the equivalent decimal and fraction for each of these percentages.

a 95%   **b** 26%

To convert a percentage to a decimal, divide by 100. This gives: **a** 0.95   **b** 0.26

To convert a percentage to a fraction, make a fraction over 100 then cancel if possible. This gives:

a 95% = $\frac{95}{100}$ = $\frac{19}{20}$ **b** 26% = $\frac{26}{100}$ = $\frac{13}{50}$

Exercise 16E

1 Copy the cross-number puzzle. Use the clues to fill it in. Then use the puzzle to fill in the missing numbers in the clues.

Across
1   71% of 300
3   73% of 200
5   107% of 200
8   58% of ……
9   88% of 400

Down
1   96% of ……
2   81% of ……
3   50% of 24
4   25% of 596
6   61% of 200
7   100% of 63

2 Copy and complete this table.

	a	b	c	d	e	f	g	h	i	j
Decimal	0.45			0.76			0.36			0.85
Fraction	$\frac{9}{20}$	$\frac{3}{5}$			$\frac{4}{25}$			$\frac{3}{50}$		
Percentage	45%		32%			37.5%			65%	

3 Calculate:
a   35% of £340
b   15% of £250
c   60% of £18
d   20% of £14.40
e   45% of £440
f   5% of £45
g   40% of £5.60
h   25% of £24.40

4 A Jumbo Jet carries 400 passengers. On one trip, 52% of the passengers were British, 17% were American, 12% were French and the rest were German.

a   How many people of each nationality were on the plane?
b   What percentage were German?

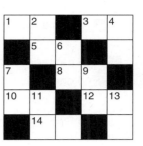

Extension **Work**

Copy the cross-number puzzle. Work out each percentage.
Then use the puzzle to fill in the missing numbers in the clues.

Across		**Down**	
1	54 out of 200	**2**	...... out of 400
3	33 out of 50	**4**	134 out of 200
5	13 out of 25	**6**	...... out of 300
8	99 out of 100	**7**	100 out of 400
10	...... out of 200	**9**	...... out of 20
12	27 out of 50	**11**	110 out of 1000
14	38 out of 200	**13**	23 out of 50

Solving problems

Below are two investigations. Before you start either of these, read the question carefully and think about how you are going to record your results. Show all your working clearly.

 ## Who wants to be a millionaire?

You have won a prize in a lottery. You have a choice of how to take the prize.

You can either:

Take £10 000 in the first year, 10% less (£9000) in the second year, 10% less than the second year's amount (£8100) in the third year, and so on for 10 years.

Or

Take £1000 in the first year, 50% more (£1500) in the second year, 50% more than the second year's amount (£1500) in the third year, and so on for 10 years.

You will probably need to use a calculator and round off the amounts to the nearest penny.

What would happen if the second method gave 40% more each year?

What would happen if the second method started with £10 000?

 ## Chocolate bars

Eight children, Alf, Betty, Charles, Des, Ethel, Fred, George and Helen, are lined up outside a room in alphabetical order.

Inside the room are three tables. Each table has eight chairs around it.

On the first table is one chocolate bar, on the second table are two chocolate bars, and on the third table are three chocolate bars.

The children go into the room one at a time and sit at one of the tables. After they are all seated they share out the chocolate bars on the table at which they are seated.

Where should Alf sit to make sure he gets the most chocolate?

4 I can use simple fractions and percentages to describe proportions of a whole.
I can add and subtract decimals to two places.

5 I can add, subtract, multiply and divide decimals.
I can use a calculator effectively.
I can calculate fractions of a quantity.
I can calculate percentages of a quantity.

6 I can convert between fractions, decimals and percentages.
I can solve more complex problems.

National Test questions

1 *2006 4–6 Paper 1*

a **Add** together 1740 and 282.

b Now **add** together 17.4 and 2.82. You can use part **a** to help you.

c 3.5 + 2.35 is **bigger** than 3.3 + 2.1.

How much bigger?

2 *2006 4–6 Paper 1*

a Add together **3.7** and **6.5**.

b Subtract **5.7** from **15.2**.

c Multiply **254** by **5**.

d Divide **342** by **6**.

3 *2004 4–6 Paper 1*

You can buy a new calculator for **£1.25**.

In 1979 the same calculator cost **22 times** as much as it costs now.

How much did the same type of calculator cost in 1979?
Show your working.

4 *2003 4–6 Paper 2*

A glass holds **225 ml**.

An adult needs about **1.8 litres** of water each day to stay healthy.

How many glasses is that?

Show your working.

225 ml

FM Running a small business – a group activity

Plan

1 You are setting up a small business to buy materials, make gadgets and sell them for profit.

Facts

2 You have £20 000 to invest in your business.

One machine to produce your gadgets costs £2500.

The machines also cost £500 per week each to maintain.

Each machine can produce 100 gadgets per day but requires two workers to use it.

Workers are paid £400 per week each.

The cost of materials to produce one gadget is £12.

Weekly sales figures

3 The number of sales depends on the selling price. The table shows maximum weekly sales for different selling prices.

Selling price	£18	£19	£20	£21
Maximum number of gadgets that can be sold per week	2000	1500	1000	500

Your aim

4 To make as much profit as possible at the end of 6 weeks.

Hints and tactics

5 Try buying different numbers of machines to start with.

Use some of your profits to buy extra machines.

Sell at the highest of the selling prices that you can.

Your **total costs** cannot be greater than the amount of money you have at the start of any week.

An example

6 Here is an example of a week if you buy one machine and employ two workers.

Be careful: If you buy four machines you cannot pay any workers to produce gadgets and will be bankrupt!

Week 1
(£20 000 available to spend)

Cost of machines bought	1 × £2500 = £2500	Income = Selling price × Number of gadgets sold
		500 × £21 = £10 500
Maintenance cost of machines	1 × £500 = £500	
Cost of workers	2 × £400 = £800	Total profit
		£10 500 − £9800 = £700
Number of gadgets produced	500	
Cost of materials	500 × £12 = £6000	
Total costs	£9800	Balance
		£20 000 + £700 = 20 700

Profit for week 1 = £700
Amount available to spend in week 2 = £20 700

This chapter is going to show you
- How to use the algebraic ideas given in previous chapters
- How to extend these ideas into more difficult problems

What you should already know
- How to solve simple equations
- How to use simple formulae and derive a formula
- How to find the term-to-term rule in a sequence
- How to plot coordinates and draw graphs
- How to use algebra to solve simple problems

Solving equations

You have already met simple equations in Chapter 6. The scales show an equation.

The left-hand pan has 3 bags and 2 marbles.

The right-hand pan has 17 marbles.

Each bag contains the same number of marbles. How many marbles are in a bag?

Let the number of marbles in a bag be x, which gives:

Take 2 marbles away from each side:

This gives:

Now, $3x$ means $3 \times x$. This is equal to 15. So:

There are 5 marbles in each bag.

$$3x + 2 = 17$$
$$3x + 2 - 2 = 17 - 2$$
$$3x = 15$$
$$x = 5$$

You will usually solve these types of equation by subtracting or adding to both sides in order to have a single term on each side of the equals sign.

Example 17.1 ▷ Solve $4x + 3 = 31$.

Subtract 3 from both sides: $4x + 3 - 3 = 31 - 3$
$$4x = 28$$
$$(4 \times ? = 28)$$
$$x = 7$$

Example 17.2 ▷ Solve $3x - 5 = 13$.

Add 5 to both sides: $3x - 5 + 5 = 13 + 5$
$$3x = 18$$
$$(3 \times ? = 18)$$
$$x = 6$$

1 Solve each of the following equations.

a	$2x + 3 = 11$	**b**	$2x + 5 = 13$	**c**	$3x + 4 = 19$	**d**	$3x + 7 = 19$
e	$4m + 1 = 21$	**f**	$5k + 6 = 21$	**g**	$4n + 9 = 17$	**h**	$2x + 7 = 27$
i	$6h + 5 = 23$	**j**	$3t + 5 = 26$	**k**	$8x + 3 = 35$	**l**	$5y + 3 = 28$
m	$7x + 3 = 10$	**n**	$4t + 7 = 39$	**o**	$3x + 8 = 20$	**p**	$8m + 5 = 21$

2 Solve each of the following equations.

a	$3x - 2 = 13$	**b**	$2m - 5 = 1$	**c**	$4x - 1 = 11$	**d**	$5t - 3 = 17$
e	$2x - 3 = 13$	**f**	$4m - 5 = 19$	**g**	$3m - 2 = 10$	**h**	$7x - 3 = 25$
i	$5m - 2 = 18$	**j**	$3k - 4 = 5$	**k**	$8x - 5 = 11$	**l**	$2t - 3 = 7$
m	$4x - 3 = 5$	**n**	$8y - 3 = 29$	**o**	$5x - 4 = 11$	**p**	$3m - 1 = 17$

3 Solve each of the following equations.

a	$3x + 4 = 10$	**b**	$5x - 1 = 29$	**c**	$4x - 3 = 25$	**d**	$3m - 2 = 13$
e	$5m + 4 = 49$	**f**	$7m + 3 = 24$	**g**	$4m - 5 = 23$	**h**	$6k + 1 = 25$
i	$5k - 3 = 2$	**j**	$3k - 1 = 23$	**k**	$2k + 5 = 15$	**l**	$7x - 3 = 18$
m	$4x + 3 = 43$	**n**	$5x + 6 = 31$	**o**	$9x - 4 = 68$		

4 Solve the following equations.

a	$12x + 3 = 87$		**b**	$13x + 4 = 56$
c	$15x - 1 = 194$		**d**	$14x - 3 = 137$
e	$13m - 2 = 24$		**f**	$15m + 4 = 184$
g	$17m + 3 = 105$		**h**	$14m - 5 = 219$
i	$16k + 1 = 129$		**j**	$15k - 3 = 162$
k	$13k - 1 = 38$		**l**	$12k + 5 = 173$
m	$17x - 4 = 285$		**n**	$14x + 3 = 73$
o	$15x + 6 = 231$		**p**	$19x - 4 = 167$

Extension Work

Solve the following equations.

a	$\dfrac{x + 3}{2} = 5$	**b**	$\dfrac{x - 1}{3} = 9$	**c**	$\dfrac{x + 6}{5} = 5$
d	$\dfrac{x - 2}{5} = 8$	**e**	$\dfrac{x + 5}{6} = 3$	**f**	$\dfrac{x + 1}{4} = 3$
g	$\dfrac{x - 7}{5} = 4$	**h**	$\dfrac{x - 3}{4} = 8$	**i**	$\dfrac{x - 6}{7} = 2$

Formulae

Formulae occur in many situations, some of which you have already met. You need to be able to use formulae to calculate a variety of quantities.

Example 17.3

One rule to find the area of a triangle is to take half of the length of its base and multiply it by the vertical height of the triangle. This rule, written as a formula is:

$$A = \tfrac{1}{2}bh$$

where A = area, b = base length, and h = vertical height.

Using this formula to calculate the area of a triangle with a base length of 7 cm and a vertical height of 16 cm gives:

$$\text{Area} = \tfrac{1}{2} \times 7 \times 16 = 56 \text{ cm}^2$$

Exercise 17B

1 The average of three numbers is given by the formula:

$$A = \frac{m + n + p}{3}$$

where A is the average and m, n and p are the numbers.

a Use the formula to find the average of 4, 8 and 15.
b What is the average of 32, 43 and 54?

2 The perimeter of a rectangle is given by the formula:

$$P = 2(m + n)$$

where P is the perimeter, m is the length and n is the width.

a Use the formula to find the perimeter of a rectangle 5 cm by 8 cm.
b Use the formula to find the perimeter of a rectangle 13 cm by 18 cm.

3 The average speed of a car is given by the formula:

$$A = \frac{d}{t}$$

where A is the average speed in miles per hour, d is the number of miles travelled, and t is the number of hours taken for the journey.

a Find the average speed of a car which travels 220 miles in 4 hours.
b In 8 hours a car covered 360 miles. What was the average speed?

4 The speed, v m/s, of the train t seconds after passing through a station with a speed of u m/s, is given by the formula:

$$v = u + 5t$$

a What is the speed 4 seconds after leaving a station with a speed of 12 m/s?
b What is the speed 10 seconds after leaving a station with a speed of 8 m/s?

5 The speed, v, of a land speed car can be calculated using the following formula:

$$v = u + at$$

where v is the speed after t seconds, u is the initial speed, and a is the acceleration.

a Calculate the speed of the car with 10 m/s² acceleration 8 seconds after it had a speed of 12 m/s.

b Calculate the speed of a car with 5 m/s² acceleration 12 seconds after it had a speed of 15 m/s.

 6 To change a temperature in degrees Celsius to degrees Fahrenheit, we use the formula:

$$F = 32 + 1.8C$$

where F is the temperature in degrees Fahrenheit and C is the temperature in degrees Celsius.

Change each of the following temperatures to degrees Fahrenheit.

a 45 °C **b** 40 °C **c** 65 °C **d** 100 °C

Extension Work

1 When a stone is dropped from the top of a cliff, the distance, d metres, that it falls in t seconds is given by the formula:

$$d = 4.9t^2$$

Calculate the distance a stone has fallen 8 seconds after being dropped from the top of a cliff.

2 The distance, D km, which you can see out to sea from the shore line, at a height of h metres above sea level, is given by the formula:

$$D = \sqrt{(12.5h)}$$

How far out to sea can you see from the top of a cliff, 112 metres above sea level?

Dotty investigations

Exercise 17C **1** Look at the following two shapes drawn on a dotted square grid.

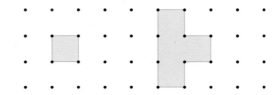

By drawing some of your own shapes (with no dots inside each shape), complete the table below, giving the number of dots on each perimeter and the area of each shape.

Number of dots on perimeter	Area of shape
4	1 cm²
6	
8	
10	4 cm²
12	
14	
16	

2 What is special about the number of dots on the perimeter of all the shapes in the table of Question 1?

3 For a shape with no dots inside, one way to calculate the area of the shape from the number of dots on the perimeter is to:

Divide the number of dots by two, then subtract 1.

a Check that this rule works for all the shapes drawn in Question 1.

b Write this rule as a formula, where A is the area of a shape and D is the number of dots on its perimeter.

4 Look at the following two shapes drawn on a dotted square grid. They both have one dot inside.

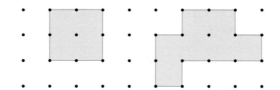

By drawing some of your own shapes (with only one dot inside each shape), complete the table below.

Number of dots on perimeter	Dots inside	Area of shape
4	1	
6	1	
8	1	4 cm²
10	1	
12	1	
14	1	
16	1	

5 For the shapes in Question 4, find a formula to connect A, the area of each shape with D, the number of dots on its perimeter.

6 **a** Draw some shapes with an even number of dots on each perimeter and two dots inside each shape.

b Find the formula connecting A, the area of each shape, with D, the number of dots on its perimeter.

7 **a** Draw some shapes with an even number of dots on each perimeter and three dots inside each shape.

b Find the formula connecting A, the area of each shape, with D, the number of dots on its perimeter.

Extension Work

Repeat these investigations but use an odd number of dots on the perimeter of each shape.

Graphs from the real world

When you fill your car with petrol, both the amount of petrol you have taken and its cost are displayed on the pump. One litre of petrol costs about 80p, but this rate does change from time to time.

The table below shows the costs of different quantities of petrol as displayed on a petrol pump.

Petrol (litres)	5	10	15	20	25	30
Cost (£)	4	8	12	16	20	24

This information can also be represented by the following ordered pairs:

(5, 4)   (10, 8)   (15, 12)   (20, 16)   (25, 20)   (30, 24)

On the right is the graph which relates the cost of petrol to the quantity bought.

This is an example of a **conversion graph**. You can use it to find the cost of any quantity of petrol, or to find how much petrol can be bought for different amounts of money.

Conversion graphs are usually straight-line graphs.

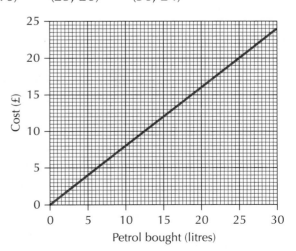

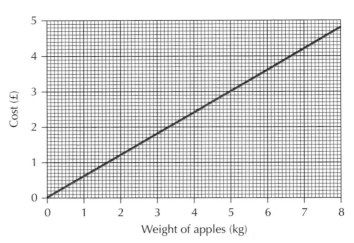

Use the graph to answer these questions:
a Find the cost of each quantity of apples.
  i 3 kg   **ii** 7 kg
b What weight of apples can be bought for:
  i £3?   **ii** £2.40?

2 The graph below shows the distance travelled by a car during an interval of 5 minutes.

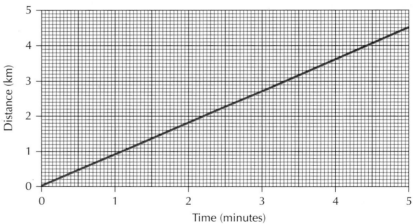

a Find the distance travelled during the second minute of the journey.
b Find the time taken to travel 3 km.

3 Here is a kilometre–mile conversion graph.

a Express each of the following distances in km.
  i 3 miles
  ii 4.5 miles
b Express each of the following distances in miles.
  i 2 km
  ii 4 km
  iii 6 km

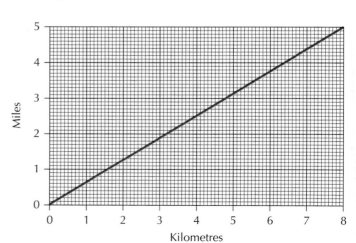

FM **4** **a** Copy and complete the following table for the exchange rate of the euro.

Euros (€)	1	5	10	15	20
Pounds (£)	0.60	3.00			

b Use the data from this table to draw a conversion graph from pounds to euros.

c Use your graph to convert each of the following to pounds.

    i €7   **ii** €16   **iii** €17.50

d Use your graph to convert each of the following to euros.

    i £9   **ii** £12   **iii** £10.80

FM **5** A box weighs 2 kg. Packets of juice, each weighing 425 g, are packed into it.

a Draw a graph to show the weight of the box plus the packets of juice and the number of packets of fruit juice put into the box.

b Find, from the graph, the number of packets of juice that make the weight of the box and packets as close to 5 kg as possible.

Extension **Work**

A taxi firm charges a basic charge of £2 plus £1 a mile.

Draw a graph to show how much the firm charges for journeys up to 10 km.

Describe the difference between this graph and the one in Exercise 17D.

Draw a graph to show the cost of gas from a supplier who charges a fixed fee of £18 plus 3p per unit of gas. Draw the horizontal axis from 0 to 500 units and the vertical axis from £0 to £35.

LEVEL BOOSTER

5 I can use formulae with more than one variable such as $A = (x + y) \div 2$, to work out the values of one variable given the values of the other variables, i.e. $A = 10$ when $x = 7$ and $y = 13$.

I can read values from conversion graphs.

6 I can solve equations with more than one operation, such as: $3x + 5 = 11$, therefore $x = 2$.

I can investigate a mathematical problem by setting up tables of values and recognising patterns.

I can set up tables of values and draw graphs to show relationships between variables.

5

FM **1** *2004 4–6 Paper 1*

A company sells books using the Internet.

The graph shows their delivery charges.

a Use the graph to find the missing values from this table.

Number of books	Delivery charge (£)
8	
9	

b For every extra book you buy, how much more must you pay for delivery?

c A second company sells books using the Internet. Its delivery charge is **£1.00 per book**.

Copy the graph and draw a line on it to show this information.

d Complete the sentence:

Delivery is cheaper with the **first** company if you buy at least …… books.

2 *2006 4–6 Paper 1*

Solve these equations:

a $2k + 3 = 11$

b $2t + 3 = -11$

3 *2006 3–5 Paper 1*

Look at this sequence of patterns made with hexagons.

       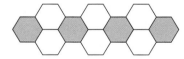

pattern number 1   pattern number 2   pattern number 3

To find the number of hexagons in pattern number **n** you can use these rules:

Number of **grey** hexagons $= n + 1$

Number of **white** hexagons $= 2n$

Altogether, what is the total number of hexagons in **pattern number 20**?

CHAPTER 18 Geometry and Measures 5

This chapter is going to show you
- The names and properties of polygons
- How to tessellate 2-D shapes
- How to make 3-D models

What you should already know
- How to reflect, rotate and translate shapes
- How to draw and measure angles
- How to calculate the angles on a straight line, in a triangle and around a point
- How to draw nets for 3-D shapes

Polygons

A **polygon** is any 2-D shape that has straight sides.

The names of the most common polygons are given in the table below.

Number of sides	Name of polygon
3	Triangle
4	Quadrilateral
5	Pentagon
6	Hexagon
7	Heptagon
8	Octagon
9	Nonagon
10	Decagon

A **convex polygon** has all its diagonals inside the polygon.

A **concave polygon** has at least one diagonal outside the polygon.

Example 18.1

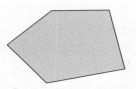

A convex pentagon
(all diagonals inside)

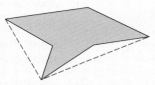

A concave hexagon
(two diagonals outside)

A **regular polygon** has all its sides equal and all its interior angles are equal.

Example 18.2 ▷ A regular octagon has eight lines of symmetry and rotational symmetry of order 8.

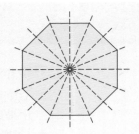

Exercise 18A

1 Which shapes below are polygons? If they are, write down their names.

a 　b 　c 　d 　e

2 Which shapes below are regular polygons?

a 　b 　c 　d 　e

3 State whether each of the shapes below is a convex polygon or a concave polygon.

a 　b 　c 　d 　e

4 Draw, if possible, a pentagon which has:

  a no reflex angles   **b** one reflex angle

  c two reflex angles   **d** three reflex angles

5 Draw hexagons which have exactly:

  a no lines of symmetry   **b** one line of symmetry

  c two lines of symmetry   **d** three lines of symmetry

6 a Write down the names of all the different shapes that can be made by overlapping two squares.

     For example: a pentagon can be made, as shown. Draw diagrams to show all the different shapes that you have made.

  b What shapes can be made by overlapping three squares?

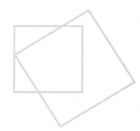

1 Construct a regular hexagon in this way.

   a Draw a circle of radius 5 cm.

   b With your compasses still set to a radius of 5 cm, go round the circumference of the circle making marks 5 cm apart.

   c Join the points where the marks cross the circle using a ruler.

2 A triangle has no diagonals. A quadrilateral has two diagonals.

 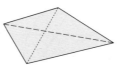

   Investigate the total number of diagonals that can be drawn inside convex polygons.

3 Use ICT to draw regular polygons.

   a Use these instructions describe a square using LOGO:

      fd 50 rt 90
      fd 50 rt 90
      fd 50 rt 90
      fd 50 rt 90

   b Use these instructions describe a regular pentagon using LOGO:

      repeat 5 [fd 50 rt 72]

4 Investigate how to draw other regular polygons using LOGO.

Tessellations

A **tessellation** is a pattern made by fitting together the same shapes without leaving any gaps.

When drawing a tessellation, use a square or a triangular grid, as in the examples below.

To show a tessellation, it is usual to draw up to about ten repeating shapes.

Example 18.3

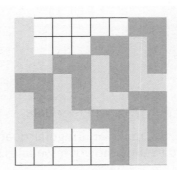

Example 18.4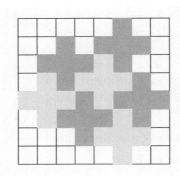

Example 18.5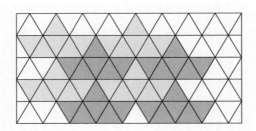

Exercise 18B

1 Make a tessellation for each of the following shapes. Use a square grid.

a    **b**    **c**   **d**

2 Make a tessellation for each of the following shapes. Use a triangular grid.

a   **b**   **c**   **d**

Extension **Work**

1 Design a tessellation of your own. Working in pairs or groups, make an attractive poster to show all your different tessellations.

2 Here is a tessellation which uses curves. Can you design a different curved tessellation?

3 Investigate which of the regular polygons will tessellate.

4 Any quadrilateral will tessellate. So, make an irregular quadrilateral tile cut from card. Then use your tile to show how it tessellates.

Constructing 3-D shapes

Construct one or more of the 3-D shapes given in Exercise 18C. For each shape, you start by drawing its net accurately on card.

Make sure that you have the following equipment before you start to draw a net: a sharp pencil, a ruler, a protractor, a pair of scissors and a glue-stick or adhesive tape.

The tabs have been included to make it easier if you decide to glue the edges together. The tabs can be left off if you decide to use adhesive tape.

Before folding a net, score the card using the scissors and a ruler along the fold lines. When constructing a shape, keep one face of the net free of tabs and secure this face last.

Exercise 18C Draw each of the following nets accurately on card. Cut out the net and construct the 3-D shape.

1 Regular tetrahedron

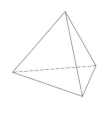 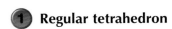

Each equilateral triangle has these measurements:

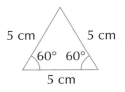

5 cm   5 cm

60°   60°

5 cm

2 Square-based pyramid

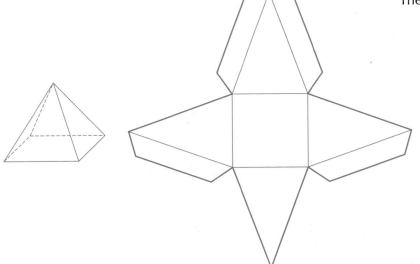

The square has these measurements:

5 cm

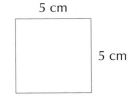

5 cm

The isosceles triangle has these measurements:

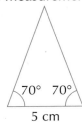

70°   70°

5 cm

3 **Triangular prism**

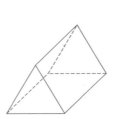

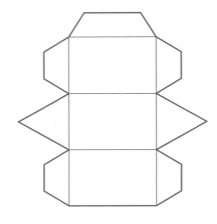

Each rectangle has these measurements:

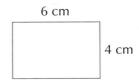

6 cm

4 cm

Each equilateral triangle has these measurements

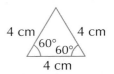

4 cm 4 cm

60° 60°

4 cm

Extension Work

The following nets are for more complex 3-D shapes. Choose suitable measurements and make each shape from card.

1 Octahedron

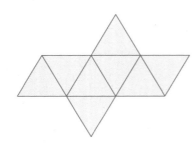

2 Regular hexagonal prism

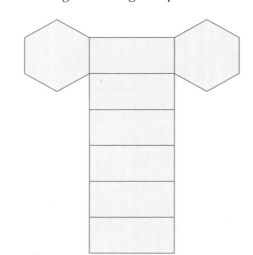

3 Truncated square-based pyramid

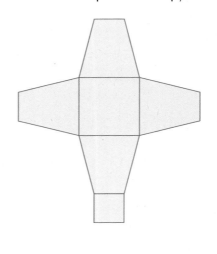

LEVEL BOOSTER

4 I know the names of and can draw common 2-D shapes.

5 I can identify all the symmetrical properties of 2-D shapes.
I know how to tessellate a 2-D shape.
I can make 3-D models from a net.

1 *2006 4–6 Paper 2*

I use two congruent trapeziums to make the shapes below.

Which of these shapes are **hexagons**?

a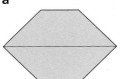

b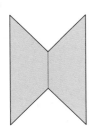

c

d

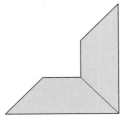

2 *2004 4–6 Paper 2*

The square grid below shows a **quadrilateral** that has **four right angles.**

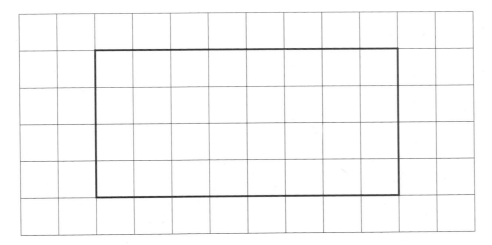

a On a similar square grid, draw a quadrilateral that has exactly **two** right angles.

b On a similar square grid, draw a quadrilateral that has exactly **one** right angle.

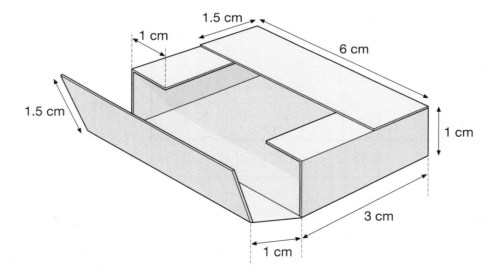

3 *2000 Paper 1*

The sketch shows the net of a triangular prism.

The net is folded up and glued to make the prism.

a Which edge is tab 1 glued to? On a copy of the diagram, label this edge A.

b Which edge is tab 2 glued to? Label this edge B.

c The corner marked ● meets two other corners. Label these two other corners ●.

4 *2001 Paper 1*

The diagram shows a box. Draw the net for the box on a square grid.

Index

William Collins' dream of knowledge for all began with the publication of his first book in 1819. A self-educated mill worker, he not only enriched millions of lives, but also founded a flourishing publishing house. Today, staying true to this spirit, Collins books are packed with inspiration, innovation and practical expertise. They place you at the centre of a world of possibility and give you exactly what you need to explore it.

Collins. Do more.

Published by Collins
An imprint of HarperCollins*Publishers*
77–85 Fulham Palace Road
Hammersmith
London
W6 8JB

Browse the complete Collins catalogue at
www.collinseducation.com

Keith Gordon, Kevin Evans, Brian Speed and Trevor Senior assert their moral rights to be identified as the authors of this work.

British Library Cataloguing in Publication Data
A Catalogue record for this publication is available from the British Library.

Commissioned by Melanie Hoffman and Katie Sergeant
Project management by Priya Govindan
Edited by Brian Ashbury
Proofread by Amanda Dickson
Design and typesetting by Jordan Publishing Design
Covers by Oculus Design and Communications
Functional maths spreads and covers management by Laura Deacon
Illustrations by Nigel Jordan and Tony Wilkins
Printed and bound by Martins the Printers, Berwick-upon-Tweed
Production by Simon Moore

Acknowledgments
The publishers thank the Qualifications and Curriculum Authority for granting permission to reproduce questions from past National Curriculum Test papers for Key Stage 3 Maths.

The publishers wish to thank the following for permission to reproduce photographs:

p.12–13 (main image) © Jon Hicks / Corbis, p.40–41 (main image) © Van Hilversum / Alamy, p.41 (football image) © istockphoto.com, p.70–71 (main image) © istockphoto.com, p.70 (inset image) © istockphoto.com, p.82–83 (main and inset images) Ted Levine / zefa / Corbis, p.82–83 (inset images) © istockphoto.com, p.104–105 (main image) © Jeff Morgan food and drink / Alamy, p. 104–105 (all inset images) © istockphoto.com, p.122–123 (main image) © Science Photo Library, p. 122–123 (all inset images) © istockphoto.com, p.152–153 (main image) © Stephen Vowles / Alamy, p.162–163 (main image) © Sean Justice / Corbis, p.176–177 (all images) © istockphoto.com, p.200–201 (main and inset images) © istockphoto.com

Every effort has been made to trace copyright holders and to obtain their permission for the use of copyright material. The authors and publishers will gladly receive any information enabling them to rectify any error or omission at the first opportunity.

**St Saviour's & St Olave's School
New Kent Road
London SE1 4AN**

Mixed Sources
Product group from well-managed forests and other controlled sources
www.fsc.org Cert no. SW-COC-1806
© 1996 Forest Stewardship Council

FSC is a non-profit international organisation established to promote the responsible management of the world's forests. Products carrying the FSC label are independently certified to assure consumers that they come from forests that are managed to meet the social, economic and ecological needs of present and future generations.

Find out more about HarperCollins and the environment at
www.harpercollins.co.uk/green